HOMICIDE in HARDCOVER

A Bibliophile Mystery

Murder is always
a bestseller.

New York Times Bestselling Author

Kate Carlisle

BERKLEY

$7.99 USA
$10.99 CAN

S EAN

ISBN 978-0-451-22615-0

9 780451 226150

5 0 7 9 9

Praise for *Homicide in Hardcover*

"Saucy, sassy, and smart—a fun read with a great sense of humor and a soupçon of suspense. Enjoy!"
—Nancy Atherton, author of the
Aunt Dimity mysteries

"A cursed book, a dead mentor, and a snarky rival send book restorer Brooklyn Wainwright on a chase for clues—and fine food and wine—in Kate Carlisle's fun and funny, delightful debut." —Lorna Barrett, author of the
Booktown Mystery series

"Who'd have thought book restoration could be so exciting? When Brooklyn Wainwright inherits the job of restoring the priceless copy of Goethe's *Faust* from her murdered mentor, her studio is ransacked, she's stalked, and the bodies pile up around her. Is it the famous *Faust* curse? I'm not tellin'. But trust me, you'll have fun finding out. *Homicide in Hardcover* is good reading in any binding." —Parnell Hall, author of the Puzzle Lady
Crossword Puzzle mysteries

"Brooklyn is my kind of detective! She loves books, wine, chocolate—and solving mysteries! Kate Carlisle has crafted a fabulous new series with great food, great books, and lots of fun."
—Maureen Child, author of *Bedeviled*

"Beautiful and brilliant Brooklyn Wainwright thought bookbinding was a low-risk occupation, but she soon discovers her mistake in Kate Carlisle's smart and sophisticated page-turner."
—Leslie Meier, author of *Candy Cane Murder*

"Welcome to the fresh and funny world of bookbinder Brooklyn Wainwright. A delicious mix of San Francisco, book restoration, and a lingering counterculture beset by murder. Who knew leather and vellum could be so captivating?"
—Jo Dereske, author of the Miss Zukas mysteries

TITLES BY KATE CARLISLE

Bibliophile Mysteries
Homicide in Hardcover
If Books Could Kill
The Lies That Bind
Murder Under Cover
Pages of Sin
(an eNovella)
One Book in the Grave
Peril in Paperback
A Cookbook Conspiracy
The Book Stops Here
Ripped from the Pages
Books of a Feather
Once upon a Spine
Buried in Books

Fixer-Upper Mysteries
A High-End Finish
This Old Homicide
Crowned and Moldering
Deck the Hallways
Eaves of Destruction
A Wrench in the Works

HOMICIDE
in HARDCOVER

A Bibliophile Mystery

Kate Carlisle

BERKLEY PRIME CRIME
New York

BERKLEY PRIME CRIME
Published by Berkley
An imprint of Penguin Random House LLC
375 Hudson Street, New York, New York 10014

Copyright © 2009 by Kathleen Beaver
Penguin Random House supports copyright. Copyright fuels creativity, encourages
diverse voices, promotes free speech, and creates a vibrant culture. Thank you for buying
an authorized edition of this book and for complying with copyright laws by not
reproducing, scanning, or distributing any part of it in any form without permission.
You are supporting writers and allowing Penguin Random House to continue to
publish books for every reader.

BERKLEY and the BERKLEY & B colophon are registered trademarks and
BERKLEY PRIME CRIME is a trademark of Penguin Random House LLC.

ISBN: 978-0-451-22615-0

Berkley Prime Crime mass-market edition / February 2009

Printed in the United States of America
20   19   18   17   16

To Don, who always believed this day would come

Acknowledgments

As this is my first book, I owe a debt of gratitude to so many people I can't begin to name, but please indulge me as I mention a special few.

My agents, Christina Hogrebe and Kelly Harms of the Jane Rotrosen Agency, for great advice, wonderful enthusiasm, and consummate skill at guiding this new author along the bumpy path to publication. And thanks to my editor, Kristen Weber, whose positive energy calmed all fears and helped make my book shine. Thank you as well to NAL's art department for creating the most beautiful cover ever.

Maureen Child for your friendship, love, honesty, and support, and Susan Mallery for your wisdom, encouragement, and excellent taste in wine. I am deeply grateful to call you my dear friends and fellow plotters, and I can never thank you enough for all that you've given me.

Muchas gracias to the remarkable writers who make up the Romance Bandits (http://romancebandits.blog spot.com), whose collective wit, kindness, and dedication to the cause have made this journey so exciting.

I am also grateful to Romance Writers of America and Sisters in Crime for opening doors and providing opportunities to develop friendships and gather knowledge.

Thanks to master bookbinder Bruce Levy, who first introduced me to the art of bookbinding, and to the San Francisco Center for the Book and bookbinding expert Ann Lindsey for giving me the skills and knowledge necessary to create beautiful books using classic nineteenth-century methods. Also, many thanks to book artist Wendy Poma for teaching me so many different binding techniques, all in one afternoon. Any mistakes with regard to these methods and techniques are my own.

Finally, I am profoundly indebted to my wonderful family—my husband, mother, brothers, sisters, nieces, nephews, aunts, uncles, cousins, in-laws, and outlaws—for your love, support, and enduring humor. I swear, any resemblance between you and the characters within these pages is purely coincidental.

Books have the same enemies as people: fire, humidity, animals, weather, and their own content.

—Paul Valéry

Chapter 1

My teacher always told me that in order to save a patient you'd have to kill him first. Not the most child-friendly way of explaining his theory of book restoration to his eight-year-old apprentice, but it worked. I grew up determined to save them all.

As I studied the faded, brittle, leather-bound volume that lay near death on the worktable before me, I knew I could bring it back to life, too. But it wouldn't be easy. With six hundred pages of crusty, smelly pulp, the book's once-elegant, gilded spine was nearly severed from its body.

"Sorry, old thing, but I'm not letting you die on my watch." I dusted its hinges with a soft brush, then ran a finger along the spine. It came away covered in red powder. Red rot had set in. The leather binding was terminal.

I picked up my scalpel and pierced the frail calfskin along the aged brown hinge, extricating the bits of thready sinew still clinging to the sticky bits of leather.

Despite my mother's misgivings, I was grateful I'd bypassed medical school, because let's face it, if this book were human, I'd be drenched in blood up to my elbows and probably unconscious. I didn't do so well around blood.

I heard a sharp intake of breath. "That's disgusting!"

I flinched and the scalpel flew from my hand. I looked up and saw my best friend, Robin Tully, staring at the flaky leather chunks and moldy paper splayed across the table.

"I didn't hear you come in," I said, patting my heart.

"Apparently not," she said as she retrieved the scalpel off the floor and placed it safely on the table. "A bomb could go off and you wouldn't notice."

I ignored that, jumped off the high stool and grabbed her in a tight hug. "You're early, aren't you?"

She checked her watch. "Actually, I'm right on time, which I suppose is early in your world."

I smiled, then held up my camera. "Do you mind? I need another few minutes to map and shoot this stuff."

"Procrastinate all you want. I'm in no hurry." She pulled off her fuzzy black jacket and fluffed her hair.

"I'm not procrastinating." I took several close-up shots of the decomposing front foredge, then looked up and caught Robin's look of profound pity. "What?"

She held up her hands. "I said nothing."

"I can hear you judging me." I put the camera down and grabbed a handful of chocolate-swirled caramel kisses, a product I personally considered a miracle of modern technology. I popped a few pieces into my mouth, tried to enjoy the warm burst of flavors, but finally threw my hands up in defeat. "Okay, I'm procrastinating. Can you blame me? I could be walking into a trap tonight."

She laughed. "We're going to the library, not sneaking down a dark alley."

"I know it." I scowled. Tonight was a private showing of the most important book collection to open at the Covington Library in years. And the man being honored tonight, the man responsible for the restoration of the rare antiquarian books on exhibit, was Abraham Karastovsky, my lifelong teacher and mentor.

And nemesis?

I didn't know. We hadn't spoken in six months and I was frankly nervous about seeing him after being estranged for so long.

Six months ago, after years of indecision, I'd finally given Abraham notice that I'd be moving out from under his shadow to start my own business. He hadn't taken the news well. He'd never been good at accepting change. He was old school, settled in his ways, determined to fight the modern trends in both book restoration and life in general. When I went off to college to study book restoration and conservation, he declared it was a useless waste of time and I'd learn more on the job, working with him.

Despite his gruff ways it had been a difficult decision to leave him, even though I'd essentially been working independently for years. Abraham had been furious and had said some things I hoped he might regret now.

What would happen when we met face-to-face again? Would he treat me like an enemy? Cut me off without a word? Ridicule me in front of friends and colleagues? I was beyond worried. Could anyone blame me for procrastinating?

"He sent you an invitation," Robin said. "That proves he wants to see you. He's not the best communicator, but he loves you, Brooklyn. You know that."

I felt tears spring up and I prayed she was right. It was both comforting and annoying to know she usually was.

We'd been best friends since the age of seven, when my parents joined a spiritual commune up in the wine country north of San Francisco. My mom and dad had dragged me and my five young siblings off to experience the excitement of growing our own vegetables, wearing clothing made of hemp and sharing in the harmony and oneness of nature. I did not go quietly.

When we arrived at the commune, the first person I noticed among the crowd of strangers was a dark-haired girl about my age, defiantly clutching a bald-headed Barbie doll clad in a red satin dress and black stiletto heels. That was Robin. We bonded immediately, despite the fact that we were opposites in so many ways.

These days Robin comes across as a glamorous, carefree society girl. You'd never guess she runs her own tour and travel business and is also a brilliant sculptor. She is a curvy brunette with almond eyes and an uncanny ability to cause men to wander off sidewalks into oncoming traffic.

I, on the other hand, am serious, blond, tall, still barely out of my gangly stage and occasionally have men ask me about my revolutionary technique for stretching leather. Sounds kinky but sadly, it's not.

I was wearing a somber yet elegant black suit while Robin looked simply smashing, all dressed up for a splashy art opening in a sassy cocktail dress and spiky black heels, her only accessory a classic strand of pearls she'd inherited from her great-grandmother.

Unfortunately, we weren't going to a splashy art opening.

"Why are you so dressed up?" I asked, carefully removing my dust-covered lab coat. Tonight's private showing for the Covington Library Founders' Circle would be a quiet affair attended by the library trustees, past and present donors, the board of directors and the wealthiest members of San Francisco society.

"Hey, there may be nothing but wall-to-wall old farts tonight, but I'm still there to par-tay."

"Ah." I hung the lab coat up in the small closet near the front door. "I thought maybe you'd forgotten where we're going."

"How could I forget?" she said, steering clear of the table, which was covered with brittle hunks of leather and swollen manuscript pages. "Abraham called me again this afternoon to make sure I was coming tonight. He was almost hyperventilating, he was so excited."

"He's been calling you?" I felt a tug of resentment that Abraham had contacted her. But why wouldn't he? He'd been a commune member as long as Robin and I had lived there. We were all very close, but I'd always been his favorite. Now I didn't know what I was to him.

"He never used to call me," Robin pointed out. "I figure it's his way of keeping tabs on you."

"Maybe."

"And he never asks directly about you, but I always end up talking more about you than me. Go figure."

I refused to get my hopes up. "So, he's anxious about tonight?"

"*Frantic* would be a more accurate word," she said, as she sat down at my desk. "I guess one of the most important books in the show isn't finished yet."

"The *Faust*," I murmured. It was all I could do to keep the woefully bitter jealousy that was yapping inside me from creeping into my voice. "I hear it's really something."

That might've been the understatement of the year.

Here I sat, toiling away on a set of lovely but anonymous old medical treatises, while Abraham had snagged the dream commission of the century—the legendary Heinrich Winslow collection of rare antiquarian books and prints.

The Winslow book collection was considered one of the finest in the world, and the crowning glory was said to be a jewel-encrusted, gilded edition of Goethe's masterwork, *Faust*, commissioned by Kaiser Wilhelm in 1880.

And it was cursed.

Some attributed the curse to the fact that it had briefly belonged to Adolf Hitler, who apparently had little appreciation for books—no big surprise. Der Führer had passed the priceless *Faust* on to Heinrich Winslow's wife as a token gift for a dinner party thrown in his honor.

Shortly after that fateful dinner, Heinrich Winslow was poisoned and died a gruesome death. The books were distributed among the Winslow brothers, and several other family members died after taking the *Faust* into their homes. No wonder they thought it was cursed.

Nobody loved a good book curse more than I did. I was so jealous of Abraham that I could barely think straight.

"Hallooo? Brooklyn? I come with food?"

My eyes lit up as a pretty young Indian woman poked her head inside the doorway.

"Hey, Vinnie, come on in," I said.

Her torn 501s and clunky biker-chick boots belied her chirpy voice and delicate features as she walked in carrying a shopping bag stuffed with little white cartons. "I don't wish to interrupt but Suzie and I agreed you would like our leftover Chinese food. This is true?"

"God, yes," I said, practically drooling as the tempting scent of orange chicken and beef with broccoli sauce wafted my way. I turned to Robin. "Vinnie's one of my neighbors." To Vinnie I said, "This is my friend Robin."

"Nice to meet you," Robin said.

Vinnie bowed her head. "I am Vinamra Patel, but please call me Vinnie."

Vinnie and her girlfriend, Suzie Stein, lived in a loft down the hall from me. They were wood sculptors and animal activists. Until I moved here, I'd never actually seen two chain-saw-wielding lesbians go to town on a three-hundred-pound hunk of redwood burl. It was impressive.

"This is really sweet, Vinnie," I said, staring into the stuffed shopping bag. "Thanks."

"We leave tonight for the Sierra Festival and didn't want to throw food away," she explained to Robin. "It will not go to waste here."

Robin shot me a look. "They know you so well."

My eyes narrowed. "They're attentive neighbors."

"She is a good little eater," Vinnie said with a soft smile. "I will put this in the kitchen." She disappeared down the hall that led to my living area.

Robin laughed. "No wonder you love this place."

She also knew me well. Yes, I liked to eat. A lot. I wasn't picky. I loved everything. Especially chocolate. And pizza. Oh, and red meat. I loved a good steak. I blamed it on my parents and the two-year "vegan phase" they'd foisted on me and my siblings during our formative years. I still had the emotional scars and enjoyed reminding them of the pain whenever they lit up the barbecue grill.

"Everything is in the fridge," Vinnie said in her singsong voice as she handed me a cluster of keys. Her eyes widened as she noticed the lumpy shards of leather and paper on my table. "This is your new work?"

"Yes," I said proudly.

Her gaze darted to Robin and her forehead creased in distaste. "It is . . . very nice."

Robin snorted. "You mean 'It's a pile of rancid crap'?"

Vinnie nodded. "As you say."

"Thanks so much for the food, Vinnie," I said, shaking the key ring. "You and Suzie enjoy the art festival. I'll take good care of Pookie and Splinters."

Vinnie didn't seem concerned about the fate of her

cats. She just stared at the decrepit book parts as if she were hypnotized or something.

I jiggled the keys again and she blinked. "You are most kind to attend to our darlings." Then she bowed one last time and took off.

Robin's brown eyes sparkled with amusement. "She left you in charge of her pets?"

"I can handle two cats for three days."

She laughed. "Famous last words from the woman with the largest plot at the commune pet cemetery."

"That's not fair." I grimaced. "I had goldfish. Goldfish always die."

"Come on. They banned you from the pet store."

"Shut up, please." I grabbed my purse. "Let's go."

She glanced down at my feet and her eyes widened. "Oh my God. You can take the girl out of the commune . . ."

"Oh dear." I kicked off my comfy sandals and slid into the pair of black pumps I'd left by the door. "Better?"

"Marginally."

"Such a bitch."

She laughed as she opened the door. "Okay, I love the suit and the heels are definitely an improvement. But I can't believe you still wear Birkenstocks."

"Just when I'm working." I sighed. "It's like my feet are molded to their shape."

Robin snorted delicately. "Like a geisha, only not."

"Sad but true." I turned off the light. "But for Abraham, I'll bite the bullet and wear heels."

"Don't worry; you look great," she said over her shoulder. "He's just going to die when he sees you."

Chapter 2

If I hadn't already decided by the age of eight to work with books, my first visit to the Covington Library would've sealed the deal.

The stately Italianate mansion with its museum and lovely gardens dominated two square blocks at the top of Pacific Heights. Walking through the immense iron doors of the Covington was like entering a Gothic cathedral. You could almost hear the secrets of the universe being whispered by the spirits that inhabited the massive, mahogany-lined room and all the books that sat within its walls.

There was magic here. Whether or not anyone walking inside would admit to a belief in the sacredness of the room, they would instinctively speak in hushed tones as they wound their way through the various rooms and exhibits.

The Covington Library collection was one of the largest and finest in the world. It boasted twelve of Shakespeare's folios on permanent display, as well as Walt Whitman's letters and one of the first Gutenberg Bibles. There were shimmering illuminations painted by medieval monks, sixteenth-century correspondence between Queen Elizabeth I and the third earl of Covington, and printed accounts of explorers from Christopher Columbus onward.

Those items shared space with rare first editions of works by Mary Shelley, Hans Christian Andersen, Agatha Christie and Henry David Thoreau. Faulkner, Hemingway and Kingsley Amis shared space with John Lennon's drawings, Stephen King's rejection letters, Kurt Cobain's diaries and an amazing collection of vintage baseball cards. The Covington collection was diverse and often quirky to say the least. To me, that was a major part of its appeal.

After a rollicking ride through the City, Robin dropped me off out front, then drove away to find a safe parking place for her beloved Porsche Speedster. I didn't bother to wait for her because I knew she'd take her time and make a grand entrance. I just wanted to get inside and see Abraham and the books.

I made my way through the crowd of well-dressed, chatty people gathered in the wide, marble-floored foyer, finally breaking through to the main exhibit room, where I almost slammed right into Abraham.

His eyes widened when he realized it was me. "Punkin Pie!" He grabbed me in a bear hug so tight I almost passed out, but at least he seemed happy to see me. "I'm so glad you made it."

"Me, too," I said, gasping for air. The man was bigger than a bull and twice as genteel. Tonight he wore a subdued dark suit that couldn't begin to tame the wild man within—or the unruly mop of hair that grew in a thick black mass of curls. My father always said Abraham's hair should have its own zip code.

Abraham was a force of nature, occasionally blustering, sometimes destructive, always stubborn and brilliant. He smelled of musty books and peppermint tea, and I clung to him for an extra moment just to enjoy his scent.

I'd missed him, loved him like a favorite uncle. This was the first time I'd seen him since severing our business relationship, but he was acting as if we'd never been apart. It was a little weird, but I was happy.

With his arm still around my shoulder, he waved madly to a woman standing a few feet away. My entire body shook as he cried out, "Doris, come meet Punkin—er, Brooklyn!"

A petite, frail woman in a black and gold Chanel suit waved back absently before continuing her conversation with the tall, balding man next to her.

"She can do wonders for your career, Punkin," he whispered loudly.

As we waited for Doris, I had a few more seconds to catch my breath, look around and try to forget that he'd used that horrid childhood nickname of mine three times now. Yes, I'd once had a little obsession with pumpkin pie at Thanksgiving. Hadn't everyone?

I guess I could forgive him as long as he was about to introduce me to someone who could help my business. That was enough to tell me he'd let go of his anger at my leaving him. Not that I expected him to actually discuss it. Abraham was a male from the old school—strong, silent, occasionally brooding. Except when he was ranting about something. Then he was anything but silent.

Smiling, I gazed up at Abraham. "How have you been?"

"Ah, life is good, Brooklyn," he said, squeezing me again briefly. "I didn't think it could get any better, but it can."

"Really?" I'd never heard my grumpy mentor sound so upbeat. "I'm thrilled for you."

From sômewhere above us, a string quartet began to play a Haydn serenade. I gazed up at the three-story-high coffered ceiling and the delicate wrought-iron balconies of the second and third floors. The musicians were seated on the third floor, overlooking the main hall, with acres of bookshelves providing the backdrop. On both of the higher floors, tall shelves of books circumnavigated the main hall, broken up by narrow aisles of more books leading back into cozy reading rooms and study corners. There were more nooks and crannies than a hobbit hole and I could still picture myself as an eight-year-old book lover, visiting for the first time and wandering the elaborate mazes. No wonder I fell for the place.

More guests were moving into the main hall and filling the space with lively conversation and elegant evening wear. Laughter competed with the music as tuxedoed waiters emerged with trays of champagne-filled flutes and delicate hors d'oeuvres. I rubbed Abraham's arm affectionately. "Everything looks fabulous. It's so exciting."

"Thanks, sweetheart," he said. "You're looking especially nifty tonight."

I sighed. *Nifty?* Who said that anymore? I liked it.

His arm muscles tightened and he swore under his breath. I glanced up and saw that his face had turned ashen.

"What is it, Abraham? What's wrong?"

"Baldacchio!" he whispered angrily. "I can't believe that two-faced crook had the balls to show up here tonight."

"You're kidding." I started to turn but he grabbed me.

"Don't look!" he cried. "I don't want him to see we're wasting breath talking about him."

"Tell me when."

He gripped my arm. "Okay. Over your left shoulder. Wait. Okay, now."

I tried to be casual as I turned to stare across the crowded space. At first I barely recognized the greasy-haired, shrunken man in the corner, but then he grinned slyly and there was no doubt it was Enrico Baldacchio, Abraham's most detested archrival in the small world that was bookbinding. Over the years, they had undermined each other's reputations by spreading gossip and stealing lucrative commissions out from under each other.

"I'd heard you were working together again on some project for the Book Guild," I said. "Was that just a vicious rumor?"

"No." Abraham looked ready to spit nails. "The Book Guild begged me to do it and I tried, but had to cut him loose again. The man can't be trusted. He's a liar and a thief."

I snuck another peek across the room. Baldacchio was talking animatedly to Ian McCullough, the Covington's head curator and an old college friend of my brother Austin—and my ex-fiancé. A woman stood at Ian's side with her arm tucked into his. When she turned her head, I gasped and looked away.

"What is it, Punk?" Abraham asked.

"Minka LaBoeuf."

I appreciated Abraham's quick frown. "I'm surprised she's here tonight."

Abraham knew Minka LaBoeuf?

Oh yes, bookbinding was a small world. She had a lot of nerve showing up anywhere within two city blocks of me. I silently fumed. Of all the bitches in all the world . . .

Years ago, Minka and I had been grad school classmates in the art and architecture department at Harvard. I didn't know her well, but whenever our paths crossed, I would catch a weird vibe of anger or contempt—for me. It was disconcerting but I did my best to ignore her.

One day, after I was singled out for my superior gold-finishing work by a professor in a papermaking class, Minka walked over to my worktable to see my work, or so I thought. Instead, she'd concealed a skiving knife, a very sharp tool used for paring leather, with which she tried to spear my hand. She barely missed my radial artery as well as several vital nerves and muscles, and swore it was an accident, but I'd seen the calculation and derision in her shifty eyes.

I found out later that she was crazy in love with my boyfriend at the time. Crazy in a bad, bad way. She'd been trying to find a way to get me out of the picture. Fortunately, soon after the knife incident, she dropped out and I went on to get my Master's degree.

Our paths crossed again the semester I taught a leaf attachment course at the University of Texas at Austin. She tried to audit my class and I was unnerved enough to think she still might be stalking me. Call me cuckoo, but after finding two flat tires on my car, then discovering a dead cat on my front porch, I went to the administrative offices and got her removed from the class. I seriously feared for my safety, and even imagined her trying to jam my head between the boards of a book press or something.

Now here she was at the Covington, clinging to Ian. Did she know I'd been engaged to him a few years back? It wasn't a secret. What game was she playing now?

"You know her," I said flatly.

"Not well," he admitted. "She's part-time staff, so I used her for some of the Winslow restoration work. She came across as charming and efficient, but problems erupted as soon as she started. Two of my best people threatened to quit, so I took her off the project."

I could barely watch as she laughed and yakked like an intimate friend of both Ian's and Baldacchio's. On tonight of all nights, the opening of Abraham's exhibition. I had to wonder, was she here because of me? Everyone in the business knew he'd been my teacher and mentor. Was I completely paranoid?

I would've loved to pursue the topic of Minka's shortcomings and find out how in the world she'd finagled a job at the Covington in the first place, but Abraham's friend Doris interrupted us just then, grabbing Abraham's arm and giving it a vigorous shake.

"Now, what were you yelling about, old man?" she said.

I almost snorted.

"Doris Bondurant," Abraham said formally, "I'd like to introduce my former assistant and now my greatest competition, Brooklyn Wainwright. Brooklyn, this is my old friend Doris Bondurant."

"Watch who you're calling old, buster," she said, and elbowed Abraham in the stomach. She turned to me and shook my hand. "Hello, dear."

"It's such a pleasure to meet you," I said. Along with being Covington Library trustees, Doris and Theodore Bondurant were on the board of at least a half dozen charitable organizations around San Francisco, and their names were synonymous with the arts and high society. On a good day they were probably worth a few billion dollars, so Doris could afford to be feisty.

Her hand was gnarled and covered in age spots, but her handshake was strong enough to make me cry uncle.

"I've heard a potful of good things about you from this guy, missy," she said, pointing her thumb at Abraham. "I'd like to see some of your work around here one of these days." Her voice had the gravelly character of a lifelong smoker's.

"Thank you, Mrs. Bondurant. That's very kind of you."

She wagged a finger at me. "First of all, I'm not kind. And second, you call me Doris."

I smiled. "All right, Doris."

She winked. "That's better. Now, look, people think I'm a mucky-muck around here, but mostly I just love books."

"Me, too."

"Glad to hear it," she said. "Now, this big lug tells me you know your way around a bookbinding, so I'm going to send you some business."

I sent Abraham a grateful look and he waggled his eyebrows at me. "I'd be honored."

"Do you have a business card?"

"Um, sure." I fumbled in my bag, found my cards and handed one to her. She peered at it for a few seconds before nodding.

"I'll call you." She slipped my card into her clutch purse, glanced around the room, then patted Abraham's barrel chest. "I'm going to track down Teddy and hit the bar before it gets too crowded, but then I want that behind-the-scenes tour you promised me."

"Yes, ma'am," Abraham said, grinning.

She winked at me, smacked Abraham's arm and wiggled her fingers good-bye as she walked away.

I turned to Abraham. "I love her."

"She's a classic, all right." He checked his watch and swore under his breath. "I'd better run. I've got some business to attend to."

"Of course. I won't keep you."

"Look, why don't you mingle for an hour or so, then come downstairs to my workshop? I'll give you a sneak preview of the *Faust*." He leaned in close and wiggled his eyebrows. "Don't tell me you're not dying to see it."

I grinned. "I'd love to see it."

"It's spectacular, trust me."

"I do, Abraham."

He gave me another quick squeeze. "You're my good girl."

Tears stung my eyes. The first time he'd ever said that to me, I was eight years old and miserable. My stupid brothers had used my favorite book, *The Secret Garden*, as a football and I'd found it lying in the dirt, its front cover hanging by threads and half the pages ripped or shredded. My mother suggested I go see the commune's bookbinder to get it fixed.

Abraham took one look and ordered my brothers into the studio, where he promised them any number of chilling reprisals if they ever damaged another book again. After scaring the bejeezus out of them, he sat them down and gave them a quick lesson in book arts and history—the kid-friendly version—followed by an explanation of what family meant and why they should cherish and honor their sister by respecting what was precious to her.

I fell in love with Abraham that day.

Now I sniffed back tears and said, "Abraham, I just wish we—"

"Not another word." He gripped my shoulders. "I admit I've been a stubborn old fool, but I've recently learned a valuable lesson."

"You have?"

"Yes," he said with a firm nod. "Life's too damn short to spend time regretting or wishing for what might've been. From now on, I plan to live in the present and enjoy every minute."

My throat was tight but I managed to whisper, "I've missed you, Abraham."

He pulled me in for one last hug. "Ah, Punkin, that's music to these old ears." He let me go, but added, "We won't be strangers anymore, agreed?"

"Absolutely."

"Good. I'll see you downstairs in a while."

"I'll be there."

He walked away and would've vanished in the crowd, but his mop of hair was like a beacon. I watched him until he slipped through the doorway leading to the small West Gallery and disappeared.

I knew the West Gallery led to a series of smaller

display rooms that finally ended at the stairway that led to the basement where his temporary studio was located. One of the perks of working on a Covington exhibit was the free use of their state-of-the-art on-site workshops—if you could find your way through the jumbled warren of galleries and halls and stairways. Of course, if you were going to get lost, this was a great place to do it.

My heart felt as though a weight had been lifted. Abraham and I could go forward as friends and colleagues instead of the distant rivals I was afraid we'd become.

Feeling lighter, I moved toward the exhibit of Walt Whitman letters and photographs. The main hall was now filled to capacity with the cream of San Francisco society. Wall-to-wall old farts, as promised.

Thinking of old farts made me think of Robin, which in turn reminded me that I didn't have a drink in my hand.

As I scanned the room in search of the bar, my attention was drawn to the far side of the hall. Near a large panel of original Audubon paintings, one man stood alone, leaning against the wall, a wary stranger in this swarm of friends and fellow book lovers. He sipped a drink as he observed the crowd, the exhibits, the ambiance, yet he seemed to hold himself apart from it all.

I'd never seen him before. I would've remembered. He was over six feet tall and his hair was dark and closely cropped. His leanly muscled build exuded tough-guy strength, almost as if he'd just as soon use his fists as his charm to get what he wanted. I could appreciate that. There was pure male arrogance and more than a few secrets in his dark eyes as he glanced around the room.

When his gaze met mine, his eyes narrowed and he frowned. Directly at me. I wasn't mistaken. What was that all about?

His apparent disapproval was such an unexpected affront that I glowered right back at him. He didn't look away, continued to stare, and there was no way I was going to look away first. But the room began to shrink and I had to grip the railing in front of the Walt Whitman exhibit for a second.

I might've blinked. I hope not. But in that instant his frown disappeared, replaced by a look of bland disinterest as he once again surveyed the crowd.

He didn't look back at me. A good thing because I probably looked like a fool, heaving and panting for air.

I really needed to get out more.

More than a little annoyed with myself, I pushed my way through the crowd and by the time I made it to the bar, I was relatively sane again—until I saw who was pouring the drinks.

"Dad?"

"Hi, sweetie," he said as though this were an everyday occurrence, his tending bar at a high-society opening, pouring me a glass of cabernet sauvignon without asking whether I wanted one. Weird.

Well, of course I wanted the wine. That wasn't the weird part.

"Dad, what are you doing here?"

He nudged his eyeglasses up (they had a tendency

to slide down his nose), then handed me the wine. He poured two glasses of chardonnay and passed them off to another patron before turning back to me.

"Hey, babe, isn't this a gas?" he said, grinning. "Abraham swung this gig. The Covington's agreed to feature our wines at all their events from now on. Robson's totally psyched. Can you dig it?"

He went back to pouring and explaining the complexities of the wines to the others gathered around the bar while I took two deep swigs of excellent cabernet sauvignon. It wasn't the best way to savor a fine wine, but who could blame me? I'd been here less than half an hour and I was already wrung out.

Back in the seventies, my parents and Robin's parents and a few hundred of their closest friends, fellow Deadheads and seekers of wisdom, had followed their spiritual leader, Avatar Robson Benedict—or Guru Bob, as my siblings and I called him—to Sonoma County, where they created the Fellowship for Spiritual Enlightenment and Higher Artistic Consciousness. I couldn't say whether higher consciousness had anything to do with it, but it turned out to be a good investment. The commune lay on sixteen hundred acres of lush farmland, most of which were eventually turned into vineyards.

Dad had been a trust-fund baby disinherited by his father, who disapproved of my dad's free and easy lifestyle. By the time Grandfather decided to put Dad back in his will, it was too late to change his evil ways. Dad loved the low life, as he liked to call it.

It was no surprise how well he took to the wine-making life. He was a bon vivant down to his toes.

Nowadays, Dad ran the commune winery with my

older brother, Austin, and my sister Savannah. My brother Jackson was in charge of the vineyards. I wondered whether they were here tonight as well.

"How's the cab, Brooks?" Dad asked.

"Mm, perfect," I mumbled, taking a smaller sip of wine and properly rolling it around in my mouth as I scanned the crowd, looking for Robin. That was my story, anyway, until I couldn't take it anymore and finally took a peek back at the corner where I'd last seen the frowning man. He'd moved away from the Audubon exhibit, but I tracked him down easily enough over by the circular Shakespearean display.

I watched as he prowled the exterior edge of the wide room, studying the crowd, casting an occasional look at the exhibits, taking it all in. He moved like a panther stalking its prey. I tried to look away but couldn't. I'm sorry, but he was incredibly hot and sexy. You didn't find that at the library every day.

I watched him raise one eyebrow and bite back a smile. Intrigued, I followed the direction of his gaze across the room to the open doorway where Robin stood with one hand on her hip, checking out the crowd, looking sassy and vivacious as she finally made her splashy grand entrance.

It figured. I'd earned a foul-tempered frown from Mr. Hot 'n' Sexy, while Robin got a raised eyebrow and a smiley face. I hated to be a whiner but sometimes life sucked a lot.

I sighed, held my glass out and Dad automatically filled it. Sometimes it really helped to have friends in high places. Like behind the bar, pouring drinks.

I left my dad charming the guests and with my wineglass full, I darted in and around the displays, enjoying the pretty music as I greeted some people I knew. It looked as though Abraham had invited every bookbinder in Northern California tonight. I couldn't blame him. This show was a triumph, right down to the salmon- and crème-fraiche-topped blini I munched as I wandered.

A large corner of the main library room had been set aside for the Winslow exhibit, and a tasteful banner pronounced it ONE HERO'S LITERARY JOURNEY: GERMAN LITERATURE AND PHILOSOPHY FROM THE 17TH CENTURY THROUGH THE 20TH CENTURY—THE COLLECTION OF HEINRICH WINSLOW.

The displays told in letters, photos and museum placards the story of Heinrich Winslow, who had owned a large construction firm in Nazi Germany and used his powerful position to save more than seven hundred Jews from being shipped off to concentration camps. It was all eerily similar to that of Oskar Schindler's "List." It made me wonder how many other ordinary German citizens had dared to defy Hitler and the Nazis.

Heinrich's life had recently been the subject of a History Channel special, and I assumed that unexpected coup would bring even more interest to the exhibit.

I strolled along the rows, checking out the other books in the Winslow collection, notably the 1812 first edition of the Grimm brothers' fairy tales with its elegant, hand-painted illustrations, and several of Wagner's original opera scores with his notes penciled in the margins.

There were also letters from Holocaust victims and survivors along with photographs from that time. The presentation was emotional and disturbing, yet uplifting at the same time.

Despite the subject matter, the crowd was vivacious and friendly. The music soared above the hullabaloo of conversation, and the food and alcohol flowed.

It had been more than an hour since I'd last seen Abraham, so I decided to venture downstairs to view the *Faust*. After stopping to refresh my wine, I slipped down a quiet hall to find the ladies' room and freshen my lipstick.

Revived and refreshed, I passed the alcove that led to the public telephones and heard a man whisper heatedly, "That lousy son of a bitch won't get away with this."

"Please don't do anything foolish," a woman said, her voice simmering with worry.

"I never do anything foolish," he said. "I leave that to you women."

"Oh, Daddy," a younger woman said, her voice high and whiny.

"Unfortunately, dear, Daddy's right," the older woman said. "Let's not forget how this fiasco got started."

"At least you admit it," the man said bitterly. "Now I've got to figure out the best way to handle this asshole and the bind he's put us in."

"Language, dear," the woman cautioned.

"She's heard worse," he argued.

"Look," the woman said, "let's just forget the problems with the book and try to have a nice time tonight."

"Can I leave?" the girl asked. "This is so boring."

"Your legacy is boring?" the man said, his voice

rising. The trio marched out of the alcove, saw me and stopped dead.

I recognized them. Conrad and Sylvia Winslow and their lovely daughter, Meredith, San Francisco's answer to Paris Hilton. They were the present owners of the Winslow collection and wealthy beyond belief, but unlike Abraham's friends, Doris and Teddy Bondurant, the Winslows liked to flaunt their money, creating daily fodder for the local paparazzi.

I prayed I didn't look like a deer caught in the headlights as I smiled, said a gracious "Good evening" and kept walking. When in doubt, act as if you own the damn place.

As they strutted off, I wondered who might be the "son of a bitch" Mr. Winslow had been referring to. And what was his wife talking about when she said there were "problems with the book"? If there were any problems with any books, Abraham would know. I quickly headed for the West Gallery.

I realized I'd lost track of both Robin and the frowning man. It was just as well, since the last thing I wanted to see was the two of them flirting with each other. And how silly did that make me sound? I'd never even met the man.

Temporary insanity. Too many long hours spent in the company of moldy old books. Whatever. I took another gulp of wine as I popped through the West Gallery door and headed for the basement stairs to find Abraham.

The stairwell lighting was low and the stairs were narrow and steep. My high heels didn't help matters, so I took each step slowly, clutching the rail with one hand and my wineglass with the other as I descended.

Below me, I could hear staccato footsteps ascending quickly toward me. As I rounded the landing, a woman jerked to a stop to avoid barging into me.

I gasped in shock. She looked at me.

And screamed.

Chapter 3

"Mother?"

"Whoa!" My mom laughed nervously and the sound echoed in the stairwell. "Brooklyn! Whew, I'm glad it's you and not your father."

Not the greeting I'd expected. But nothing was meeting my expectations this evening.

She clung to the stair rail, catching her breath. She wasn't exactly dressed for a high-society art opening in her pink and white jogging outfit and gym shoes. Her dark blond hair was pulled back in a ponytail and her skin glistened with moisture as though she'd been working out for the last hour.

"Mother, what're you doing here?"

She glanced anxiously over her shoulder. I did, too, suddenly paranoid. Assured we were alone, she whispered, "I needed to see Abraham privately."

"Tonight?" I frowned. "It's kind of the opposite of private around here, Mom. What's going on?"

She bit her lip. "Nothing."

I almost laughed. "Nothing?"

"That's right, nothing." She fisted her hand on her hip, annoyed. "He stood me up."

"What? Who stood you up? Abraham?"

"I can't talk about it."

"But Mom, you—"

She held up her hand to shut me up, then closed her eyes, rolled her shoulders and put her palms together, yoga-style. I recognized the move. She was finding her center, calming herself, aligning her chakras, balancing her core. She was one with the universe. Good grief.

"Earth to Mom."

She slowly opened her eyes and bowed her head. "All is well."

"No, Mom, all is *weird*. What're you—"

"Om shanti shanti shanti," she chanted, as she reached out and touched the center of my forehead, my third eye, the seat of higher consciousness where inner peace reigned.

"Mother." There was a warning note to my voice.

"Brooklyn, breathe. You worry too much." She rubbed her fingers lightly across the frown lines of my forehead, then smiled sweetly. "Peace, baby girl."

I almost groaned. She'd passed through to another place and now wore what my siblings and I liked to call her Sunny Bunny face. When she clicked on that eerie, happy mask, all battles were over.

I shook my head in defeat. Nothing penetrated the Sunny Bunny face.

"We're not finished here, mom," I said. "I want to know what's going on."

"Perhaps, in time." She glanced around again. "Do me a favor, sweetie."

"Okay." I said it hesitantly.

She patted my cheek. "Don't tell your father you saw me here."

"What?"

"*Namasté*, honey. Gotta go."

Before I could stop her, she zigzagged around me and raced away, up the stairs. My yoga mom was speedy when she wanted to be.

I stared at the empty stairway for a few seconds. So, it was official: My mother had gone insane. The upside was, back at the commune, nobody would notice.

But seriously, what the heck was that all about?

I took a big sip of wine, tried to lighten up, align my own chakras, whatever, and continued downstairs.

My mother was the most open, honest person I knew. She couldn't keep a secret to save her life, or so I'd always thought. Was something going on between her and Abraham? Clearly the answer was yes. The real question was—*what* was going on between her and Abraham?

And did I really want to know the answer?

"Nothing's going on," I told myself, then repeated it a few times. Of course there was nothing going on. Mom and Dad had been sweethearts ever since they'd met at the tie-dyed T-shirt booth during a Grateful Dead weekend blowout at the Ventura Fairgrounds in 1972. We'd heard the story often enough to recite it by heart.

Mom was nineteen, Dad was twenty-two. Mom wore frayed, button-fly cutoffs with a short, tight T-shirt that read like an advertisement for a local motel. BED & BECKY, it said. And yes, Mom's name is

Becky. We all figured Dad was probably stoned, not to mention turned on, but he insisted he was enchanted by her sweet, natural spirit.

They made their early years together sound like ·a fairy tale. But the bottom line was, my parents were still lovey-dovey to this day. They'd stayed together through good times and bad, through six kids and major moves and family issues and commune politics. The very idea that Mom and Abraham were . . . no. Ugh. Not that I didn't love Abraham but . . . no, forget it.

I know it sounds sappy, but deep down inside, I liked to think my parents represented the possibility of everlasting love. Meaning, maybe someday, I might experience my own version of that. It had eluded me so far, but it could happen.

I took another fortifying gulp of wine, banished all thoughts of Mom and . . . you know, and kept going.

When I reached the basement level, I followed the signs and arrows pointing the way to Conservation and Restoration. After several series of switchbacks and two sets of double doors, I finally ended up at one end of a long, deserted hallway. There were doors on both sides of the hall, probably twenty all together. These were the book restorers' workrooms. Every door was closed.

"Abraham?" I called.

Nothing.

I supposed he was intent on keeping the priceless *Faust* under wraps and behind closed doors, so I would have to hunt him down. I finished off the glass of wine before trying the handle on the first door. It was locked. Same for the next three. The fifth door was unlocked but the room was completely empty.

The next door opened easily.

Every light was on full blast. The room was glaringly bright. Papers were scattered everywhere. Tools and brushes lay in disarray on the counters and on the floor. Cabinet drawers were pulled out and upturned. A high stool lay on the floor next to the center worktable.

What a mess. I stepped inside to look around.

That was when I saw Abraham, lying on the cold cement floor. A pool of dark liquid seeped from under him.

"Oh my God." My glass slipped from my hand and shattered on the floor. Spots began to spin in front of my eyes. I sucked in a breath, ran over and fell on my knees by his side.

"Abraham!"

His arms were wrapped tightly around his chest. Alive? *Please, God, alive.*

I was screaming, couldn't help it.

"Abraham. Wake up." I tried to pull him into my arms, but he was so heavy I couldn't budge him. "Oh, please don't die."

I grabbed his shoulders and shook him hard before I realized that was a bad idea. I leaned over and held him close to me. "I'm sorry. Did I hurt you? Oh God, I'm sorry, so sorry."

I felt him stir.

His eyelids fluttered, and I almost fainted with relief. "Oh God, you're alive. Thank you. I'll get help. Don't worry."

He gazed up at me, his eyes blurry. He coughed, then muttered something.

I leaned closer. "What?"

"De-vil," he whispered. His arms relaxed around his chest and his jacket loosened.

"What are you saying?"

He coughed again. "Remember . . . the . . . devil."

A thick, heavy book slipped out from inside his jacket. I quickly snatched it before it slid onto the bloody floor. Instinct, I guess, ingrained in me from childhood. Save the book. I gaped at the faded black leather binding. Once-elegant gold tooling created a pale border of fleur-de-lis around the front edges of the cover, and each flower point was studded with bloodred gems. Rubies? Ornate but rusted brass clasps in the shape of claws held the book closed.

Goethe's *Faust*.

My gaze darted back to Abraham. His lips trembled as he formed a slight smile.

I shoved the book inside my suit jacket.

He nodded his head in approval. At least, I thought it was a nod. Then his eyes glazed over and flickered closed.

"No." I grabbed his jacket. "No. Don't you dare. Abraham. Wake up. Oh God. Don't—"

His head slumped to the side.

"No! No, please—"

"Let him go."

"Yikes!" I snatched my hands away. Abraham sagged to the floor. I stared at my hands. They were covered in blood. I screamed again.

"That's enough. Stand up and move away from him."

I whipped my head around. The frowning man from upstairs stood at the door holding a gun pointed directly at me.

And yeah, he was still frowning.

I stared, unable to move. The lights were too bright. Shards of color twirled like kaleidoscopes at the edges of my vision. Frowning Man waved the gun as if to catch my attention, but he was getting blurry.

I felt myself sway. And everything faded to black.

Calloused hands pushed my hair back from my forehead.

"Women," a male voice muttered in scorn.

I groaned.

"Wake up, now." The voice was clipped, British, impatient. It had to be the frowning man. Who else? From his tone I imagined he wasn't exactly beaming at me.

He patted my cheek. "Come on, snap out of it." He smelled like heaven. Manly and warm with a hint of green forest and a touch of leather and—

He slapped my cheek a little too vigorously. "I know you're awake. Come on now. That's it. Come about."

Come about?

"I'm not a boat," I grumbled, and shifted away from him. There were cushions beneath me. A couch. How'd I get on a couch?

"Good, you're awake." He gave me another smack for good measure and I managed to reach up and grab his hand.

With one eye opened, I glared at him. "Stop hitting me."

"Ah. You're feeling better."

"No thanks to you." I pushed my way up to a sitting position. "Where am I?"

"Two doors down from where I found you."

He'd found me with Abraham. The memory came rushing back. My tears welled up and spilled over.

"Oh, for God's sake." He reached in his breast pocket and thrust his white linen handkerchief into my hand. Then he stood and began to pace.

I was about to thank him for the handkerchief when he said, "You'd better sit all the way up or you'll likely drown yourself."

"Oh, be quiet." Then I blew my nose and dabbed away the tears, determined not to cry anymore in front of this insensitive jerk. I sat straighter and folded my arms tightly around my chest—and realized with alarm that the book I'd been hiding was gone.

I jumped off the couch. "Where's my—"

"Looking for this?" He held up the black leather-bound *Faust*, clutching it with a white dust cloth.

"That's mine," I blurted.

"Yours?"

"What I mean is, it's not yours."

"It's not?"

"It belongs to the Winslow collection. Abraham gave it to me."

"Gave it to you?"

I clenched my fists. "Stop repeating my words."

"Repeating?" He pursed his lips in a smirk.

I no longer cared that he was sexy and smelled good. He was too incredibly annoying.

I took a deep breath. "Abraham gave the book to me for safekeeping."

"Of course he did."

"You don't need to be sarcastic," I said, glaring at him. "He really did give it to me."

He grunted. "Right."

"Who the hell are you?"

He carefully placed the book down on the side counter. "We'll get to that."

"We'll get to it right now or I'm leaving." I swept my hair back from my face and said, "Why am I even talking to you? I'm out of here."

He stepped in front of me. "You're not going anywhere. The police arrived just moments ago and they'll want to question you."

"Fine. I want to talk to them, too."

"You won't have long to wait. They're upstairs handling the crowd right now. They'll be down shortly to survey the murder scene and then they'll have a little talk with you."

I gulped and sat back down on the couch. Why did that phrase make this horrible night feel even worse? "Murder scene?"

"Oh, that's very well played," he said. "Should've known you'd be trouble the moment I saw you."

I scowled. "What are you talking about?"

"This innocent routine." He strolled about the room with his hands in his pockets. "I'm certain the local police will be impressed with your little fainting act, but I saw you in that room with Karastovsky."

Appalled, I pushed myself off the couch and cornered him. "You think I killed Abraham?"

"You have his blood on your hands."

I looked at my hands. Maybe I wavered because he grabbed me by the shoulders, shook me and said, "Oh no, you don't. No more fainting."

I slapped his hands away. "Let go of me. I'm not going to faint."

"Then stop breathing so heavily."

"What is wrong with you?"

He leaned back against the counter and crossed his ankles nonchalantly. "You killed a man and there's something wrong with *me*?"

"I didn't kill anyone!"

"Tell it to the cops."

"How dare you?" I sucked in a much-needed breath before continuing. "You don't even know me. Abraham Karastovsky was my friend. My teacher. He—he was like my uncle. We talked tonight and he was so happy and—and then I found him in that room. He died in my arms." I felt my throat close and had to stop. I put my hand over my eyes.

"Oh, here we go again," he said. "I'm sure the local cops will be properly hoodwinked."

I shrieked. I admit it. Then I gritted my teeth, looked him in the eye and said, "First of all, I never faint. Well, except for tonight. It was the blood. I have this thing about blood. Never mind, why am I explaining myself to you?"

"I have no idea."

I paced away, then whipped around. "Second, I don't give a damn what you think. I did not kill Abraham Karastovsky. I know the truth and that's all that matters. And by the way, I'm thinking the cops are going to be interested in hearing your alibi, too, pal."

He snorted with contempt.

"And third," I continued, "no one says hoodwinked anymore."

His eyes narrowed to angry pinpoints as he leaned closer. "Hoodwinked. It means to trick, deceive, dupe."

I jabbed his lapel. "I know what it means, but nobody uses it outside of a Dickens novel."

We stared at each other with suspicion and ire.

I shook my head. "Why am I even talking to you? You're obviously just another insane person carrying a gun." Oh, crap, he was carrying a gun. He could've used it to kill Abraham. I felt sick all over again.

"Never mind," I said. "Nice talking to you. See you around."

He blocked my path again. "You're not going anywhere."

"And you're going to stop me?"

"It appears I already have," he said with another one of his smirks.

I threw up my hands and stormed around the room. "You are the most annoying man I've ever met." I turned and pointed at him. "No, wait. I haven't actually met you, have I? I don't have a clue who you are and yet you slander and falsely imprison me just because—"

"Enough already." He pulled a sterling silver card holder from the breast pocket of his expensive black suit and handed it to me. "Derek Stone."

I read it aloud. "Stone Security. Derek Stone, Principal." Underneath his name it said COMMANDER, ROYAL NAVY, RET. On the next line it said SECURITY AND INVESTIGATIONS. and in smaller letters in the lower left-hand corner the card said A DIVISION OF CAUSEWAY CORNWALL INTERNATIONAL.

I looked up at him. "Causeway Cornwall is the underwriter for the Winslow exhibition."

"Exactly." He nodded at me as if I were a particularly bright three-year-old. "And Stone Security specializes in arts and antiquities. There were certain security issues that required my team's presence at the opening tonight. We're working hand in hand with the local police."

I resisted groaning. "So why didn't you just say so, Commander?"

He shrugged. "I was having such a good time, it must've slipped my mind."

I rolled my eyes, stuck his business card in my pocket, took a breath and cautiously held out my hand. "I'm Brooklyn Wainwright."

He started to take my hand, but stopped abruptly. I looked down and again saw the blood caked on my fingers.

The door swung open with a bang.

"Brooklyn, there you are! Oh my God!" Robin, tears streaming, ran across the room and pulled me into her arms. "I just heard about Abraham. It can't be true."

"It's true," I whispered, and lost it for real. I sobbed on her shoulder, finally releasing all the tears that had been choking me.

We stayed like that, hugging and rocking back and forth, for a few minutes, until Robin sniffled and said in a low voice, "Leave it to Abraham to make this exhibit unforgettable."

I gave her a watery smile. "He always was a showman."

She hiccupped and we both laughed; then fresh tears erupted.

"Forgive me, ladies," Derek interrupted. I'd forgotten he was still there, observing our emotional waterworks. I refused to care what he thought of us.

"Who's Double-Oh-Seven?" Robin whispered in my ear.

I sniffed. "Security."

"Extremely hot," she said.

"A jerk," I countered. "And touchy."

"I like the sound of that."

Derek coughed discreetly. "The local police will question you now, Ms. Wainwright."

Oh boy.

"Why are they questioning you?" Robin asked.

"I—I found him," I said, and stared at my hands.

She shrank back. "Oh my God! Brooklyn, no! Is that his blood? Oh my God."

I felt my lip trembling and looked up at Derek. "Can I wash my hands first?"

"It's evidence," he said, his voice cool. "Leave it."

Homicide inspector Nathan Jaglow, tall, probably in his fifties, with short, curly gray hair and a sad smile, was a very patient man. His partner, Inspector Janice Lee, was Asian American, pretty but painfully thin, with long, lustrous black hair. They took notes, asked questions and occasionally made me repeat myself, just so they could write my words down exactly as I'd stated them.

They'd commandeered another binder's workroom and they sat across from me at a high worktable. I didn't know whether they were both pretending to play good cop until someone else showed up to play bad cop, but I liked them. Unlike Derek Stone, they seemed to believe me when I insisted I hadn't killed Abraham. However, that didn't keep them from asking me to go over my story in minute detail several times.

Early on, a crime scene technician swabbed my hands in order to test the blood to see if it matched Abraham's. I was allowed to wash my hands in the workroom sink, which made me feel somewhat better. I could now look at my hands without sliding to the floor.

Jaglow held up a large Ziploc baggie. Inside was a ten-inch knife with a wide, rounded blade. "Can you tell me what this is?"

The knife was smeared with blood.

And there went my stomach again.

"Deep breaths, Ms. Wainwright," Inspector Lee said, her gravelly voice calm and strangely seductive. "I know it's difficult but we really need your expertise right now. Take your time."

I inhaled deeply, then exhaled, and repeated that several times, telling myself to relax.

"It's called a—a Japanese paper knife," I said, my voice sounding hoarse. "It's made in Japan." Duh, I thought. I took a sip of water and continued. "It's used to cut paper." Again, duh. I could no longer think straight.

"You're doing great," Inspector Jaglow said. "So this is a tool used for cutting paper. Paper used in making or repairing books, I presume."

I nodded. "Is that what killed him?"

He paused for a moment, then said, "We still need to determine that."

"He was shot, Ms. Wainwright," Inspector Lee said evenly.

"But the blood on the knife . . ." I gulped.

"He might've grabbed it," she said, apparently unconcerned that her partner was glowering at her. "Do you own a gun, Ms. Wainwright?"

"What? No." The only gun I'd seen lately belonged to Derek Stone, but he was one of them. Or so he'd said.

Jaglow's eyes narrowed in on me. "What are you thinking, Ms. Wainwright?"

I chewed my lip, unsure what to say next. They'd worn out my last nerve. All I could picture was Abraham, so happy tonight, so glad we were friends again. I wanted to hug him and hear him laugh. Against my will, tears sprang to my eyes.

The two cops exchanged glances.

"I guess that's enough for tonight," Jaglow said as he stood and slipped his notebook into his back pocket. The action pulled his jacket back and I could see his gun in the holster under his arm. Yet another reminder that I wasn't in Kansas anymore. "We've got your contact information and I assume you're not leaving town anytime soon?"

Was that cop humor? I'd probably laugh about it later.

"No, I'm not going anywhere."

"Good. I'm sure we'll have more questions for you."

"That's fine," I said, sliding off the stool. "Really. Anything you want to know, please call me. I want to help find whoever did this."

"We appreciate that." They led me out of the workroom and pointed the way back down the hall to the room where I'd left Robin and Derek Stone.

Derek came out into the hall just then, and as he passed me, he whispered, "I'll be watching you like a hawk, Ms. Wainwright."

My stomach knotted up. I didn't know where to turn. Uniformed police officers stood guard in front of several of the doors to the different studios. Yellow crime scene tape was strewn across the double doors at the far end.

"Commander," Inspector Lee called. "We'd like to meet in here if that's acceptable to you."

I turned in disbelief. They actually called him Commander? And cared about his preferences? I'd thought he might be lying, but he really was working with the local cops. I was so screwed.

I surreptitiously clenched my fists as I continued the long walk down the hall. It wasn't pleasant to recall how many ways I'd insulted the commander, but at least those thoughts distracted me from the highly disturbing fact that I'd blatantly lied to two San Francisco homicide inspectors tonight.

Okay, maybe I hadn't exactly *lied*, but if omission was a sin, I was guilty as charged. Not once, but twice.

First of all, I'd never mentioned to Inspectors Jaglow and Lee the words Abraham said before he died. I tried to convince myself the reason I'd left out that little detail was that I couldn't be sure exactly what Abraham had said.

But that was me, lying to myself. He'd said, "Remember the devil." I'd never forget it. But what did he mean? Maybe he'd been referring to the book. *Faust* was the story of a man who sold his soul to the devil. Did I need to read the book? Maybe there was something in there that would give me the first clue to what he'd been talking about. Who was the devil? And why was I supposed to remember him?

My mind was spinning and I realized I was seriously exhausted. I would need a good night's sleep before I could begin to figure out what the words meant.

I stopped, leaned against the wall of the overly bright hallway, closed my eyes and faced the truth. Omitting Abraham's last words to the inspector had nothing to do with the real reason why I felt truly sick with guilt.

No, the real sin of omission occurred when I'd neglected to tell the police that I had seen and spoken to the one person who had the means and opportunity to actually murder Abraham Karastovsky.

My mother.

Chapter 4

Standing by myself in the long hall, I was abruptly aware of a disturbance in the Force. Chilled, I scanned the hallway in both directions. I'd felt this way before and knew that Minka LaBoeuf was somewhere in the vicinity. I couldn't see her but it didn't matter. She was close. Too close. I could smell the sulfur.

Then she walked out of the workroom two doors down from Abraham's and spied me through the crowd of police officers milling around. Adrenaline spiked. The exhaustion I'd felt seconds ago was history as an overwhelming urge to attack her, to punch her in the stomach and run, took over. It totally irked me that the woman could fuel my rage faster than anyone I'd ever known, just by walking into the room.

As she walked toward me, Minka twirled a strand of hair around her middle finger, something she'd always done when she was nervous. Good to know she wasn't as confident as she tried to appear to be. And how had I missed the fact that under her short black leather jacket she wore a skintight black catsuit tucked into thigh-high black boots?

Was the world ready for Minka the Dominatrix?

Her lips were slathered in coral lipstick and she'd ringed her eyes with black kohl. As she came closer, I could see the body suit straining at the seams near her stomach. Was it wrong to be gleeful over the fact that she'd put on weight?

"Well, if it isn't Ms. High-and-Mighty herself," she said in that distinctively whiny voice that never failed to boil my blood. "Karma's a real bitch, isn't it?"

"You ought to know," I said. As comebacks went, that one sucked, but I was off my game.

She giggled and I shuddered. Her smile had always caused me more apprehension than her animosity did. It wasn't her fault, but the left side of her upper lip naturally curled up so that when she smiled, she looked like a snarling dingo.

Fear was a perfectly reasonable reaction, but I tried not to show it.

She studied me. "I probably shouldn't be seen chatting with you, now that you're a murder suspect. It could ruin my reputation."

"We're not chatting, and your reputation was ruined a long time ago." I sighed. Seriously, if I was going to trade barbs with Minka LaBoeuf, I needed to regroup.

"What are you doing down here, Minka?" I asked wearily.

"I work here," she said with a sneer. "That's more than I can say for you. I belong here. You don't. So you're not the one calling the shots this time. This time it's *your* ass on the hot seat. How does that make you feel, Brooks?"

"Don't call me Brooks," I snapped. Brooks was the nickname my family and close friends used. Like my old college boyfriend. The same boyfriend Minka had been so obsessed with that she'd picked up a wide-blade X-Acto knife and stabbed me in the hand.

"Whatever," she said.

I noticed some of her coral lipstick had migrated to her tooth and it gave me the strength to lob another round of insults her way.

"I know reality isn't your forte," I said. "But let me remind you that Abraham Karastovsky fired you from the Winslow job and I know that pissed you off."

"And your point, as if I care?"

"Now you're stuck in archives and we all know that's the bottom of the barrel."

"It's not so bad."

"Right. But see, here on earth we call that *motive* and I'm sure the police would love to hear all about it."

Her upper lip twitched and curled as her self-assurance slipped. She moved even closer and snapped her fingers back and forth in front of my face like some jive diva. "And I am so sure they would love to know who Abraham was hooking up with in his workshop earlier tonight."

Every nerve ending in my body jumped into high alert. Had she seen my mother down here? But Mom had insisted that Abraham didn't show up, so what was Minka talking about?

I grabbed her arm and whispered through clenched teeth, "Be careful, Minka."

She pulled away from me. "Or what? You'll kill me, too?"

"Don't be ridiculous." But I could see how someone could be pushed to the brink with her.

"Really? We both know you'd like nothing better than to—"

"Brooklyn?"

We both jumped back as Ian approached from down the hall. "Just the person I was looking for. Oh, hi, Minka."

Minka made a sound of disgust, then took off in the opposite direction, her shoulders rigid, the heels of her hooker boots pounding the hardwood surface as she fled.

"Where's she going?" Ian asked, frowning as he watched her stalk away.

"Straight to hell, I hope."

We both watched as a uniformed officer stopped Minka from going any farther. After a few tense words back and forth, he escorted her into a workroom, for questioning, I assumed. I didn't know whether to be pleased or worried, but decided to go with worried.

I turned to Ian. "What a horrible night, huh?"

"Huh?" He looked at me in complete surprise as though he hadn't realized I was standing there. This was the charmingly befuddled Ian I knew and loved.

We'd been engaged several years ago for almost six months until I took pity on him and broke it off. Thankfully, we were still good friends and if he was being honest, he'd concede he'd never been in love with me.

He'd professed his so-called love shortly after watching me produce an exact copy of a Dubuisson binding, right down to the gilded imprinting of one of Dubuisson's "one o'clock birds." Ian was easily impressed, though I must admit I was damn good.

See, Pierre-Paul Dubuisson was an eighteenth-century bookbinder, the royal binder to Louis XV of France. And one of his most celebrated signature designs was that of a bird with wings extended, facing one o'clock. The "one o'clock birds."

Only a fellow book geek would get excited about something like that, and Ian was geekier than most. I could picture our kids, scary little Poindexter types with leather-stained hands and annoying tics and constant questions. No, I'd done us all a favor by breaking up with him.

"Brooklyn?"

"Huh?" I blinked up at him. "Sorry, I zoned out." Did I tell you we were a pair? "What's up?"

"It's about the *Faust*."

I shivered. "What about it?"

"I need you to take over the restoration. Can you start tomorrow?"

"But . . ." What could I say? Images of Abraham passed like a slide show in my head. The party atmosphere earlier. The hugs. The shared laughter. Doris Bondurant playfully slugging him. Then the fear. Finding him dying. The whispered phrase. The book slipping out of his jacket. Then death. And blood. So much blood.

The curse.

"Ian, you know I would help if I could, but . . ."

His expression was sorrowful. "I know, I know. I hate to even ask."

He slung his arm around my shoulder and led me down the hall, away from the curious glances of the police. "The Winslows are threatening to pull the book from the exhibit if it's not ready by next week's official opening. I really need to know if you can do it."

"Of course I can do it," I said quickly. "That's not the issue. There's, you know, Abraham to consider."

It seemed to me, stepping in to take the place of a murdered friend carried a fairly high creep factor with it.

"I know, babe," he said, running both hands through his hair in frustration. "But there's no one else I can count on."

"The Winslows can't pull the book, can they?"

"You haven't met them, have you?" he asked warily.

"Yes. No." I stopped walking and looked up at him. "But the *Faust* is the most important book in the collection. It doesn't matter if it's restored or not. It's already a work of art. Display it as is."

"Believe me, I'd love to, but they don't see it that way. Mrs. Winslow said she wants it to look pretty." He shook his head in disgust. "Civilians."

He had a point. On the other hand, if there weren't "civilians" out there wanting me to make their old books look pretty, I'd be out of work.

"You'll be paid well," he said.

"You know I don't care about that."

Then he quoted the salary he was willing to pay me and I knew I'd be a complete idiot not to take it. Yes, the timing was unfortunate. And yes, I was about to sacrifice my principles for money. So sue me, but the job needed to be done and I wasn't about to let it go to somebody else.

I smiled tightly. "Of course I'll do it."

He let out a relieved breath. "Thank you. I knew I could count on you."

"Always."

He grinned and gave me a chuck on the chin. "Good stuff, you."

It was a classic Ian thing to do and say, and it brought home the fact that Ian wasn't a laid-back Californian but an upper-crust, old-school Bostonian, out of his element in the land of fruits and nuts. I imagined he grew up in a stately home where his parents and siblings greeted one another with cries of "hail, fellow" and "pip-pip" and "cheerio, old bean."

"Do you mind if we discuss the details tomorrow?" I asked. "I'm really beat."

He gave in with a nod. "Sure. Why don't you come by my office around ten tomorrow morning and we'll talk?" Then he surprised me by pulling me close for a hug. My eyes began tearing up again, so I took a deep breath and stepped back.

"I'll see you tomorrow," I said.

He slugged my arm gently. "Thanks, kiddo."

While Robin took a shower in my guest bathroom, I did what I always did when I was completely at my wits' end and unsure what to do next.

I worked.

Robin had kindly insisted on spending the night and I was frankly grateful for the company. So now I focused my camera lens on the medical treatise I'd been working on this afternoon, trying to get a good shot of the book's tattered foredge.

"How can you concentrate on work?" she asked as she came into the room rubbing a towel over her wet hair. I had to marvel that even in my old chenille bathrobe, she looked like a party girl.

And since I was closer to her than I was to my own two sisters, I didn't mind confessing, "I'm working so I can keep from seeing him dying over and over again in my mind."

"Oh, honey." She gave me a tight hug. "Keep working, then. I'll just wander."

"Help yourself to wine if you want."

She disappeared down the hall and was back in two minutes with glasses for both of us.

"Your place is great," she said as she strolled through the room, moving from window to window to check the view from the sixth floor of what was formerly a corset warehouse, now converted to trendy artists' lofts.

"It's great, isn't it?" I glanced around with more than a little pride. I'd fallen in love with the place six months ago after I'd decided to concentrate on my own book restoration and conservation business. The wa-a-ay South of Market Street neighborhood was, hmm, eclectic, as my mother would say instead of admitting it was downright scary and no place for her daughter to live.

Despite Mom's fears, I'd taken the plunge and was now the very proud owner of one-eighth of the top floor of the six-story brick building. The open, sunny, warehouse-sized front room was perfect for my studio. It was filled with all my book presses and worktables and benches and tool racks and leather rolls and supply cabinets and bookshelves, along with an office desk and chair.

My living area in back had massive skylights, lots

of windows, a huge bathroom and a view of the bay so breathtaking it made the slightly seedy environs and semiweekly frantic phone calls from my mother completely worth enduring. Add a mere six-block walk to the Giants' ballpark and that was enough to sway my father's opinion in my favor.

And so far, I loved all my neighbors. How often did that happen?

I watched as Robin checked that the front door was still locked. A minute later, I could hear her fiddling around in the kitchen.

While she was gone I had another troubling vision of Abraham dying in front of me and felt more disturbed than ever. I wondered how I was supposed to sleep, tonight or ever again.

I tried to feel some pleasure and satisfaction that Ian had singled me out to restore the *Faust*. But at what cost? I hated that Abraham and I had repaired our friendship only to have him die in my arms.

At that moment, I vowed that I wouldn't rest easy until I'd brought his killer to justice. Even if the police never found the bastard, I swore I would track him down and make him pay.

Robin returned with a small plate of cheese, crackers and olives.

"Hey, thanks."

"I know you were dreaming of Chinese food, but this will be healthier."

I acknowledged the truth with a grunt and a sip of wine as she cruised back to the front window and checked the street scene below. A few seconds later, I heard her gasp.

"What's wrong?"

She whipped around. "Don't panic. But Derek Stone followed us home."

I almost choked on my wine. "What're you talking about?"

"Did I stutter? Brooklyn, the man followed us home."

"What—why?"

"Because he got lost? Because he's a jerk? Because he's a serial killer? Never mind. Come here and see for yourself. That's his car parked across the street."

I jumped off the high chair and turned the lights out, then joined her at the window. She'd pulled the curtain back so I could stare out at the well-lighted street. A couple was just leaving Pho Kim, the Vietnamese restaurant across the street. I ate there all the time. Incredible prawns and Bahn Hoi to die for, but that probably wasn't relevant just now.

I watched two people staring at the display in the window of the Afro-Pop Bookstore. A woman walked her dog nearby. It was a comfortable, diverse neighborhood where people walked and shopped and lived and worked and generally didn't worry about strange men sitting alone in ridiculously expensive cars.

"Okay, there's definitely a black car parked there." I didn't know a Bentley from a baboon, so I wasn't willing to admit more than that. "How do you know it's him?"

"Oh, please." She put her fist on her hip. "A brand-new black Continental GT Bentley does not escape my notice, nor does the driver."

"I get that." Robin did know her status symbols. "But how do you know that Derek Stone is driving that particular car?"

"Just how many people do we know who drive Bentleys?"

"None?"

"Exactly." She smiled. "And I happened to see him take off as we were leaving the Covington, so I know he drives that car." She stared down at the street. "And if you wait a few seconds, you can see his profile when the headlights hit him just right."

"Oh dear." It was Derek Stone, all right. I might not know cars but I knew that rugged profile.

"I guess he wasn't kidding when he said he was going to watch you like a hawk," Robin mused.

"You talked to him?"

"Yeah." She sipped her wine. "When the police took you away for questioning, I was pretty much stuck with him."

I let the front curtain go, leaned against the bookcase and sipped my wine. "So, what else did he say about me?"

"You're joking, right?" There was a hint of disbelief in her voice. "Um, gee. He said he's going to ask you to the prom. What is up with you?"

"Nothing." I put the wineglass down on the worktable and paced nervously. "He's a jerk. I just meant, I hope he didn't, you know, bug you."

She started to laugh. "Oh God. You like him."

"What? No."

"You do."

"Don't be ridiculous."

She held her arms out. "Hey, why not? He's totally hot, I'll give him that much. Great car, too."

"Oh yeah, it's all about the car. Are you insane?" I waved my arm toward the street. "He's a—a stalker."

"And as stalkers go, he's a hot one."

"Oh, I'm so flattered." I grabbed my wine and took a gulp. "The man has no sense of humor and he thinks I'm a murderer."

"Sounds like love to me."

I groaned. "Shut up." I turned the lights up and headed back to the worktable. At least my personal stalker had given me something else to think about besides Abraham's murder.

Robin chuckled as she backed away from the window and followed me across the room. "So, how's the putrid pile of caca doing?"

The smell of mold and ancient leather and old paper wafted up and I've got to say, I loved it.

"It is nasty, isn't it?" I said with a satisfied smile. "But this is my version of heaven."

"You can actually fix all this?"

"Of course I can," I said, turning the cover over. "I'm a genius, haven't you heard? And I'll earn every penny on this job because some of the damage is dismal. Will you look at this?" I pointed to a jagged rip on the end plate.

She squinted. "Is that duct tape?"

"Yes." I shook my head in disgust. "On a John Brindley binding! Can you imagine?"

"The horror."

"It gets worse." I held out a stiff column of mottled, torn leather for her closer examination. "Rats. They nibbled straight through the—"

She jumped back a foot. "Oh, good God. Rat cooties on top of everything else? Get that disgusting thing away from me."

"Wimp."

"Freak." Robin laughed again and shook her head. "Come on, it's time to sleep."

"I'm hungry."

"I'm shocked. Good night."

"Good night." I gave her a hug. "Thanks again for staying."

"I loved the old coot, too, you know. And I didn't want to be alone, either," she admitted, as she toddled off toward the guest bedroom. "Don't forget to feed the cats."

"I'll feed them in the morning."

"You already forgot, didn't you?"

What? Was she a mind reader? "No, I didn't."

"Don't make me have to call PETA," Robin said with a laugh.

Disgusted, I rummaged in the kitchen junk drawer, found a yellow stickie, wrote *Feed cats* and stuck it to the refrigerator door. "There, are you happy?"

"Yeah. Now don't forget to read the note."

"Go to bed."

"Nighty-night."

I stuck my wineglass in the sink, debated whether to break into the bag of leftover Chinese food, but took the high road. I poured water into the automatic coffeemaker and added three scoops of Peet's Blend 101 for the morning, then headed off to bed.

Eight hours later I awoke feeling strangely refreshed and amazed I'd been able to sleep even a wink. The smell of freshly brewed coffee assailed me, so I jumped out of bed and checked the guest bedroom. Robin was already up and gone, but when I got to the kitchen, I saw that she'd taken ten or twelve stickies and drawn arrows pointing to the one in the middle that said *Feed cats*.

"Very funny," I growled as I grabbed a cup of coffee. I savored it for a few minutes, then called Ian and confirmed our ten o'clock meeting at the Covington before wandering off to take a quick shower. Afterward, I blow-dried my hair, then dressed in black jeans, black boots, and a black turtleneck sweater. I glanced in the mirror and felt depressed by all the black, so I added a cheerful green jacket for color. After a few quick swipes of mascara and some lip gloss, I microwaved a bowl of Vinnie's Shanghai noodles and slurped them down, followed by two caramel chocolate kisses from the new bag I'd opened. Not exactly the breakfast of champions, but the noodles were incredibly delicious and helped raise my mood a few more notches.

I was down in the garage, jogging to my car, when I remembered Pookie and Splinters.

"Oh, crap." I smacked the innocent car door. I really wasn't cut out to be a caretaker of other living creatures.

Riddled with guilt, I calculated exactly how late I could afford to be this morning. I supposed the cats could live out the day without food and water, but did I want to take that chance? What if Vinnie and Suzie came home early and found the food bowl empty and two emaciated kitties listlessly mewing for their lives? We would no longer be friends and they wouldn't tell me where they got those Shanghai noodles. And lest I forget, those women owned chain saws.

And worse, Robin would have a field day with the news. That convinced me to take the high road.

Ten minutes later, with the cats fed and me feeling guilt free, I fired up the car. As I exited the parking garage, I glanced across the street, half expecting to see a black Bentley parked there. It was gone. Good. The man had no business following me around when there was a murderer running free in the City. Apparently, Derek Stone had come to the same conclusion at some point during the night. I hoped he suffered some mild frostbite before driving off to his cozy hotel room.

I headed west on Brannan to Ninth Street and over to Hayes in order to skirt the Civic Center mess, then turned right on Franklin. From there it was a straight shot up to Pacific Heights and the Covington.

I parked in the adjacent lot and followed the tree-lined walkway to the library, pulling my jacket a little tighter around me as I walked. It was a glorious February morning, the air crystal clear and brisk. From here at the top of Pacific Heights, I could see the amazing span of the Golden Gate Bridge stretching across the whitecapped bay to meet the rolling green hills of Marin County on the far side.

Once inside, I went straight to Ian's office, where his secretary told me he was already downstairs. I detoured through a small side gallery and down to the basement studio area. I was a little creeped out to see that despite the yellow crime scene tape still strewn across the entrance to Abraham's workroom, the door itself was open.

I peeked around the doorsill to find Derek Stone, kneeling on the concrete floor, studying the blood spill.

I must've made a noise because he saw me and

jumped up, then ducked under the yellow tape and hustled me down the hall.

"I won't pass out," I insisted, almost stumbling from the bum's rush he gave me.

"So you were whimpering on general principle?"

"I never whimper," I said with a sniff.

From two rooms down, Ian popped his head out. "You made it." He approached and wrapped his arm around my shoulders, pulling me close for a quick hug; then he walked me to the new workroom. "You're working in here."

"Okay," I said, and hated that my voice trembled. Seeing that dark red blob brought back all the horrors of the night before.

The new room was identical to Abraham's in every way—except for that pesky bloodstain on the concrete floor.

I eyed Derek Stone over Ian's shoulder as he followed us into the room. He stared right back at me. Today he was dressed in a black turtleneck sweater, black tailored trousers and a dark pine green cashmere jacket. Essentially, we were dressed alike, although his outfit probably cost several thousand dollars more than mine. Show-off. Not that I cared, but I guessed security paid more than your run-of-the-mill cop salary.

Ian turned to me. "I understand you two have already met."

"I've had the distinct pleasure," he said, his mouth twisting in a wry grin.

My stomach tingled and I could've smacked myself. Yes, okay, he was indeed gorgeous as honey-baked sin, but that didn't mean I was the least bit interested in a man who considered me capable of killing someone in cold blood. It just wasn't flattering, and my self-esteem was healthier than that. I hoped.

I wasn't surprised to find myself attracted to Derek Stone since I clearly had no clue when it came to choosing appropriate men. Recently, my own family had forbidden me to act alone when it came to dating, simply because I'd been engaged three times without closing the deal. I don't know what the big deal was. So I picked the wrong men. Who didn't?

I avoided looking at him as I walked the perimeter of the room, testing the book press and opening cupboards and drawers to check out supplies. I fiddled with the light switches to find the best possible lighting.

The two men ignored me, talking quietly as they sat in the tall, comfortable chairs that lined one side of the high worktable. I moved to the opposite side, slipped off my jacket and pulled up a backless stool. That was when I noticed the Winslow *Faust* lying on a white cloth in the middle of the table.

First I pulled my camera out of my bag. Then I reached for the cloth, holding my breath as I tugged the whole thing closer to me.

Even with its slightly faded gilding, clouded gemstones, tarnished clasps and cracked leather binding, the Winslow *Faust* was exquisite. Swirls of pale gold were embossed along the outer edges of the cover. In the center of the cover was an elaborately tooled, rather bold and angry eagle holding a shield, a globe and a sword, all deeply etched in gold. But there was something else. Dripping from the eagle's left wing was blood, so thick and crimson, it almost looked real.

I touched it. It was real, all right. There was blood on the book. Abraham's blood? Oh God.

I was going to be sick. I dropped the book and tried to push away from the table. The legs of the high stool stuck and tottered beneath me and I flew backward with nowhere to go but down.

Chapter 5

Derek was on his feet and around the table before my head could hit the floor. My stool clattered to the floor as he swooped me up and clutched me securely in his arms.

I stared at him, unable to catch my breath.

He stared back. His mouth was too close to mine and my heart raced in my chest. To say I was embarrassed didn't begin to describe it. *Mortified* worked better.

I panted for more breath, thinking this might be a great time for me to find that portal into another dimension. Yes, I was grateful for Derek's speed and strength, but really, this wasn't exactly the most professional position I'd ever found myself in.

On the other hand, he seemed to have absolutely no problem hoisting a grown woman into his arms—not that I weighed a ton or anything. He appeared perfectly at ease, as if he were holding a cup of tea and carrying on a lovely conversation with the Queen.

"Must I always be saving you from near disaster?" he murmured.

"No," I whispered. "That won't be necessary." But all things considered—and despite the fact that he continued to stare to the point where I was certain my face was as hot and red as a radish—I'd rather have ended up in his arms than in a coma or a back brace from colliding with the concrete floor.

"Thank you," I said in as dignified a tone as I could muster, what with my throat gone dry and all. "You can put me down."

"Are you sure?" He grinned, showing off his straight white teeth and some adorable little crinkles around his cobalt blue eyes, not that I really noticed or anything.

"I'm sure."

"You fall with alarming regularity."

"I don't," I insisted. "But I've had a bad week."

He scanned the length of me. "You look quite fine now."

I frowned. "You need to put me down."

"Of course." He got me back on my feet and stepped away. "Good as new."

Ian stepped around my British knight in shining Armani and grasped my shoulders. "Are you okay?"

"Yes, thanks." I eased away and self-consciously straightened my sweater.

"Are you sure?" Ian persisted. "What happened?"

Derek picked up the stool and placed it on the other side, then pulled one of the more comfortable high chairs into position for me. He met my gaze, patted the seat and said, "Sit."

"Thank you." I maneuvered my way back onto the chair and forced myself to focus on the book. The blood was still there.

Struggling to retrieve some authority, I glared from Ian to Derek and said, "There's blood on this book cover."

Ian cocked his head. "Beg your pardon?"

Derek's mouth curved in a frown. "What blood?"

"On the eagle's wing." I held up the book and pointed. "Why didn't the police take this into evidence?"

While Ian's forehead creased in confusion, Derek went with inscrutability.

I sighed. "The police never saw it, did they? You never told them Abraham gave it to me, did you? Why?"

"Apparently, you didn't find it necessary to reveal that fact, either," he countered; then, without another word, he picked up my camera and snapped off several photos of the book cover. Putting the camera down, he pulled a white linen handkerchief from inside his jacket and dabbed at the blood, then scrubbed it. He put the book back on the table and folded the handkerchief. "There. I'll take this to the police for analysis. In the meantime, you can get to work."

I stared in disbelief. "Are you insane?"

Ian craned his neck to get a look at the cover. "Is it gone?"

"Pretty much," Derek said, tucking the handkerchief back in his pocket.

"Good work, Stone," Ian said, visibly relieved. "Guess that takes care of it, then."

I whipped around and slugged his arm. "That was evidence!"

"Hey," he protested, rubbing his arm. "It won't bring Abraham back, so why should it matter?"

"It matters," I repeated, slightly more shrill than required.

Derek shook his head firmly. "Not if it means turning the book over to the police."

"They need to see it!"

"Why?" Ian asked.

I whirled to face him. "What if it's not Abraham's blood? What if he attacked his assailant and that's the killer's blood on the book? What if—"

"Jeez, Brooklyn," Ian said. "Chill out."

Derek held up his hand to stop the argument. "I'm tasked with keeping this book secure. I fully intend to turn over those photos and have them examine the blood on this handkerchief."

"But what about the book itself? The police—"

"Will destroy it in their zeal to investigate combined with their typical cloddish incompetence," Derek said with a dismissive wave.

"I thought you were working with them."

"I am, but that doesn't mean I'll allow them to bollix a priceless work of art I'm determined to protect." He picked up the book again and held it at an angle to check that he'd cleaned it thoroughly.

"Oh, give me the damn book," I said.

He returned it to its place on the white cloth, then pulled the cloth until the book was directly in front of me.

"I knew you'd see reason," he said.

"Oh, please." I jabbed my finger at him. "I want to hear the results of that handkerchief analysis."

"Yes, ma'am." He raised an eyebrow, looked at Ian. "Prickly thing."

Ian nodded. "Always has been."

"Not funny." But apparently they didn't care. "Don't you both have somewhere else to be?"

Derek thought for a few seconds. "Not really."

"Me, neither," Ian said, checking his watch.

I huffed out a breath. They were worse than my brothers now that they had a shared bond, namely, the joy of tormenting me.

Not that I'd ever let these guys know, but I didn't want to see the *Faust* covered in slimy black fingerprint dust, either. At the same time, a twinge of guilt rippled through me. I wanted Abraham's killer caught, but I wanted the book to be protected, too. I tried to convince myself that Abraham would've felt the same way.

I ignored my peanut gallery and pulled a pair of reading glasses, a notebook and a pen from my bag to take a closer look at the book and figure out what tools and supplies I would need to bring in from my own studio.

The Winslow *Faust* was large, probably about fourteen inches tall and ten inches wide. I would need my metal gauge to get an accurate measurement, but that was my educated guess. Gathering the corners of the cloth around the book, I hefted it a few inches off the table. It was heavy, perhaps four, maybe five pounds. I stared at the thickness. Three inches? At least. I added the metal gauge to the list of supplies, along with my table-mounted hands-free magnifying glass.

The two clasps used to keep the book tightly closed were made of brass and shaped to form what looked like stylized eagle claws, each approximately one inch wide and two inches long. They slid through two brass bridges welded to the front cover, then clicked into place, essentially locking the book closed. The brass claws were affixed to one-inch-thick leather straps that were fitted seamlessly into the back cover leather.

My shoulders twitched. I could hear Ian breathing. I turned and found him and Derek inches from my back, watching my every move.

"Want to give me a little room here, guys?"

Ian stepped back immediately but Derek stood his ground.

I sighed and picked up the magnifying glass to examine the red rubies embedded in each leaf point of the fleur-de-lis border. There were thirty rubies total, all clouded and dusty. They would need to be removed for cleaning, then reset.

With the jewels and the elaborate gilding and the strange brass claws all vying for attention, the book should've appeared gaudy and crude. Instead, it was a masterpiece. Anyone would feel humbled and privileged to be gazing at such an incredible work of art. Or maybe it was just me, the book nerd.

"Where will you start?" Ian asked.

"Not sure yet," I muttered, staring at the corded spine.

"*When* will you start?" Derek asked.

I gave him my best dirty look, then spent a few more minutes studying and admiring the tooling and cording along the spine before I carefully unclasped the brass eagle claws and opened the book.

The pungent smell of warm, musty, aged vellum blended with the scent of rich Morocco leather. I closed my eyes to let the glorious scent of age and elegance cloud my senses and engulf my brain.

I had to blink a few times to clear my vision. Okay, yes, I tended to get a bit emotional about my work, but as I gazed down at the inside cover, all I could think was, wow. Nothing I'd seen before could've prepared me for this.

Instead of the usual marbled end papers typical of books from the same period, some divine artist had painted a spectacular battle scene on the scale of Armageddon—and yet, it was all done in miniature. The detail was astounding. Clouds swirled in the heavens as battalions of charging angels descended in full battle regalia, wielding shiny swords in a valiant effort to restore righteousness to a world gone to the dark side.

Rising from the ground to meet them were an equal number of black-clad, malevolent horned creatures, brandishing evil-looking clubs and other instruments of destruction. These were the warriors sent by Mephistopheles to destroy their heavenly rivals.

In the midst of the clashing forces, yet somehow removed from the action, stood a handsome man of wealth, dressed in the elegant attire of nineteenth-century nobility. His face was a mask of revulsion and confusion as he watched the battle wage and the bodies fall around him.

This was Faust, Goethe's tragically misguided hero.

"This is amazing," I whispered.

"Beautiful," Ian concurred. "I've never seen anything quite like it."

Again, the wild colors and dramatic illumination should've come across as garish and melodramatic, but instead, this was a stunning work of art all on its own.

It wasn't signed, so I had no idea who the artist was or if it was the same person who'd created the book itself. I intended to find out.

Abruptly I wondered how in the world the Covington might display the book to show so many aspects of it.

"You should display this inside a glass cube at eye level," I said, my excitement growing. "People need to be able to walk all the way around and see the different parts. You could clip it open to show some of the text, and have another clip here so that this painting is displayed, and you've got to be able to see the binding, too. I could fashion some brass clips that would blend with—"

"Sounds great," Ian said. "Can you finish it in a week?"

I winced. "I hope so."

He smiled. "So you like the book?"

"Magnificent," I said with a sigh, then glanced up and met Derek's dark stare. I shouldn't have been surprised to see him staring at me, but the look on his face in that moment made me feel somewhat akin to a juicy steak and he was a starving carnivore.

My reaction must've been obvious because he instantly schooled his features and appeared only blandly interested in the book.

Okay, maybe I'd imagined that hungry look, but I hadn't imagined my reaction. My heart was still stuttering and butterflies flitted around my stomach. How many times did I have to remind myself that Derek Stone was a big jerk and still considered me a suspect? Why else would he be here if not to keep an eye on me?

Well, I was over it. I cleared my throat. "Ian, would you mind raising the lights up a level?"

"No problem," he said, and crossed the room to fiddle with the lighting panel.

I turned to Derek and whispered, "Stop staring at me."

He leaned in close. "Don't flatter yourself."

"What would you call it, then?"

"I'm watching you."

My hand fisted and I had to fight the urge to pop him one. "You can't seriously think I would kill—"

"Better?" Ian said as he stared up at the ceiling, gauging the light level, blissfully unaware of the tension occurring under his nose.

"Perfect," I said, beaming at him. "Thanks." I flashed one more stern look at Derek, who smirked, causing my fists to twitch. I was itching to break something, preferably his nose. Too bad I was such a loving pacifist.

"I'm off to a meeting," Ian announced. He took a minute to hash out a work schedule for me; then he handed me keys and a parking card. As he walked to the door, he reminded me to stop by his office to fill out an employment contract before I left for the day. Just like that, I was a Covington employee.

Derek stood and stretched his arms out. "Guess I'll leave you to your work."

"Oh, thanks so much."

He shot me a look of warning. "For now." Then he winked at me—*winked* at me!—and walked out.

Blissfully alone, without Derek Stone sucking the oxygen from the room, I ran both hands through my hair and shook my head and shoulders to get rid of all this built-up frustration. It was Derek Stone's fault I was feeling all this tension. I laid the blame directly at his feet.

And what kind of a name was Derek Stone, anyway? It sounded like some James Bond wannabe. Of course, I was the last person to criticize someone's given name, having been named after the New York borough where, legend has it, I was conceived in the balcony between acts of a Grateful Dead show at the now defunct Beacon Theatre. And if that weren't lowering enough, my evil brothers used to call me the Bronx.

But I digress. No matter what his name was, Derek Stone exuded more animal magnetism than all those Bond men combined. The man paid attention, and he was strong. I thought of the way those lean muscles of his arms had bunched and tensed as they caught and held me. Impressive, to say the least.

Was it getting warm in here or what?

"And this is helping me concentrate *how*?" With a deep inhalation of breath, I grabbed a bag of peppermint patties from my purse and consumed three as fast as I could. Refreshed, I squared my shoulders, grabbed my handheld magnifying glass and continued checking out the *Faust*.

I'd thought at first that the Armageddon painting inside the cover had been produced on a thin sheet of canvas. Now I could see it was high-quality vellum, which felt more like parchment even though it was actually fine calfskin that had been stretched and treated to allow for printing—or in this case, painting.

If the artist was also the bookbinder, he had to have known the chance he was taking, using this astonishing painting as a pastedown. Given the nineteenth-century style of applying liberal amounts of wheat starch paste to affix paper and leather to the boards, it was remarkable that the paint's vibrancy and the vellum itself had survived.

"Uh-oh." I moved the magnifying glass closer and as if to prove the point, I noticed a significant portion of the painting had peeled away from the top of the inside front cover.

I ran my finger along the loose edge. The underside was still tacky.

"Hello," I said. The painting hadn't peeled away on its own. Someone had helped it along, creating a pocket between the vellum and the board. By angling the book toward me, I could see something wedged in between.

"What's this?" I reached in my bag for my thin tweezers and an X-Acto knife and carefully, meticulously pried more of the painting away from the board.

I maneuvered the tweezers into the space and secured the item, then tugged, ever so slightly, since I had no idea what was in there. What if I tore it? What if it crumbled to dust from the pressure?

But the thing slid easily from its hiding place. I was surprised and somewhat disappointed to find a simple piece of contemporary card stock, maybe four inches square. A note card. Expensive. Sturdy, quality stock.

In the center of the card, written in pencil, was a squiggled "AK," and a notation, "GW1941."

The "AK" was obviously Abraham's initials, but the notation was a mystery, easily solved if I could track down his journal for this job. Abraham had always kept copious notes as he worked, so I had no doubt he'd have an explanation for the note card and his scribbled notation.

It would be a leap to assume that Abraham had slipped the note card into the slender pocket to keep the vellum from fusing to the board, but that's what I would've done. So for now, that was my working theory. So the question was, what had Abraham found in the space behind the painted vellum? And another question: What did "GW1941" mean?

My imagination conjured a secret letter written by Kaiser Wilhelm himself on the German emperor's royal stationery. Maybe it was a denunciation of some government official and its contents were so inflammatory it had to be hidden away from prying eyes. Or maybe it was a scorching love letter to the emperor from his mistress, assuming he had one. Of course he had one. He was an emperor. Maybe he'd tucked the sexy letter away inside the book as a secret keepsake.

And maybe I was being a twit.

Given Abraham's notation, the missing item was dated 1941, so an artifact from Kaiser Wilhelm was probably out of the question. Whatever it turned out to be, I hoped it would make a noteworthy piece of Winslow family memorabilia for the exhibition as well as add credibility to the provenance of the book itself.

Most likely, what was missing was something more prosaic, perhaps a receipt or maybe the bookbinder's description of the materials used to make the book. I didn't care what it was; I just wanted to see it.

"Abraham, what was it?" I asked, glancing around the tidy workroom. "What did you find?"

I heard a cupboard slam in a nearby workroom and smiled. It was comforting to know there were other binders at work today. Another cupboard thumped shut. My curiosity piqued, I walked out into the hall to meet my neighbors. Another drawer banged shut and I followed the noise to Abraham's door. It was still closed up with yellow crime scene tape draped across it.

Someone was inside.

I pushed the unlocked door open and saw Minka on tiptoe, peering into one of the cupboards above the sideboard.

"Why am I not surprised?" I said.

She gasped and whipped around. That was when I noticed the little pile of supplies she'd amassed on the worktable.

"Pilfering?" I asked cheerily.

"What the hell do you want?"

I slipped under the crime scene tape and came inside to take a closer look at what she'd found.

"Get out of here!" she cried.

"I'm just looking," I said, and picked up a polished wood box with the initials "AK" engraved on the top.

Abraham's personalized set of Peachey knives.

"I have dibs on those," she said. "Get your dirty meat hooks off them."

I shook my head at her. "You're a pathetic thief."

"Those are mine."

"No, these belong to Abraham."

She lunged for the box and I whipped my hand away.

"You're such a bitch!"

"That may be true," I said. "But these still don't belong to you."

"He can't use them and I found them first."

My eyes widened. I couldn't help it. Her lack of a moral compass never failed to shock me. "That doesn't mean they belong to you."

"God, I hate you," she said through clenched teeth. She swept the rest of her booty to her chest and stomped out. Then she turned back and glared at me. "I hope you die."

"Back atcha," I yelled after her.

I let go of the breath I'd been holding. The woman was so toxic. I had to wonder, not for the first time, how anyone in their right mind would hire her.

"Hey, you shouldn't be in here." Ian stood at the door, frowning at me.

I laughed without humor. "Where were you when I needed you?"

"What do you mean?"

"Minka was in here. I caught her pilfering Abraham's stuff."

"Oh." His frown deepened. "Well, we've got tools everywhere. She must've been looking for something."

"No, Ian. She was stealing Abraham's stuff." I dipped under the yellow tape and closed the door, then handed him the box of Peachey knives. "She was going to take this."

He examined it, handed it back, then shrugged. "It's just a box of knives, Brooklyn. I'm sure it was completely innocent. You're just a little sensitive. Come on."

In my moment of stunned disbelief, he was able to wrap his arm around my shoulder and lead me back to my room.

It was déjà vu all over again. My college boyfriend

had refused to believe Minka was capable of attacking me. It was why we'd eventually broken up. He'd said I was just being overly emotional because my hand was all bandaged up and hurting. It was an accident, he'd insisted, and I needed to lighten up.

Back in my workroom, as Ian pulled the high chair out and helped me sit, I felt like Ingrid Bergman in *Gaslight*. And not for the first time. Here I was again, trying to prove that Minka was a pathological liar and dangerous to my health while all anyone else could see was that Minka was an innocent bystander and I was a wrathful bitch.

At that moment I realized Minka could get away with murder.

I tried to work for another twenty minutes, but it was useless. Between Minka throwing me off my game and the missing artifact from the *Faust*, I couldn't concentrate.

I circled the room, stared out the high windows at the blue sky and wondered what that missing artifact might be.

"And where in the world did you hide it?" I asked out loud.

Abraham had hounded me from the earliest age to always keep notes of my work. At every stage, it was important to photograph and map everything, not just the physical work, the paper, the boards, the binding, the threads, but also my own impressions and thoughts and problems and theories regarding the project. He likened the job to that of an archaeologist or a crime scene investigator. If Abraham had found something inside that hidden pocket, he would've slipped the item into a clear plastic sleeve and clipped it into a binder for protection and reference.

"A book is a piece of living history." I could hear him say it as clearly as though he were here in the room with me.

"So what the hell did you do with this piece?" I wondered aloud. "And where'd you put your damn journal?"

My eyes narrowed as I scanned the compact space again. It was identical to Abraham's workroom two doors down. Modular shelving and cabinets in a blond wood veneer lined three walls, and the large worktable and stools filled the remaining middle space. The ceiling was high, the lighting decent. It was a clean and orderly room with everything neatly arranged.

Abraham, however, had always been a whirlwind of creative energy, an artist who left his mark wherever he went. In other words, he was a slob. As I looked around at this assigned space, I realized the man never would've kept anything important here. He might've been forced to work in this room, but he didn't live here, didn't create here, didn't leave his mark here.

The man I knew had kept every notebook and journal he'd ever written on every project he'd ever worked. He was a pack rat. So where were all the papers and notebooks and journals the Winslow project would've generated?

Had someone stolen them? Was that why he was killed?

Taking one more glance around, I realized I wouldn't find the answers here.

There was only one place I could think of looking

and that was at Abraham's rambling home studio at the commune in Sonoma. I still had a key to the place.

My stomach growled. I checked my watch and realized it was almost noon. As I tidied up, I calculated that if I could make it to my car within ten minutes, I'd have time to go to the drive-through at Speedy Grill and get a junior double cheeseburger, mega fries and an Oreo milk shake, and still make it to Sonoma by two o'clock.

Chapter 6

It was almost twelve thirty when I passed the busy Presidio toll plaza and drove onto the Golden Gate Bridge. I'd made decent time from the Covington, despite the noontime drive-through stop at not-so-Speedy Grill. It was worth the wait, though, because there was no better cheeseburger in the world. Theirs was made with Niman Ranch beef, slices of heirloom tomato and sweet Walla Walla onion, a fluffy homemade bun and an aioli-based secret sauce worthy of a Cordon Bleu chef. Critics insisted and I concurred, it was the best in the City.

Sadly, I was so hungry that by the time I hit the bridge, the burger was a vague, happy memory. Luckily, I still had some fries and most of my milk shake left for the rest of the trip north.

My hands clutched the steering wheel a little too tightly as I played back my latest run-in with Derek Stone before leaving the library. I'd tried to track down Ian, but he'd left his office and I wasn't willing to trust the Winslow *Faust* to anyone else but Derek.

But did he appreciate my concern? No. He demanded to know where the hell I was going and when I told him I needed to visit my mother, he snatched the book away and made an annoying crack about my lackadaisical working hours. My sad comeback was something along the lines of "bite me."

I forced him out of my head and tried to enjoy the drive. The Golden Gate Bridge and the view of the bay never failed to impress me. The sky was still a gorgeous blue, but it was colder and the crosswinds were gusty.

Stop-and-go traffic plagued the southbound drivers, but I was able to zip along at the forty-five-mile-an-hour speed limit after carefully dodging an ancient pop-top minivan that appeared to be readying for liftoff. Two little boys in the back were sticking out their tongues and making naughty finger gestures that the harried, white-knuckled driver—their mother, I presumed—wouldn't have approved of. But Mom seemed oblivious of the little monsters, too busy fight ing to keep the car grounded against the buffeting winds.

Two minutes later, I was off the bridge and safely back on terra firma in Marin County. I drove through the rainbow tunnel and as I whizzed past the first San Rafael turnoff, my cell phone bleated out a generic sound, meaning I had no clue who was calling. I grabbed the phone anyway and fumbled for the button. "Hello?"

"You left without signing the papers." It was Ian.

Damn. The Covington employment contract.

"Sorry, but I tried to find you," I said. Then I went rigid. "You got the *Faust*, right?"

"Yeah, thanks."

I let out a breath. "Good."

"But I wish you'd stuck around," he said. "The Winslows were here. They wanted to meet you."

"Oh, darn."

"Something wrong?" he asked, unexpectedly attuned to my dripping sarcasm.

"No, everything's great," I said, pumping up my enthusiasm. "I'm sorry I missed them but my mother called."

"Is she okay?"

"Oh yeah. But she needed me to, um, pick something up for her."

Not too clever as excuses went, but I wasn't ready to tell him what I'd discovered inside the *Faust*—or rather, what I had *not* discovered—until I actually found whatever it was. And I didn't want the Winslows to know what I was looking for. Which wouldn't be a problem since I didn't have a clue what I was looking for, anyway.

I frowned. Even I was confused.

"Well, say hi to your mom for me," Ian said.

"Ah," I said, remembering where I was and who I was talking to. "I will. Hey, you should come up for dinner one of these days. Austin thinks this year's pinot is bordering on world class. He's forcing everyone to taste it."

"That bastard."

I laughed. Since Ian had been Austin's college buddy as well as my short-term fiancé, he was no stranger to my family and the commune.

"I know my parents would love to see you," I said, steering around an idiot in red spandex riding a ten-speed. On the freeway? But it was Marin, after all.

"I'd love to see everyone," he said, sounding wistful. "I'll give them a call soon."

"Great." I slammed on my brakes to avoid sideswiping a vintage copper Mustang whose driver thought he owned the road. Cool car. Dumb driver. "I'll try to get back there later today," I added, knowing it was a lie.

"Don't bother," he said. "You can sign everything tomorrow. You'll be here tomorrow, right?"

"Of course," I said, feeling the pressure of employment all of a sudden. This was why I owned my own business. I didn't work well in captivity. "I'll be there every day until the book's done, I promise. This was just, you know, an extenuating circumstance."

"No problem, kiddo. I'll call the Winslows and let them know to come by tomorrow."

"Dandy," I lied. Again. "See you tomorrow."

"Good-o," he said, and signed off.

I hung up. The good news about Ian's call was that it had helped me ignore the cheesy condo-clogged hillsides of Sausalito and all the minimalls and car lots that lined the freeway through San Rafael.

The bad news was that I'd have to deal with the Winslows tomorrow. I wondered again whether the conversation I'd overheard the night of Abraham's murder had something to do with his death. I tried to recall their words.

"Son of a bitch." "Problem with a book." "I took care of it."

It all sounded suspicious. Without thinking, I checked my rearview mirror. I had the abrupt and uncomfortable feeling that someone was following me.

I took the turnoff to Route 37 and for the next few

miles there was little but wide-open marshland that spread clear to the eastern side of the bay. I could see no sinister cars behind me. And no black Bentley, either.

Miles later, grassy hills melded into vineyards. I finally made it through Glen Ellen, the southern boundary of the region known locally as the Valley of the Moon. Three miles beyond town, I turned onto Montana Ridge Road and headed for Dharma.

The day we moved here so many years ago, Montana Ridge Road had been a pitted, one-lane gravel road bordered by rickety wood fences and rusted chain link. We'd driven past broken-down barns, funky farmhouses and tarnished trailers. Most front lawns featured the requisite bullet-riddled washing machine. Lots of tarnished RVs were parked on the driveways as extra housing for the in-laws.

After spending my first seven years in the quiet elegance of the St. Francis Woods neighborhood of San Francisco, I was shell-shocked by these stark surroundings and so were my siblings. As the family car bucked and bounced and we got our first depressing view of this dismal, rural neighborhood that was to be our new home, my older brother, Austin, began to quietly hum the first four bars of "Dueling Banjos."

At the time, I was too young to get the reference. But my dad got it and told Austin to pipe down.

Despite first impressions, we'd done pretty well for ourselves. For the first two years we lived up here, all eight of us were squeezed into an Airstream camper while the Fellowship members built a community and planted vineyards. Over the years, more property was acquired, more artists' studios were constructed, a restaurant was built onto the town hall and a schoolhouse was added for the kids who seemed to multiply with every season.

Within a few years, the commune had grown to almost nine hundred and Guru Bob incorporated. Now the little town of Dharma was a thriving community of chic shops and art galleries, restaurants, artisanal farms, an excellent winery, three stylish B and Bs and a world-class health and beauty spa. Not bad for a gaggle of Deadheads and freaks, as Dad always said.

Montana Ridge turned into Shakespeare Lane, signaling the beginning of the quaint, two-blocks-long Dharma shopping district. I drove past the darling shops and cafés and small storefront businesses, including Warped, my sister China's yarn and weavings shop.

Past the wide central square and town hall, I swung onto Vivaldi Way, the narrow private road that wound up the hill overlooking Dharma. I pulled into Abraham's circular drive and parked, then climbed out of the car and stretched my arms out to unkink my back and shoulders. The air up here was cooler and the sky was beginning to cloud up. I hoped it wouldn't rain before I got back to the City.

I stared at Abraham's house, an imposing two-story Spanish colonial with a great view of the town and rolling hills beyond. Not exactly the picture that leapt to mind when you heard the word *commune*, but years ago, once the commune had started making money, Guru Bob had been adamant about raising the level of impressions and lifestyle.

Abraham's patio and pool circled the back of the house and his bookbinding studio was at the far end of the property.

I grabbed my keys and bag and headed for the studio. A banner of yellow crime scene ribbon was strewn across the door, so the police had been here, too. Had they found anything incriminating?

I had a moment of indecision, then resolutely pulled the tape off and opened the door. I walked inside and was assailed by the smells of rich leather, musty parchment, inks and oils and peppermint. Almost instantly, bittersweet memories flooded my consciousness.

I could picture Abraham standing in his leather apron, his shirtsleeves shoved up his dark, muscular arms, his leather-stained hands gold-flecked as he painstakingly gilded an intricate design on the spine of a book held tightly in place by one of his antique book presses.

I'd grown up in this room, apprenticing for the man. It hadn't been easy. He'd enjoyed being a strict taskmaster and I made a lot of mistakes. But I loved the work, loved the books, loved the feeling of accomplishment that came with completing a project. I knew from the beginning I had a gift for both the art and the craft of bookbinding, even though Abraham never said so. It didn't matter. I'd overheard him telling my parents on more than one occasion that I'd done good work and it never failed to warm my heart to hear him say so.

As I rounded the room, I caught a whiff of sawdust mixed with sweat and glue and I almost lost it right there. He should've been here, working and laughing and ordering me around. I gulped, trying to ease the lump in my throat.

I dabbed away tears with my jacket sleeve as I ambled around the studio looking for anything that might tell me what had been hidden behind the endpapers of the Winslow *Faust*. A journal perhaps, or a binder, a calendar. Or maybe a sign that read "Yo, here's what you're looking for."

Abraham's studio was arranged in typical workshop fashion with three wide counters running along the walls and a high worktable in the center. The side counters were jammed with book presses and punches and other equipment. Shelves lined the walls and held hundreds of spools of threads, tools, brushes, more paper, rolls of leather and stacks of heavy cardboard.

"You were always such a mess." I straightened tools as I went, clumped loose brushes together in an empty jar, neatly restacked an unruly pile of endpapers.

I distracted myself by picking up the cordless phone from its base at the edge of the worktable. Absently, I checked the phone numbers on speed dial and recognized my own as well as my parents'. I put the phone down on the napkin it was resting on, then noticed that it was a cocktail napkin from a restaurant I recognized, the Buena Vista near Fisherman's Wharf.

I picked it up and saw a note scrawled on the back.

> You missed our appt. Are you bullshitting me? You've got one more chance. Meet me at the BV this Friday night or all bets are off.

It was signed *Anandalla*.

Anandalla? What kind of a name was Anandalla?

More important, who was she? A date? A client? The note sounded ominous. Was it written by Abraham's killer?

I was familiar with the Buena Vista, a venerable bar and restaurant near Fisherman's Wharf, down the street from Ghirardelli Square. I hadn't been there in months but it might be worth a visit this Friday night. Not that I had a clue who this Anandalla might be, but maybe she knew something about Abraham that would help me put the pieces of the puzzle together.

I stuck the cocktail napkin in my pocket and moved to the long counter against the back wall. Here, Abraham had stacked a number of newly sanded, thin birch wood panels for use as book covers, I guessed. Big chunks of bone and seashells lay in a pile next to the wood.

Months ago, Abraham had mentioned teaching a class on Zen and the art of Japanese bookbinding. I'd thought it sounded like great fun. I sifted through the bones and shells, picking out the most solid shapes, thinking they would make beautiful closure clasps. I stuck a few in my bag, neatly lined up the shells and bones, straightened the stack of birch covers, then moved to Abraham's bookshelf at the end of the counter. This was where he'd always kept his finished projects and samples, along with some of my earliest attempts at bookbinding. I leaned in to see the titles.

"Hey," I whispered, and pulled out the aged, leather-bound copy of *Wild Flowers in the Wind*.

I ran my hand over the soft blue leather and simple gilding that bordered the edges of the front cover. Abraham had allowed me to use this ratty old book as my very first restoration project. I'd chosen sky blue leather because it was so pretty.

I smiled at the memory of Abraham laughing about the book's title since he'd claimed most of the so-called flowers in the book looked like scrawny weeds. The gilded title along the spine was slightly wobbly and I remembered I'd struggled with it so desperately. It was still one of the most difficult parts of the job for me.

As I opened the book, my tears spotted the flyleaf. "Moisture destroys books."

"I know, I know." I shivered. It was as if Abraham were here in the room, giving me grief. I blotted my eyes, then stuck the Weeds book back on the shelf.

"Hey, you."

I jolted, then turned and saw my mother standing in the doorway.

"Jeez, Mom, scare me half to death, why don't you?"

"Sorry," Mom said with a grin. "I figured you heard me clomping across the patio."

I exhaled shakily. "I guess I zoned out."

She smiled indulgently. "You do that."

I bent to pick up a brush that had fallen on the floor. "What are you doing here?"

She wandered into the room. "I saw you driving up Vivaldi, but your car never made it to the house, so I figured you stopped here."

I glanced around, unsure how to explain what I was doing here. There was no need to feel guilty, but this was my mother, after all. Guilt was a mandatory response.

"Ian asked me to take over Abraham's Covington work, so I thought I'd try to find some of his notes on the books."

"Wonderful." She pulled her sweater snug around her waist and folded her arms. "Chilly in here."

I hadn't noticed until now. We were both circling around the five-hundred-pound elephant in the room, but I wasn't going to go there right now. When she was ready, she'd tell me what she was doing at the Covington the night Abraham was killed.

"Come on, Mom, I'll walk you back home."

I locked the door and left my car in Abraham's drive and we started up the hill.

"So, how is Ian?"

"Fine," I said. "I told him to come out for dinner sometime."

"That would be lovely," she said. "It's such a shame you two couldn't make a go of it."

"Oh, please." I laughed. "You know we're both better off as friends than we ever were as lovers."

She smiled. "I suppose so. It's just that Ian's alchemy and body type matched yours so perfectly."

"Yeah." I rolled my eyes. "That was the problem."

Mom placed her small hand against my sternum and closed her eyes. "Your fourth chakra was always so highly developed, even as a little girl. You need someone extremely sexual to stir your heart and passions into action."

"Oh, thanks for that." Just the conversation I wanted to have with my mother.

She took her hand away and opened her eyes. "Try adding more back bends to your exercise regime. It's a powerful way to energize the Anahata within to attract the correct sexual mate."

"I'll get right on it," I said. Nice to know she assumed I had an exercise regime.

"Good. Maybe you'll meet someone nice while you're at the Covington."

Unbidden, a picture of Derek Stone flashed through my mind and I anxiously shook the image away.

"Doubtful, Mom, but I'll keep you posted."

She patted my arm. "I'm just so proud that you're there, and you're able to make a life for yourself doing this work. I hope Abraham didn't . . . Well, I know he was hard on you."

"He taught me everything I know."

"I know." She wound her arm through mine. "And if I never loved Abraham for any other reason, I would have loved him for giving you that world."

I glanced at her. Were those tears in her eyes? She loved him? Did she mean love, as a friend? Studying Mom's face, I found it hard to read what she was feeling, thinking. And honestly, I wasn't sure I wanted to know. I felt my stomach churn and doubted it had anything to do with the Speedy burger.

I lasted forty-five minutes at my parents' house. While Austin coerced me into trying short tastes of the pinot he was so psyched about along with the newest cabernet they'd just barreled, Dad filled me in on plans for Abraham's memorial service that would be held this Saturday at the town hall.

Mom insisted on regaling me with forty or fifty new photos of my sister London's infant twins. I didn't say anything to Mom, but for God's sake, those babies were barely three months old and this made something like six thousand pictures London had sent Mom to ogle and giggle over. Could infants be blinded by overexposure? Could they develop flashbulb dependency?

I endured the picture show grudgingly. London had always been the competitive one, always trying to one-up me with Mom. You didn't see me foisting shots of my moldy old books onto my mother, did you? Figures London would give birth to twins. I wasn't about to compete with that.

I finally managed to say good-bye without succumbing to the pot roast dinner my mother tried to tempt me with. The fact that I would turn down my mom's incredible cooking said something about my desperate need to get back to the City before it rained. I really hated driving in the rain.

I hiked down the hill to Abraham's where I'd left my car. On a whim, I detoured back to his studio, thinking I'd grab some more of those shells for my own use. Abraham wouldn't miss them and I wanted to experiment with an Asian-influenced accordion-style album I was designing for a client.

There was just enough moonlight that I didn't turn the studio light on, just zipped inside and headed straight for the shells. I stumbled over something hard but caught myself, barely.

"Nice going, Your Grace," I berated myself. I moved forward slowly in the dark and found the back worktable. I fumbled around, grabbed a handful of shells and carefully placed them in the side pocket of my bag.

As I started back toward the door, I realized that what I really wanted was my *Weeds* book. It would be a sweet reminder of my early years working with Abraham and I wanted it for my own studio.

I headed for the bookshelf and my foot crunched over something. It was probably another shell. I thought I'd picked them all up off the floor, but I guess I missed one.

I made it to the darkened bookshelf and looked closely for a moment before distinguishing the blue leather cover from the others. I pulled the book off the shelf and slipped it into my bag, just as the studio light flipped on and the world lit up.

Chapter 7

"Stealing books again?"

My heart nearly jumped out of my chest. "Oh my God."

"Call me Derek," he said with a sardonic chuckle, amused by his little joke. He stood in the doorway, not quite inside the room, so the light didn't reach his face. But even if he hadn't announced himself, I would've recognized that lithe, muscular figure anywhere.

I had to slap my chest a few times to get my heart pumping before I could squeak intelligibly. "What are you doing here? You scared the crap out of me."

"That's always a nice side benefit," Derek remarked as he strolled toward me. "I recall watching the police seal this room."

"It was sealed? I hadn't noticed." I took a step back. "You followed me here."

"Of course I did." He splayed his hands out as though he were holding some special gift I'd always wanted. "You left the Covington in too much of a hurry to be up to any good."

"Well, you're late. I'm leaving now."

"I saw you in here earlier, but your mother arrived so I decided to wait. And sure enough, you're back, skulking around in the dark."

"If this is about me being a murder suspect, get over it." I rubbed my temples to stave off the headache he was giving me. "You've wasted time tracking me halfway across Northern California while the real killer is getting away with murder."

"I don't think you're a murder suspect," he said as he picked up a birch board and ran one hand across the smooth surface, his clever fingers stroking the wood back and forth across the grain.

Good grief.

His words slowly filtered through my clogged brain. "Wait. You *don't* think I killed Abraham? Then why are you here?"

He shoved his hands in his pockets. "I assumed you'd try something stupid. Turns out I was right."

"You—what?"

"I said, I assumed you'd—"

"I heard you," I snapped. "Can you get any more insulting?"

He grinned. "I can try."

I stifled a shriek, inhaled deeply and let the air out slowly. "So you followed me because you think I'm *stupid*?"

"I don't think you're stupid but I do think you might *do* something stupid." He leaned back against the worktable and crossed his ankles.

I shook my head. "Sounds like the same thing to me."

"It's not."

"I appreciate that you think there's a difference, but I don't—"

"Are you, or are you not, trying to track down a killer by yourself?"

I licked my lips. A tell? "No."

"I believe you are."

I laughed but it sounded tinny. "That's ridiculous. I came up here looking for Abraham's journals to help with the work I'm doing on the *Faust*. I went to visit my parents up the street and stopped back here to get a book that belongs to me."

I glanced around as I said it and suddenly realized something was very wrong.

Abraham's studio was a mess. I mean, a real mess. Torn apart. Things were tossed across the countertops and on the floor. A heavy punching cradle was upended on the floor, the hard object I'd stumbled over. There were papers pulled from drawers and reams of book cloth strewn around the room. Several glass jars used to mix PVA glue were shattered on the floor.

"Look at this mess," I said in alarm. "Somebody's been here."

His eyes narrowed. "What do you mean, somebody's been here?"

I waved my hands around frantically. "Everything's tossed every which way."

He looked around. "I assumed Karastovsky liked it this way."

I stomped my foot. "No! I was just here an hour ago and it was fine. Somebody's been here and done this. You were waiting for me. Did you see anyone?"

He scowled. "No. I followed you up the hill to your mother's and missed catching whoever did this."

I sagged against the counter.

"Don't touch anything else." He rubbed his jaw in frustration. "I'll call the police."

Derek didn't have to follow me home but he did it anyway. When I detoured and pulled into the Whole Foods parking lot, he insisted on accompanying me inside, then carried my bags out to the car when I was finished.

I had a tendency to eat when I was overly nervous, and tonight's mood qualified.

Derek had called Inspector Jaglow to tell him the news of the break-in at Abraham's. We'd dutifully waited the hour and a half it took him to get there with one of his crime scene investigators. Jaglow had asked a few questions, then cleared us to leave the premises.

Halfway across the Golden Gate Bridge it had occurred to me that if my timing were different, I might've run right into Abraham's killer.

What had the killer been searching for? Was it the missing item from the secret pocket inside the *Faust*? Something else? A book? Gems? If I could find Abraham's journals, I might have a better idea what it was that was worth killing for.

"You're an intense shopper," Derek said.

"It calms my nerves. You didn't have to follow me here."

"I needed a few things as well."

He carried six grocery bags, five of which were mine.

"I suppose you're going back up there to look for Karastovsky's journals," Derek said as I punched the security button and unlocked my car.

"Of course," I said more boldly than I felt, then opened my trunk. "I don't want to duplicate his work and he may have some thoughts and insights I haven't considered." That was a lie, of course. All I wanted was the missing piece of paper, whatever it was.

"I'll help you look for them."

"Oh, thanks." Sweet, but awkward. I didn't want him in the studio while I searched for the missing item, especially since I had no clue what it was. Could this get more convoluted?

"But it won't be necessary," I added lightly. "I've got to go up for the memorial service anyway, so I'll have the whole afternoon to find the journals."

"You really are an appalling liar," he said conversationally, as he loaded the shopping bags into my trunk.

"I'm not lying," I lied. Could he see my face turning red in the dim light of the parking lot? He was right. I really was bad at lying. I needed to take lessons from Robin. If there were a baseball team for liars, she would be the cleanup hitter. And she would consider that a compliment.

"You're lying about something," he countered cheerfully as he shoved the last of the bags into the space. "But not to worry. I'll be heading up for the service as well, and I *will* help you look."

I bit my lip to keep from groaning. "Cool."

He stared at the plethora of bags in my trunk. "You're actually going to consume all this swill?"

Why did an insult uttered with a sexy British accent

have less of a sting? "If you're referring to my pur-chases, it's not swill; it's perfectly good food."

Slamming the trunk shut, he folded his arms. "I counted six frozen pizzas, eight bags of chocolate and a gallon of ice cream."

"Ice cream is an excellent source of calcium."

"It's swill."

"Nutritious swill," I pointed out.

"If you're a fourteen-year-old boy."

"You're getting offensive again."

"It's a gift." He brushed his hands together. "Get in your car. I'll follow you home."

I held up my hand. "That's not necessary."

"It is."

"Okay, first of all, I'm not a killer, remember? So you need to stop following me. And second, seriously, you should get a hobby or something. What about sports? Is there a gym near your hotel? You could work out more often."

He just smiled and waited. It was exasperating. And seeing as how we were standing in the middle of the parking lot of Whole Foods Market, it was also ridic-ulous.

I sighed. "I'm going straight home to feed my neigh-bors' cats and watch some TV. As strongly as you may believe to the contrary, I assure you I'm not a foolish person."

"Your eating habits betray you." He gave a signifi-cant nod to the back of my car where my bags of swill were stashed.

"I happen to have a speedy metabolism."

"That can't last forever."

"Oh, thanks for that." I threw up my hands in defeat. "Fine. Follow me. Whatever."

He shooed me toward the driver's door. "Off you go, then."

"You're incredibly annoying," I said. "But thank you for carrying my grocery bags."

"I assure you it was pure entertainment."

I jogged around to the driver's side, climbed in and slammed the door shut, then started up the engine. I looked over and gave him a weak smile.

The gaze he gave me was anything but weak. I gulped, then drove away, watching in my rearview mirror as he jumped into the Bentley, started it up and followed me out of the lot.

I tossed and turned all night and woke up the next morning feeling groggy and out of sorts, with a dull headache accompanied by an impending sense of doom. I wasn't sure whether to blame Derek Stone or the pint of Coney Island Waffle Cone Crunch I'd consumed the night before while watching *Survivor: East L.A.*

I was happier blaming Derek, I decided, as I stumbled to the kitchen to grab my first cup of strong coffee before heading for the shower.

I stared at the contents of my closet and remembered I'd most likely be meeting the Winslows today. I chose a semiconservative, fitted gray pin-striped suit with a short flared skirt, crisp white shirt with a stand-up collar and black heels.

Robin had insisted I buy this suit because it made me look like a defrocked postulant. I'd figured it was a compliment but later had to Google the word *postu-*

lant. I'd found a Web site of a nunnery in Indiana filled with photos of happy young women bowing their heads in prayer as they answered the heavenly call to become brides of Christ.

There were no photos of the defrocked variety, but it no longer mattered. Sometimes it was better not to examine Robin's words too closely.

After I poured my second cup of coffee, I went next door to check on the cats. Somehow I'd forgotten to feed them last night, another offense I would lay at the feet of Derek Stone. I washed their kitty bowls and gave them fresh water and some mushy food from a can mixed with kibble bits.

Pookie and Splinters were in a playful mood, so I stuck around for ten minutes to keep them company as they careened around a massive redwood log and a couple of hunks of burl, then zoomed up the tower of their deluxe carpeted cathouse and back down again.

As the cats chased each other and their tails, I thought about last night at Abraham's studio. I'd barely avoided meeting a murderer. He'd been there— whoever he was—carrying on a hasty search while I'd blissfully visited with my family a few hundred yards up the hill.

Creepy.

I couldn't put a face to whoever it was. I wondered again whether he'd been looking for the same missing item I was after. Or was it something else? Had Abraham been hiding other secrets?

And speaking of secrets, I hadn't told Derek Stone about the cocktail napkin I'd found with the scrawled note from someone named Anandalla. I wondered

guiltily whether I should've told him, then shook my
head. There were only so many sins I could deal with
at one time. I'd tell him about the note later.

It wouldn't hurt to stop at the Buena Vista tonight,
chat up the bartenders and ask whether they knew
someone named Anandalla. It was a long shot. I
couldn't describe her.

Did the cocktail napkin note even matter? Was I
picking at nits? Possibly. Nevertheless, I was overcome
by a sudden desire for Irish coffee. I could tag Robin
to come with me if she didn't have a date. She probably had a date. Fine. I could go alone.

Maybe Derek Stone was available. He seemed to
have nothing better to do than follow me around, so
why not include him?

"It's not like it's a date or anything," I muttered
aloud. "More like an outing."

Pookie hopped onto the couch and gave my thigh
a much-needed head butt.

"Come here," I murmured, and settled the cat in
my lap, where he proceeded to lick and groom himself. Splinters paced in front of my feet and meowed
loudly.

"I thought cats were supposed to be aloof," I said,
scratching Pookie's ear. "You're embarrassing Splinters."

Pookie apparently got the message because he leapt
off the couch to rejoin Splinters in their chasing game.
I watched them for another minute, chuckling and
wondering if maybe I should get myself a cat. Then I
caught a whiff of something horrendous and remembered I hadn't cleaned out their litter box.

"Oh, mercy." I grabbed a plastic bag, covered my nose and approached the offending box.

So maybe I didn't need a pet right now.

As I walked back to my place, I realized my headache was gone. I packed leftover Chinese food for lunch, collected the tools I would need for the day along with some leather and paper samples, then locked up and took off across town.

When I got to the Covington, I headed straight for Ian's elegantly masculine office to sign all the necessary papers to become an official independent contractor for the Covington Library.

"You won't be leaving early today, right?" Ian asked, as he walked to a large Renaissance painting of a nude woman lounging on a bed and holding an orange shawl that did nothing to cover her lush body. He pulled the frame away from the wall, revealing a wall safe. "I'd hate to disappoint the Winslows two days in a row."

"I'll be here," I assured him, then added lightly, "I guess they're used to everyone kowtowing to them."

He turned. "The Winslows are our largest benefactors, so it's in our best interests to kowtow our butts off to make them happy."

I grimaced inwardly but said, "Kowtowing here, boss."

He smirked. "I like the sound of that. So you'll stick around?"

"Of course, don't worry." But it still annoyed the hell out of me that the Winslows got away with making everyone bend over backward to accommodate them.

I shouldn't have been so irritated, but after over-hearing that suspicious discussion the night Abraham was killed, I couldn't help feeling that they weren't nice people. Had one of them killed Abraham?

I had to say, it gave me a warm feeling to picture Meredith Winslow spending twenty years or so in an ill-fitting orange jumpsuit, cozying up to a great big gal named Beulah.

"Here you go." Ian removed the *Faust* from the wall safe and handed it to me. The book was still wrapped in the white cloth I'd secured it in yesterday when I left it with Derek.

"Thanks." I gripped it close to my chest, feeling a strange urge to protect it. I had a sudden picture of Abraham clutching the book inside his jacket as he died.

A pounding wave of grief washed over me and I had to fight the urge to curl up and cry. I wondered how many other painful memories the book had been witness to. Could a book hold memory within its covers? When I peeled away its covers, would the pain seep out and hurt me? Was I going a little crazy?

Maybe it was a good thing Ian kept it in the safe.

He was watching me closely, I realized. Were all my feelings showing on my face?

"Guess I'll be downstairs," I said.

He smiled uncertainly. "Have a productive day, Brooklyn."

Productive. Right. Get to work.

"Ciao," I said, and rushed out of his office.

"First, do no harm" was not just for doctors. In book restoration, the same was true. The less manipulation and disturbance of the original work, the better. As I stared at the thick black leather cover where the spine was mildly cracked along the front seam, I determined exactly how to proceed, step by step, and made notes accordingly.

Of course, I wouldn't take any steps until the Winslows had come and gone. I didn't mind an audience when I worked, but I drew the line at book owners. For some reason, they rarely handled it well. It was as if they were watching me destroy their baby, pulling the little darling apart and spreading its tiny limbs and body parts out across the work space.

Plus, owners had opinions—which they were entitled to, of course, but that didn't mean I wanted to hear them.

So while I waited, I pulled out my camera and photographed the book from every possible angle. I took shots of the interior pages and the gorgeous Armageddon painting that was just as staggering on second view as it had been yesterday. I zoomed in on the brass eagle's claw clasps in both latched and unlatched positions and got close-up shots of each, then photographed the embedded jewels from several angles to catch their many facets.

"Why is she taking pictures of our stuff?"

I should've been used to people sneaking up on me by now, but no. I almost dropped my camera.

Meredith Winslow stood just inside the room, wearing a petulant frown and a perky yellow wool minidress. Meredith's mother and father stood close behind her, making a perfect family portrait. *American Gothic* with snotty offspring.

I had an insane urge to shout, "Say cheese!" and

snap their photo, but I resisted. Instead, I pasted a smile on my face and said, "Come on in. I'm just doing some preliminary work before I start the restoration."

Meredith didn't move but continued to glare at me with her bottom lip stuck out in a pout. She looked exactly as I'd seen her in hundreds of tabloid photos taken over the years. I wondered why she was looking at me as if I'd stolen her favorite puppy or something.

"Come on, Merry, you're holding up the show," Conrad Winslow said jovially as he grabbed hold of his daughter's arm and steered her into the room. I hadn't noticed the other night, but he spoke with a slight German accent.

"Daddy," Meredith protested, and tugged her arm away. Her cheeks turned pink. She seemed embarrassed by her dad and obviously pissed off about being dragged in here to meet me.

"I'm Brooklyn," I said as I casually spread the white cloth over the *Faust*. I still felt a little protective about the book.

"We've heard all about you, Brooklyn," Mrs. Winslow said. Her smile was so genuine, I almost relaxed.

"I can explain some of the work I'll be doing if you'd like."

"We'd love it," Mrs. Winslow said.

I pulled the book closer and took off the cloth, and they all jostled for position around me.

"It's so fascinating," Mrs. Winslow said.

"Whole other world," Conrad agreed.

Ian walked in and grinned. "There you are."

"Hi, Ian," Meredith said, batting her eyelashes.

"Hi, Meredith." He gave her a slight smile. "Allow me to make the official introductions." He formally introduced us, then said, "Brooklyn is one of the finest rare book experts in the country. She'll be completing the work on the *Faust* for the official opening next week."

"It's great to meet you all," I said, flustered by Ian's praise as I stood to shake hands with everyone. I was at least half a foot taller than Meredith, but she still gave the impression of looking down on me. Screw it, I'd been looked down on by better bitches than this one. Besides, her handshake had all the clout of a dead trout.

Mrs. Winslow shook my hand and said, "It's lovely to officially meet you, Brooklyn. You come so highly regarded, I know you'll do us proud."

I smiled. "Thanks, Mrs. Winslow. I hope you'll be pleased."

"Oh, honey," she said with just a hint of a soft Southern accent as she patted the top of my hand affectionately. "I don't have a worry in the world. And you call me Sylvia."

I smiled for real. "Thanks, Sylvia."

"We're just so grateful to have you working for us, under the circumstances."

"Yah, it's great to meet you, young lady," Mr. Winslow said genially, edging around his wife to grab my hand and pump it briskly. "Conrad Winslow, at your service."

He was solidly built, about six feet tall, with reddish hair going gray at the temples. His navy suit probably cost three thousand dollars, but his white shirt was coming untucked and his tie was askew. And his eyes were slightly red. I had the fleeting thought that he'd probably had a drink with breakfast.

I was shocked to realize I liked him. I liked his wife, too. These were the people that less than a day ago I'd considered most likely to fry for killing Abraham.

Of course, my altered opinion didn't stretch to little Meredith. She was a stone-cold ice maiden.

How had two fairly normal people spawned someone like her?

"It's just so fascinating, what you do," Sylvia said, moving closer to the table. "Can you explain some of your processes?"

"Sure," I said, and turned back to the table in time to see Meredith reach for the book.

"No," I said, moving the book away.

"What?" She looked astonished. "It's *our* property."

"I'm sorry," I said immediately. "Of course it's your property. I meant no insult. It just needs to be handled carefully; that's all. I can show you."

"Forget it."

"Meredith, please," Sylvia said. "I'm sure Brooklyn didn't—"

"Fine, take her side." She crossed her arms and slumped against the side counter. "It's just a stupid book."

"That's more than enough, Meredith," Sylvia said through clenched teeth, then turned to me. "Brooklyn is such an interesting name. Are you named for the borough? Do people call you Brook?"

"Well," I began, "most people call me—"

"Sylvia, don't badger the girl," Mr. Winslow said with a hearty laugh. "Let her get back to work."

Sylvia laughed and patted my arm. "I don't mean to pester you." She glanced at her daughter. "Meredith, please don't slouch."

"You're not pestering me at all," I insisted with a smile. "It's a pleasure to talk to you." I glanced at Ian to make sure he noticed all the happy kowtowing going on. "Please come by anytime."

"It's nice to see a young person with such focus." She gave her daughter a pointed look.

Oh boy.

Meredith clenched her teeth. "We should let the working girl get back to work."

"Good idea," Ian said quickly.

Conrad rocked on his heels. "You do a good job and there might be a little bonus in it for you."

I smiled at him. "That's not necessary, Mr. Winslow. I'm just doing my job and I love my work."

"Nothing wrong with being well paid for a job well-done, is there?" He winked. "I've found that money greases a lot of wheels."

He laughed and I chuckled at his cheery candor. I didn't mean it to be a private moment between us, but that was how he seemed to take it. And so did Meredith. Her eyes narrowed on me like a death ray. Not to be a wimp, but she seriously creeped me out.

I hadn't noticed the other night, but up close, Meredith Winslow, despite her petite stature, had an almost predatory thing going on. Like a cat, but not a nice kitty. The tabloid press had often called her frivolous, a dumb blonde, but I had the distinct impression there was a lot more going on under those expertly high-lighted tresses than most people gave her credit for.

Dumb wasn't the word I'd use for Meredith Winslow.

Scary came a lot closer.

Chapter 8

I supposed Meredith Winslow and I would never go shopping together, but Mr. and Mrs. Winslow were a couple of pips, as my dad would say. Nice, charming and nothing like what I'd expected, especially after overhearing that argument the other night.

As I began work on the *Faust*, first prying away the pastedowns from the cover boards, I recalled what I'd overheard of the Winslows' conversation the night of the murder.

They hadn't actually mentioned Abraham's name, so maybe they'd been talking about someone else. But they'd definitely said something about a problem with a book. It had to be connected to their book collection and probably the exhibition.

Could they have meant Ian? I hoped not. The Covington Library had employed an entire crew to work on the Winslow collection. I could ask Ian for the names of everyone on staff, then talk to each of them. But why? Was this me, playing detective? Was this where Derek Stone would step in and call me an idiot for trying to flush out a killer?

"I'm not an idiot," I grumbled, then realized I was gripping the knife handle so hard it was digging into my palm. I quickly relaxed my grip before I drew blood and broke one of the top ten rules of bookbinding. Don't bleed on the books.

Maybe I could satisfy my curiosity by calling the police. Just to touch base, find out how the investigation was going. Unfortunately, I still had a few secrets of my own I wasn't ready to give up, so how could I wangle information out of them if I wasn't willing to spill my guts in return?

I couldn't tell them about the Winslows' conversation I'd overheard the night of the murder because I didn't even know who they'd been talking about.

And there was my mother showing up at the Covington that same night and acting very strangely. I wasn't about to mention that to the cops.

There was something missing from inside the *Faust*. But until I knew what it was, what could I tell the police?

There was the splotch of blood found on the cover of the book, wiped clean by none other than Derek Stone.

"A suspicious move on his part," I added aloud, then made a note to follow up with Derek about whose blood it was.

I also hadn't mentioned to the police that I'd found Anandalla's cocktail napkin note in Abraham's ransacked studio. But I didn't know who she was or whether she had anything to do with anything. She could be Abraham's accountant or his manicurist or someone equally innocuous.

Let's face it, all I had were theories and maybes

and possibilities. No wonder my head was spinning. I guess I wouldn't be calling the police anytime soon.

The gilded eagle on the cover of the *Faust* stared up at me with its one good eye. Was it thinking I should get my butt back to work and earn my inflated salary?

"My salary is not inflated, and you're not even a real bird," I protested. But I picked up my brush and got back to work anyway. I worked page by page, using the stiff, dry brush to remove microscopic grains of dirt and film and making notes of any damage as I went.

The book hadn't been stored well, but it wasn't the worst I'd ever seen. I'd have to detach the signatures—the pages—from the spine and clean and resew them back together more securely. The front and back boards had come loose at the hinges and would need reinforcement. There was some mild insect damage on the tops of a number of pages. And I'd have to clean and resct the gems on the front cover.

I got up from my chair and tested the workroom's double-screw book press to see if it was in workable condition. I would use it to hold the book, spine end up, to resew the signatures and do the gluing and possibly regild the spine titles and "make it look pretty," per the clients' orders. The screws on the press needed oiling, but otherwise, it was a decent piece of hardware. This type of press, with its two independent screws, was ideal for books that had suffered water and mildew damage because they were often bloated and uneven along the sides.

I studied the fanciful text as I worked. The book

was written entirely in German, of course. I could make out a number of basic words, having spent two weeks skiing in Garmisch-Partenkirchen during college. Unfortunately, I didn't see any references to swilling cheap German lager or extreme snowboarding, which I would've been able to translate impeccably. I made a note to buy a German dictionary and a paperback version of *Faust* and read Goethe's version of the man who sold his soul to the devil.

The *devil*.

My hands froze on the page as Abraham's last words came rushing back into my head. *Remember the devil*. I felt a wave of dismay that I still didn't have a clue what they meant.

"Knock, knock."

"Oh!" I looked up and saw Conrad Winslow standing at the door. "Mr. Winslow. You caught me off guard. Come in."

He was alone, thank goodness. I didn't think I could take another round of dodge-the-poison-dart vibes with darling Meredith.

"I'm sorry, my dear." He looked a little embarrassed as he walked in.

"That's okay, I get lost in my work sometimes."

"You must love what you do."

"I do," I said. "How can I help you?" It sounded obsequious to my ears, but as Ian had pointed out earlier, Mr. Winslow was the boss and kowtowing was the word of the day.

He stared at the *Faust* for a long moment. "It's something, isn't it?"

I smiled. "Yes, it is."

With a shy smile, he said, "I've never been much of a book reader. Sports page and financial section are more my speed. So how did I end up with all these books?" He chuckled. "That is irony."

"It just figures, doesn't it?" I turned a page and ran the brush along the seam. "But it's a beautiful collection and the *Faust* is fantastic."

"Yah, well." He looked around the room, then back at the book, not meeting my gaze. Then he stepped a few inches back from the table. "You've heard it's cursed."

I scribbled a note to myself about the foxing on the next page. "Yes, of course. Fascinating, isn't it?"

He stared hard at me. "You don't mind working on something that might kill you?"

My smile faded. "Mr. Winslow, that's just a legend. A book can't—"

"No legend," he said firmly. "The thing is cursed. My grandfather was given the book and died of poisoning a few days later. It was passed on to my great-uncle, who barely had it a week before he died, crushed under a trolley. Two cousins met a similar fate. It is no legend."

"But that's—"

"They found one cousin swinging from a rope. He was not suicidal." Mr. Winslow pulled a handkerchief from his breast pocket and swiped his brow. "Now Karastovsky's dead because of it. I want to pull it from the exhibition before someone else suffers."

"But you can't," I insisted, closing the book and stroking the rich, jewel-encrusted leather cover. "Look at this. It's priceless, exquisite. It's the centerpiece of your collection for good reason. It's an extremely important work of art, both historically and aestheti- cally. You can't pull it. It would be a crime to—"

"It's just a book," he said sharply. His German ac- cent grew thicker and he jabbed his finger in the air for emphasis. "Do you want to die over a stupid book?"

I edged back. "Abraham may be dead but this book didn't kill him."

Easy for me to say.

He stared at me, looked at the book, then up at the ceiling, frowning all the while.

"Hell, you're right," he finally said.

I was?

He weighed his words before speaking. "Karastov- sky called me the afternoon of the opening, said he needed to meet with me that night. Had something to show me. I told him I couldn't make it." He shrugged. "I didn't like him, so I put him off."

"You didn't like Abraham?"

"No. A personality conflict, I suppose. And I over- heard a shouting match between him and McCullough that sealed my opinion."

Abraham and Ian had argued?

"What was the argument about?" I asked.

He frowned. "You don't want to hear about that."

"If it has anything to do with the books, I do."

He wiped the edge of his hairline and let out a breath. "Karastovsky had taken one of my grandfa- ther's Bibles and put a new binding on it, a pale pink leather, and Sylvia was thrilled with it. But McCul- lough went ballistic. He told Karastovsky he hadn't hired him to—" He stopped, gave me an apologetic look. "You'll pardon the expression, 'fuck up' a priceless collection by throwing designer leather on everything."

"Oh dear."

"Yah, he was angry."

"But Abraham was doing the Bible for your wife, right? It wasn't part of the exhibition."

"It was supposed to be," he confessed. "It belonged to my grandmother."

"I see."

"Yah," he said. "So that's why we were all very happy when Ian told us you would be taking over the work. You have ethics and respect for books."

"Thanks." I took the compliment with a smile, but now it was my turn to be uncomfortable. This problem came back to the basic argument between Abraham and me. He'd never worked with conservation methods, didn't really understand them or care about them. The conservation field was relatively new and he didn't accept it, didn't trust it.

When I'd told Abraham I was going for an advanced degree in the same field he'd worked his whole life, he'd sneered. I didn't need a diploma to know how to bring a book back to life. But I'd gone ahead and obtained double master's degrees in library science and fine art with an emphasis on conservation and restoration, along with a boatload of other certifications. Abraham, on the other hand, had learned the old-fashioned way, at his father's knee in the family bookbindery in Toronto.

"Thank you for trusting me with your book," I said. "But honestly, in spite of what you heard during that argument, Abraham was a consummate professional."

"I still like you better," he said, and winked at me. I knew he wasn't really flirting, but it was a borderline "ew" moment, seeing as how he was Meredith's father.

"Thanks," I said weakly.

"Well now, I've overstayed my welcome," he said genially.

"Not at all."

He pulled out a business card. "I want you to call me if you have any problems."

"Thanks. I will."

He nodded. "I think you've got the right attitude about this whole 'curse' business, so I'll get out of your way and let you get back to work."

"I enjoyed talking to you," I said, surprised to realize I meant it.

"Then you'll do me another favor?"

I paused, wondering what bomb he might drop this time, but then nodded. "Of course."

"Don't put a pink cover on the damn thing," he said with a wink. "It might make the ladies happy, but the book lovers will swallow their dentures."

I laughed with relief. "No pink covers, I promise."

"And one more thing."

"Sure."

"Be careful, my dear."

The next time I looked up, it was five o'clock. I'd worked for four hours straight. I dropped the dry brush on the table and rolled and stretched my fingers to ease the cramping, then raised my arms up and rolled my shoulders to work out the tightness. It was already dark outside and I knew I was probably one of the last ones left in the building. I packed up my tools and found a security guard who took the *Faust* for safekeeping.

I stepped outside and felt a chill that had nothing to do with the weather. I glanced around warily, then pulled my jacket tight and ran to my car.

Rather than sit in traffic, I had the taxi driver drop me off at Larkin and Beach and I walked a block over to the Buena Vista. Cabbing it to Fisherman's Wharf on a Friday night solved two problems for me. I wouldn't have to fight for a parking place and I'd avoid the idiocy of drinking and driving.

But speaking of idiocy, I wondered if I was nuts for hoping to find the unknown Anandalla, based on a flimsy cocktail napkin note.

"Flimsy maybe, but intriguing nonetheless," I maintained as I maneuvered my way along the crowded sidewalk, then had to cover my ears as a cable car rumbled down Hyde. It gained speed and clanged its bell loud enough to wake the dead and to alert the large crowd milling at the cable car turnaround a half block away.

Reaching the door of the Buena Vista, I stared in dismay at the standing-room-only crowd inside. Robin was going to kill me for bringing her into this madness. If I ever made it to the bar, I'd make sure to have a drink waiting for her when she showed up.

I forced my way inside and nudged people out of the way until I hit the bar. As the scents of chili and fried fish hit me, old memories poured in.

I was ten years old the first time I came here. My parents had brought our whole brood along to meet some Deadhead friends for breakfast. It was the Friday morning after Thanksgiving and we had so much fun, we insisted on making it a yearly tradition. Mom and Dad would perch at the bar, drinking Irish coffee and enjoying the fantastic view, while we six kids would pick a likely table and hover anxiously until the seated customers paid their tabs and left.

After a huge breakfast, we would pile into cars and drive out to the polo fields at Golden Gate Park where Dad and his friends and all the kids would play football for a few hours. After a few years of that, Mom and her girlfriends and my sisters and I got smart enough to pass on the football insanity and head instead to Union Square and the shopping insanity.

Within five minutes, I lucked out and grabbed a barstool. Two bartenders worked at each end of the long bar. They'd each lined up twenty Irish coffee glasses in the well of the bar. The show was about to begin.

I watched the tall, lanky bartender at my end grab a pot of hot water and move down the line, spilling hot water into each glass to warm them up. Then he quickly tossed the water out of one glass and dropped a sugar cube inside before passing to the next glass. His hands worked so fast, I could barely follow the action. After filling each glass with fresh coffee, he whisked a spoon into each one to dissolve the sugar, then added a healthy shot of Irish whiskey, followed by a large dollop of freshly whipped cream.

Classic.

There was some scattered applause. I calculated that it took both bartenders less than ninety seconds to make forty Irish coffees. Given the way the two men eyed each other, I had a feeling there was some competition involved.

I held up my hand and made eye contact with my guy. He grinned and placed an Irish on a napkin in front of me.

"Thanks," I said.

"*De nada,*" he said in a twangy Texas accent and I noticed his name tag said "Neil." He must've been a new hire because I didn't recognize him. Even though I hadn't been here in a year, I still knew the faces of most of the employees. There was very little turnover here. Seriously, they still called one busboy "the kid" and he had to be seventy years old.

I blissfully sipped my drink, drawing the hot coffee through the cream so I could taste the individual flavors without stirring it all together and losing both the coolness of the cream and the heat of the coffee.

Turning on my stool, I glanced at the thick crowd behind me and the picture-perfect view beyond. There was nothing complicated here, nothing to deal with other than the sounds of laughter and the aroma of Friday night clam chowder.

I didn't want to think about Abraham or murder or blood or books. I was tired of spinning my wheels, going around in circles and ending up back where I'd started. So instead, I spun around on my stool and ordered another drink. From here on out, I would forget about solving murders and spend my energy tracking down Abraham's journals. That was all I wanted. I didn't need to unravel any mysteries other than the mystery of the book. The police could do the rest.

"Is that so much to ask?" I wondered, and took a healthy sip of my new drink.

"Wha'd you say?" Neil, my tall bartender, asked. I did like an attentive bartender.

I smiled and took a chance. "Do you know someone named Anandalla who comes in here regularly?" I asked casually.

"Anandalla." His eyebrows squinched together, so I figured he was thinking. "You a friend of hers?"

"Sort of. She told me to meet her here tonight."

"Huh." He grabbed a wet towel and dragged it along the well where the multiple Irish coffee creation had taken place. I imagined it got pretty sticky if they didn't mop up immediately. "I haven't seen her since, hmm, must've been Wednesday."

Could I be this lucky? Could we really be talking about the same Anandalla? But seriously, how many women with that name were running around San Francisco?

"Is she out of town?" I asked.

"Nah, I don't think so." He pulled twenty glasses out of the tray the busboy left and began lining them up to make another batch. "She said something about going north for a few days."

"You mean like Canada or something?"

"Nah, she's got relatives up in the wine country. Said she might hang out there for a few days."

"Oh. Must be nice to have a place to stay up there, huh?"

"Bet your ass."

I smiled thinly. I'd have to leave a nice tip for Neil because he'd been so forthcoming, even though I still didn't know much. I still didn't know how she knew Abraham. Was she a bookseller? Another bookbinder? Was she the one who'd torn his studio apart?

"Oh, hell, maybe she's a hooker." I shook my head in disgust. Neil had given me some answers, but now I had more questions. I hated when that happened.

"Hey, you," Robin shouted, tapping me on the shoulder.

I bounced four inches off the stool and almost spilled my drink.

"Aren't you the jumpy one," she said.

"People keep sneaking up on me," I complained.

"That's got to be a problem since you're currently surrounded by a few hundred of them."

"Never mind. You want an Irish coffee?"

"Sure."

I caught Neil's eye and held up two fingers. Then I stood up and gave Robin a hug.

"Only one barstool," I said. "Do you want it?"

"You go ahead. I've been sitting all day."

Neil was waiting with our drink when I turned the stool around. The new kid was okay.

"Remind me again why we're here," Robin shouted.

"I love this place."

"So do I, but you've got to be a masochist to show up on a Friday night. I had to park three blocks away."

"Sorry about that." I filled her in on everything that had happened since we last spoke. I left nothing out. Well, except for the irritating twinge I got in my stomach whenever Derek Stone looked at me with those eyes that saw too much. I didn't mention that.

When I was finished, Robin shook her head and

ordered another round of drinks since we'd both plowed through the ones we had.

"Okay, this better be my last one," I said, toasting her.

"Famous last words," she murmured, clicked my glass with hers and drank.

"So, what do you think?" I said.

"What can I say? I think you're insane." She took another sip, then looked me up and down. "And even though you have atrocious taste in clothing and worse taste in shoes, I'll really miss you if you get yourself killed."

Chapter 9

"That's so sweet," I said, reaching out to hug her and almost falling off my stool. "I would miss you, too."

"Yes, but I'm serious."

"I know." I patted my heart. "Thank you."

"No, I mean about your atrocious taste in clothes," she said with a smirk.

I glanced down at my gray suit. "You picked out this outfit. And come on, my shoes are hot." They were killing me, too. Working in four-inch heels should be against the law.

"Okay, you look good today," she allowed. "But I still have nightmares about those Birkenstocks."

"This is San Francisco," I shouted over the din. "Everybody wears Birkenstocks."

"If everybody jumped off the bridge, would you jump, too?"

I rolled my eyes and turned on my stool to check on the bartenders. I'd lost count of the number of drinks I'd had, but that didn't mean it was time to stop, did it?

The mirror behind the bar reflected both Robin and

me as well as the burgeoning crowd and the lights of the bay behind us.

"So you didn't call me stupid and I appreciate that," I said. "But you did call my clothes stupid."

"No, I didn't. I called them atrocious." She sipped her drink. "Atrocious. I like to say that word."

I stared in horror. "Oh my God, you're drunk." I giggled. "You never get drunk."

"I'm not drunk. I don't get drunk. I'm a control freak." She downed her drink. "We should go."

"Not yet." The Irish whiskey was definitely taking effect and I couldn't quite figure out why I'd been so offended by Robin's words.

Oh yeah, my atrocious clothes. But she'd hate to see me dead, which was nice, although it implied that I was stupid enough to get myself killed.

I pointed at her. "I have no intention of getting myself killed simply because I'm looking for a few answers."

"Okay, good."

"But if you think it's a possibility that I could get myself killed, then you must think I'm stupid."

"How do you figure?" she asked.

"Is that a trick question?"

She laughed, but I knew she was trying to confuse me. And thanks to the booze, it was working. Robin thought she had the upper hand just because she was relatively sober compared to me. Maybe I was two drinks ahead of her, but I was also a Wainwright. We did all our best thinking when our brains were marinated in alcohol.

And coffee fueled the brilliance. I was fast approaching the intellectual level of Albert Einstein.

"What was the question?" I asked.

Robin laughed and sipped her drink.

"Miss?"

"He's talking to you, Brooklyn," Robin shouted.

I turned. It was the bartender, the kid. What was his name? Oh yeah, it was right on his shirt. Neil. "Yes, Neil?"

"Anandalla's at the end of the bar if you want to talk to her."

I tensed up. Here was my chance. I leaned back on the stool but couldn't see her from where I sat. Then I remembered the bar mirror. Now I could see the whole room, including the woman sitting at the end of the bar. She looked short, with dark curly hair, cute, probably in her mid-twenties. She twisted around in her stool, searching the crowd, her eyes wide, her jaw tight.

I watched her gaze drift to the mirror and her eyes suddenly met mine. She recoiled but recovered in a flash, threw some cash on the bar and disappeared in the bar crowd.

"Hey!" What was that about? Did she know me?

I jumped up. "Let's go!"

"Are you nuts?" Robin said. "I'm not finished. We haven't paid our bill."

"Hold my bag," I shouted. "I'll be back."

My heavy bag hit her in the stomach, but she managed to grab it before it slid to the floor.

"You're insane," I heard her say as I thrust myself into the horde.

Once I was out the door, I looked both ways and saw Anandalla sprinting up Hyde Street toward North Point. I took off after her, watched her reach the crest of the hill. She glanced left and right, chose right and disappeared.

The hill was unbelievably steep. Halfway up, I had to stop and hold my stomach, which was starting to cramp from the combination of alcohol, four-inch heels and a skirt that was tighter than it had been when I put it on this morning.

I leaned one hand against the building, panting and puffing like an old man.

It wasn't my best moment.

But why had she run away from me? How did she know me?

I turned and saw Robin waiting patiently at the bottom of the hill. With another heavy breath, I shuffled back down and she handed me my bag.

"I paid the bill," she said.

"Thanks."

"You owe me."

"I know."

We crossed Hyde when the signal changed. For a few minutes we strolled without speaking, enjoying the evening air. We'd walked three blocks and were passing Ripley's Believe It or Not when Robin finally spoke.

"What the hell were you thinking?"

"That was the girl I was looking for," I explained as I stared at a two-headed ferret in the Ripley's display. "That was Anandalla."

"Anandalla? The one whose note you found in Abraham's studio?"

"Right. And as soon as she saw me, she ran away."

"How do you know it was her?"

"The bartender said so." I absently studied Ripley's

poster of a pregnant man who used to be a woman. "And how many women have a name like that?"

Robin twisted her lips. "I've never heard it before."

"She looked straight at me, Robin. She recognized me. I don't know how, but she knew me. And as soon as she saw me, she raced out of there. I tried to catch up with her, but I guess I'm a little out of shape."

"You're in great shape," she said. "You're just drunk."

"Not anymore, sadly." I cast an artful glance her way. "Maybe we should have one more."

"That's one of the seven warning signs," she said.

"Okay," I conceded. But a tingling sensation along my spine made me glance around. Why did I feel as though someone was watching me? I'd felt it earlier at the Covington. I rubbed my arms briskly to ward off the icy apprehension. I'd never experienced this before. Then again, I'd never had a friend murdered in cold blood before. And I'd never been surrounded by so many suspicious characters before.

I took another look around. Was Anandalla standing in the nearby shadows, watching me?

"You're getting weird," Robin said with a sigh, and slipped her arm through mine. "Come on. We can't come this close to Ghirardelli Square and not stop for a hot fudge sundae."

I woke up in my own bed wearing my own underwear, always a good thing. I just couldn't quite remember how I got there.

I was shaking. Had I forgotten to turn on the heater? As I contemplated whether to jump out of bed and check, I considered the distinct possibility that the shaking might be a result of consuming four—five?—Irish coffees the night before.

If yes, I didn't need to turn the heater on, I just needed some aspirin and more sleep. I was going with yes.

I jumped out of bed and my legs almost crumpled under me.

"Oh Lord, that hurts."

Why did my legs feel like two lead weights? I wobbled into the bathroom, where I gulped down two aspirins, then scuffled back to bed and pulled the covers up. I had a vague memory of running up Hyde in high heels. Big mistake. I closed one eye to focus on the alarm clock and was pretty sure it said six o'clock. I really hoped that was a.m., not p.m.

The next time I opened my eyes it was nine o'clock. I threw the covers back and jumped out of bed. Then moaned and sank back down, clutching my pounding head with one hand while trying to knead my aching calves with the other.

"Oh, sweet Jerry Maguire, what did I do?"

The sudden and distinct memory of sucking down all that alcohol and caffeine did little to help my swirling stomach. I stumbled into the bathroom, turned on the hot water and stepped into the shower to do what I could to wash away the misery.

Forty minutes and two more aspirins later, after downing a cup of weak Earl Grey and a piece of dry toast, I managed to get myself down to my car and headed out of the parking garage.

I reached the Valley of the Moon in one hour and six minutes flat. Turning onto the road to Dharma, I said a silent prayer of thanks to the traffic gods, then another one to the wine gods who kept most tourists from starting their wine country tours until at least noon.

I wasn't speaking to the Irish coffee gods.

I parked the car a block from the large town hall at the top of the hill. As I walked across the blacktop parking lot, I heard a tenor from the Dharma choir sing the first tremulous notes of "In My Life."

I snuck in through one of the back doors. The arena-style auditorium had a capacity of six hundred and today it was standing room only. I stood at the back and gazed down at the backs of the colorful crowd. It only took a moment to pick out my mother and father seated three rows from center stage. My brother Jackson sat next to Mom, and my sister China sat next to Dad. Their spouses were with them, but I didn't see any of the kids. Probably a wise decision to leave them home.

On the stage, Guru Bob stood at the podium, his head lolling serenely to the music of the choir behind him. He sported a purple dashiki and matching rufi, the fez-style hat he wore on special occasions. For a tall, fair-haired man, it might've seemed an odd choice, but Guru Bob was nothing if not eclectic in his wardrobe choices. I wouldn't have been surprised to see him in anything from a formal tuxedo to a cashmere bathrobe. I think he liked to keep his flock guessing.

As I stared at the backs of the people, a disturbing question invaded the tranquility I'd begun to feel with the harmony of the music and the familiar faces and surroundings.

Was Abraham's murderer here in this room?

The thought gave me the heebie jeebies. Most of those gathered here were commune people who had known Abraham for twenty or thirty years. What would any of them have to gain from his death? The others in attendance were probably friends or business acquaintances of Abraham's. Again, where was the motive?

I glanced to the left and abruptly met Inspector Jaglow's pointed stare. He stood against the wall thirty feet away, but even from that distance I could feel the severity of his disapproval. I tried to smile at him, but his frown didn't change, so I looked away, clutching my coat more tightly around me.

What was that about? Was I in trouble? Was I going to get a ticket for being late? Maybe Derek had told him I was meddling in their investigation, which wasn't true at all. Nevertheless, I felt guilty and vaguely sick to my stomach.

I tried some deep breathing, matching my breaths to the rhythm of the music. That might've helped if I wasn't recuperating from a slight hangover, but I was, so it just made me dizzy. I leaned back against the door and waited for the room to stop spinning.

"You're not going to pass out again, are you?"

I jumped, then saw it was Derek.

"Stop sneaking up on me," I whispered irately. He merely smirked, so I ignored him as Guru Bob began to speak in measured phrases, starting off with a short but stirring cosmological lesson in how planetary body types align in order to produce conscious harmony in all things—always a favorite topic at our house.

"Today," he said, "with the loss of our dear friend, we all suffer. I remind you that with great suffering comes true purification—if we can only remember to suffer willingly and consciously. Only then can our suffering create a cosmic connection that will allow us to cross over to higher ground, higher consciousness, bridging the interval to begin a new octave."

I snuck a peek at Derek to see whether he was gagging or falling asleep, but he was attentive, his strong arms folded across his chest, his feet planted firmly on the foor. He wore black as usual, but he seemed taller. Or maybe my headache made me imagine I was shrinking.

"Brother Abraham is on the astral plane now," Guru Bob assured us, spreading his arms toward the ceiling. "He has shed his mortal coil to travel at light speed, free of all fears, free of lamentation and regret. There is only joy now. He is the sun."

The commune people nodded their heads and murmured words of encouragement and praise, but I figured most of the visitors were wondering what in the world he was talking about.

"Brother Abraham has embraced the fire and the light of true humility that may have eluded him on this earthly plane. We urge our brother, in his glorious journey along this astral plane, to embrace the wonder, the splendor, the reality of higher consciousness. And in so doing, he raises all of us to a higher plane."

There were shouts of "That's right" and "Teach, Avatar," around the room.

Derek leaned in and whispered, "Who is that guy?"

I bristled. It was fine for me to carp on Guru Bob, but nobody from the outside world got that privilege.

"Avatar Robson Benedict is a highly evolved being."

"Clearly." Derek nodded. "Very powerful."

I looked at him in surprise. Was he kidding? Most people either laughed nervously or ran off into the woods after experiencing a stirring oration from Guru Bob.

Then the service was over and Derek and I were abruptly separated by the thick stream of people exiting the hall. After a brief moment of panic, I allowed myself to be carried along in their wake. Knowing my people, I had high expectations that we would wind up at some massive buffet of food and liquid refreshment.

Sure enough, the crowd headed straight for the dining hall, where tables had been laid with every sort of finger food imaginable, from tiny cheeseburgers to miniature pigs in blankets to more gourmet fare such as toasted squares topped with caviar and salmon. Everything had an accompanying sauce or dip or spread, naturally. Guru Bob did enjoy a good spread.

A wide table at one end of the room held every kind of dessert imaginable. Chocolate éclairs, pies, cakes, puddings and flan and mousse, lemon bars and cookies everywhere.

At the other end of the hall were several long tables where five or six men poured glasses of wine. There was a huge keg at one end, and barrels stuffed with soft drinks and water bottles.

I figured it would be better to eat a little before I headed for the wine, given my slight overindulgence the night before. But as I bit into my petite chicken salad sandwich, I felt my stomach twist.

"Well, look what the cat dragged in."

Holy spoilage, Batman. What in the world was Minka LaBoeuf doing in Dharma?

I turned and saw her. She stood barely two feet

away from me, clutching a glass of red wine with one hand and Enrico Baldacchio's arm with the other. She wore another one of her dominatrix ensembles, a black leather skirt and matching vest over a white lace blouse with poufy sleeves, accessorized by leopard-patterned gloves and matching pillbox hat with a black tuft of mesh that covered most of her face.

She'd already spilled wine on her white shirt. Such a waste of good wine.

"Minka," I said, trying not to choke on the word.

"Brooklyn," she said, stretching the mesh veil back so she could actually see me. "You remember Enrico, don't you?"

Of course I remembered Enrico. He was an unpleasant little man with a tendency to sweat. And he'd been present at the Covington Library the night of Abraham's murder.

Abraham had told me they'd tried to work together again but it had ended badly. Before that, they'd barely spoken in years, beginning back when they wound up on opposite sides of a lawsuit involving a counterfeit Marlowe folio sold to the Palace of the Legion of Honor years ago.

"Hello, Enrico," I said. "It's been a long time." *Not long enough*, I thought, but didn't say aloud because I'm basically a nice person.

"Che piacere è vederti, il mio caro." He grabbed my hand and kissed it.

Minka cut in. "He's saying something like, 'How are you, my dear? Such a pleasure.' Blah, blah, blah."

"Yeah, I get it," I said, then cringed at the trail of slime Enrico left on my hand. I furtively wiped it off with my appetizer napkin.

"Che posto bello!" he cried, sweeping his arm around. *"Una montagna bella! Una montagna bella! Un giorno bello—ma che tragedia!"*

"Uh, right. It's a real tragedy." I thought that was what he said. But what was up with the Italian? With a name like Baldacchio he had to be Italian, of course, but I remembered him coming from New Jersey.

"Quite a service," Minka said, but I could see her tongue in her cheek so I knew she was lying. She viewed the crowd for a moment, then said, "Where the hell are we?"

I detested her with all of my being, but this was my town, my home, and my mother would be appalled if I treated any visitor badly, so I sucked it up and said stiffly, "Sonoma County. Really glad you could make it."

"I wouldn't have missed it for the world."

I turned to Enrico. "What are you working on now, Enrico?"

"Ah, signorina." He shrugged dramatically and fiddled with the cuffs of his dark brown shirt.

Minka slipped her arm through his. "We're working with an important collector whose name cannot be revealed."

My bullshit meter must've been showing on my face because she continued. "It's true. He made us sign a confidentiality agreement."

Who was she trying to impress? And why was she speaking for Enrico? I remembered him speaking English.

"Enrico," I persisted, "I was so glad to see you at the Covington the other night. It gave me hope that you and Abraham had become friends again. Is that true? Did you bury the hatchet, so to speak?"

"Hatchet?" His eyes widened. "No hatchet! I did not do it."

"Enrico," Minka said through gritted teeth as she tightened her hold on his arm. "That's an American joke. It means, you've made friends with Abraham." She glared at me. "Stop baiting him."

"I'm not," I protested, then said to Enrico, "I'm sorry. I meant, I'm so glad to hear you and Abraham were able to be friends again."

Minka nodded. "And his death is even more tragic because Baldacchio and Karastovsky"—she struck a dramatic pose—"the two greatest bookbinders in all the world, had once again joined together on a very important project."

Enrico pulled a silk scarf from his pocket and dabbed his dry eyes. *"Sì. È una tragedia."*

Minka's head bobbed in agreement. "The book world has suffered a double blow."

"Totally," Enrico said, blowing the Italian for a moment. He nodded rapidly, like a bobblehead. *"Sì, sì, sì, signorina."*

So not only was he faking the accent, but he was lying about his renewed friendship with Abraham, who'd told me himself that Enrico was a deceitful thief.

"That must've been such a comfort," I said. "To know that you became friends again before he died. Otherwise, you might've had to live the rest of your life feeling guilty for never repairing the friendship."

"Guilty?" he cried. *"Non sia stupido!* I do nothing!

Karastovsky! He try to ruin me! Guilty? *Siete pazzeschi!*"

He continued sputtering in outrage. I might've touched a nerve. But did he just call me *stupid*? I hated that.

"Oh, great," Minka said. "Now I'll have to listen to this crap all the way home. Thanks a lot."

"Sorry," I said flimsily.

"I need more alcohol." She stomped off, leaving me with one angry Italian. I needed alcohol, too.

"Enrico, I apologize." I grabbed his oily hand. "I'm so sorry. I did not mean to accuse you of anything."

I was starting to talk with an Italian accent.

"That's right. You donna know what you-a talking about, missy."

"I'm sure you're right." I took a deep breath and wrapped my arm through his. "Enrico, we've both lost a good friend, and today is no time to talk about business."

He seemed mollified for the moment. "You right."

I squeezed his arm. "Would you like more wine?"

"No, no." He seemed to enjoy my cozying up because he stroked my hand. "You take over Karastovsky's work at the Covington?"

"Yes, I did."

He looked left and right, then whispered, "I could-a tell you a thing or two about Karastovsky and those Winslows."

I looked around, too. "Really?"

"*Si.* They think Baldacchio's a fool but I show them. They promise me a business deal, and I make sure they donna screw me. Baldacchio, he has the last-a laugh."

"How in the world did you do that?"

"A little insurance." He rubbed his shoulder against mine. "Maybe I show you sometime."

"That would be lovely," I said softly. "Maybe we could meet next week and catch up on old times. Are you busy Monday?"

He was taken aback for a moment, then slowly grinned. "*Quello è molto buono*. You're a smart-a cookie."

His Italian came and went like the tide. I patted his arm. "I'm glad you think so. Shall I come to your studio? Say, around two o'clock Monday?"

"*Perfetto*. I show you my latest treasure." He moved even closer and I could see the comb marks in his overly gelled hair. "And maybe I show you a little something extra you will find extremely *interessante*."

"Interesting?"

"And provocative. Tell no one. We do some business together, eh?"

"I can't wait."

"You're a good girl," he said, unexpectedly avuncular; then he frowned and shook his finger at me. "But do yourself the favor and stay away from the *Faust*."

"The *Faust*?"

"The curse. I could-a lost my eye. *Quel libro maledetto*."

"Your eye? What?"

The memory seemed to cause him pain because his eye began to twitch. He rubbed his forehead, then threw up his hands dramatically. "Eh! We talk Monday. You come see me and we talk." He handed me his business card and strolled away. I saw Minka corral him by the dessert table and force him out the door.

Holy crap. What had I gone and done now? Ah well, I'd find out Monday.

"Hello, Brooklyn."

I whipped around. "Mrs. Winslow."

She looked lovely in a black Chanel suit and carried a clutch purse. She patted my arm consolingly. "I thought we should pay our respects."

"Thank you," I said, and breathed in relief. Her sincere kindness was a refreshing change from Enrico's and Minka's lies and calculations. "How are you?"

"Oh, my dear, I'm fine." She smiled sadly. "But I know what it feels like to lose a good friend, so I wanted to wish you well."

"That's very kind."

"If you're willing to hear some advice from an old gal like me, I'd recommend that you take extra good care of yourself at a time like this."

I smiled. "You're hardly an old gal and I appreciate the advice."

"I'm going to have to buy a case of that pinot," Conrad Winslow said as he joined us. "Damn fine wine."

We shared some small talk, and then they left. I was struck again by how genuinely nice the Winslows were, and how inexplicable it was that they'd managed to produce such a self-centered creature like Meredith.

I'd worked up a real appetite, so I grabbed two more tiny sandwiches, egg salad this time, then headed for the wine bar, praying the hangover gods would be gentle.

Robin sidled up to me. "You look pretty good for someone I had to pour into the cab last night."

"I'm young," I said. "I bounce back."

"Obviously." Robin turned to the bartender, a local boy who worked part-time in the Dharma vineyards. "Hi, Billy. I'll have what she's having."

We waited until she had her drink in her hand, then began to stroll the periphery of the room.

"Who was that old guy you were talking to?"

"Enrico Baldacchio," I said. "We just had a very interesting conversation." I took a sip of wine, swirled it around my mouth and swallowed. I held the glass up to the light. "This is exceptional, isn't it? Great color."

"Don't you dare change the subject. What'd he say?"

I gave her the short version as we walked.

"Do you honestly believe he's got something to show you besides his etchings?"

"Ew." But I'd had the same thought. "I guess I'll find out Monday. I made a date to meet him."

"A date?" She groaned. "What did we discuss last night?"

I frowned. "Fashion?"

"No, smartass." She stopped walking and whispered hotly, "We talked about how you shouldn't be investigating Abraham's death by yourself because you could piss off a killer. Remember?"

"Vaguely."

"We discussed how that was not a good idea. And this guy Enrico could be a killer." She took a sip of wine. "And then I called your clothes atrocious and you got miffed. Any of this ring a bell?"

I took a sip of wine. "I recall the atrocious part."

She rolled her eyes. "Good, because that was really the key point of the discussion."

"Thanks a lot." I pulled her along with me to keep strolling. "Look, I'm not investigating anything. I'm just meeting with a colleague who could someday throw some business my way."

"That is so much crap."

"I'm serious. That's all I'm going to do. Could you please relax?"

"I'll relax when Abraham's killer is behind bars."

"Me, too." I took another sip of wine and motioned toward the door. "Austin just walked in."

She whipped around so she wouldn't be caught gazing longingly at my tall, handsome older brother, the one she'd been in love with since third grade. "So what?"

I laughed. "As long as you don't deal with those deep dark feelings inside, you've got no business criticizing anything I do."

She pointed her finger at me and gave it a shake. "I have every right in the world to try and talk you out of getting yourself killed."

I put the wineglass down on a nearby table and pulled Robin into a hug. "Thank you. I appreciate it."

When I stepped back, I saw her eyes filled with tears.

I sighed. "I absolutely promise I'll be careful—"

"You'd better be."

"—if you'll do me a favor."

She sniffled. "What?"

"Go talk to Austin. He's staring right at you."

"Shut up."

"He is," I said.

"Shit."

"There's a good attitude." I grinned as I walked

away, hoping at least someone would have some fun today.

I spent the next hour helping my mother supervise the kitchen staff to keep the tables filled with food to feed the hundreds of people who'd stopped by to console and commiserate. I didn't mind putting in kitchen time since I figured it would keep me out of trouble for a while. And the sprawling commune kitchen was a warm and familiar environment for me.

All through my childhood, Mom and Dad were in charge of managing food and wine for the commune. Dad still ran the winery, but Mom was semiretired from the kitchen except on special occasions like this one. With six kids, she was a natural organizer and, more important, a first-class manipulator.

My parents' experience in food management dated back to the days when they used to travel to Grateful Dead shows in a big old UPS truck that Dad had outfitted and sectioned off into three rooms: bedroom, bathroom and kitchenette.

At the time, Dad was still out of favor with Grandfather, so he and Mom needed a way to support themselves on the road. They decided to call upon their God-given talents and created a business called Vino y Green-oh. We kids thought it was the dumbest name ever, but Deadheads and fellow campers loved it. They painted the name on the side of the truck in rainbow colors. Dad offered wine tastings at one dollar a glass and Mom made fresh green salads she sold for two dollars each, including a roll and butter.

They hooked up with several other entrepreneurs in the food trade and created a "restaurant row" in the Dead show campgrounds and parking lots. Their friends Barbara and Dexter ran a popular eatery out of their RV called Spuds 'n' Suds. Their operation was a little more complicated, requiring a deep fryer and ice for the keg.

"We need more taquitos at the Mexican station," Mom called from the doorway.

"I've got a bunch ready," Carmen, one of the cooks, answered.

"I'll take care of it," I said, and lifted the large cookie sheet stacked with corn tortillas rolled tightly around shredded beef, cheese and salsa.

"Don't forget the avocado sauce," Carmen yelled.

"Got it," I said as I balanced the bowl of creamy green sauce on top of the pile of taquitos and headed for the dining room—and nearly collided with two men.

"There you are," Derek said. "When are you—"

"Brooklyn," Ian interrupted. "I'm glad I ran into you. I've got—"

"Guys, let me put this down," I said, straining from the weight of several hundred beef taquitos. "I'll be right back."

But they weren't about to let me escape. They both followed me to the Mexican station, where I gratefully exchanged my full cookie sheet for the empty one on the table.

"Okay, so much for my break from reality," I said, smiling back and forth from one ridiculously good-looking man to the other. "What do you guys want?"

"I'll need a word with you, Ms. Wainwright."

"Hey, plenty of me to go around," I said, laughing as I turned and stared into the grim brown eyes of Inspector Jaglow.

Chapter 10

Oh, bugger, what did the police want with me? I shot a look at Derek, but he avoided my distressed gaze, turning away to chat up the closest woman available, who happened to be Mary Ellen Prescott, the manicurist at the Dharma co-op beauty salon my mother operated with a few of the commune women. He would soon find out that Mary Ellen was not a member of our commune but a shameless, serial proselytizer for the Church of the True Blood of Ogun. Served him right for ignoring me in my hour of need.

Semifrantic now, I turned to Ian and was dismayed to realize that in the few seconds it had taken me to observe Derek's betrayal, Ian had seen his chance and completely disappeared.

Suffice it to say, this was another lesson learned the hard way. Men were good for one thing only. Killing spiders. Other than that, I was on my own. It was sad, though. Where was the chivalry of yesteryear?

Inspector Jaglow coughed discreetly.

I could claim a need to use the bathroom, then sneak through the kitchen, detour out the mudroom door and be gone in seconds. There were back roads and switchbacks and hollows up here in Sonoma I could disappear into, where a hotshot City cop like Jaglow would never find me.

"Ms. Wainwright?" he said again. "This won't take long."

I sighed, gave him a wan smile and gestured for him to lead the way. Without a word, he crossed the room and exited through the wide double doors. I tried not to hyperventilate as he took the walkway around to the back, across the wide, blacktop parking lot. There were plenty of people in the hall, but nobody was out here, no witnesses to see me forced into a car or led into the woods to be brutally interrogated.

I'd never realized it before this moment, but I didn't trust the police. Here I was, completely innocent of any wrongdoing, yet I felt like a criminal as I traipsed across the blacktop with The Man.

"Over here," Jaglow said, pointing to the far corner of the lot.

That was when I saw Inspector Lee standing by a picnic table under a giant oak tree at the edge of the lot. She wore a heavy black wool coat and flat shoes. Despite the extra weight of the coat, she still looked pathetically thin. I knew I wasn't the fashion maven Robin was, but I ached to do a makeover on the inspector.

She watched us approach and I noticed she was smoking a cigarette. That was a surprise. Of course, I wasn't about to discuss the commune's recently initiated no-smoking policy. I figured it was bogus anyway since Guru Bob had been sneaking out to light up behind the winery barn for years.

"Hello, Ms. Wainwright," Inspector Lee said in her oddly authoritative voice. Now I knew where that deep, sexy tone came from. Cigarettes. It seemed like cheating, somehow. "Sorry to take you away from the service, but we had some questions that couldn't wait."

"That's okay," I said. "Did you get something to eat inside?" Always the hostess, that's me, but more important, she could use some fattening up. Maybe I'd get Carmen to put together a hearty to-go pack for her.

"I had a cookie," she allowed.

I brightened. "Did you try the Snickerdoodles? My mom makes the best—"

"Ms. Wainwright," Jaglow interrupted, thumping the page of his notebook, then looking up. "I had another conversation with, er, Minka La Burr . . . La Boo . . ." He gave up and checked his notebook. "La Beef."

"Right, La *Beef*," I said, and wanted to laugh, but sadly, even his mispronunciation of her stupid name didn't cheer me up. Minka had warned me she was going to talk to the cops. I couldn't wait to hear the lies she'd planted.

"She tells me you and Karastovsky had a big fight the night he was murdered."

"What?"

I must've shouted it because they both glared at me.

"Sorry," I said quickly. "But she's lying. Totally and completely lying. Look, Minka LaBoeuf and I have never gotten along. We go way back. It's not pretty. She's a compulsive liar and she hates me. I don't really want to get into it but—"

"Get into it," Inspector Lee said, her lips twisting sardonically.

I blew out a breath, then gave them the abbreviated version. College. Art class. Boyfriend. Obsession. Sharp knife. Vicious cut. Blood everywhere. Paramedics.

As I spoke, Jaglow wrote furiously.

"Okay, so you're not best friends," Lee said. "Why would she lie about this fight?"

"There was no fight," I insisted.

"Whatever," Lee said. "Why would she lie?"

I clenched my fists. What part of *She tried to cut off my hand* did they not understand? I counted to five slowly, then said, "It's what she does. At the very least, Minka would love to see me fired from the Covington."

"Why?" she asked.

"Because she's always hated me. Because Abraham fired her and she knows we were close. I'm the logical target."

"And at the very most?" Jaglow said, following up on my previous sentence.

Did he expect me to say the words? That Minka would love to see me arrested for murder? I wasn't going there.

Inspector Lee actually rolled her eyes. "Nate, I think Ms. Wainwright is convinced this La Beef woman's trying to implicate her in Karastovsky's murder."

She gave me a pointed look, suggesting I agree or deny it.

I hastily nodded in agreement. "Yes, exactly."

Lee nodded back, then said, "Just so we're clear, you're saying there was no fight between you and Karastovsky that night?"

"That's right. Absolutely right. No fight. We were talking and laughing; he was in a jovial mood and happy to see me. You can ask anyone—besides Minka."

"And you're saying Karastovsky fired her," Jaglow said.

Hearing Jaglow say it aloud made me remember that Minka had her own motive for murder. Hadn't I accused her of that when we first spoke in the basement hall the night of the murder? I rubbed my head. Days and conversations were getting blurred. The thing was, I seriously doubted Minka was capable or even competent enough to commit murder, but I was almost giddy with relief that the spotlight was off me. Now it was time to return the favor and kick Minka under the tires.

"Yes," I said firmly. "Minka had been hired by the Covington to work with Abraham on the Winslow collection. He fired her from the project within a week. Frankly, if it had been up to him, he never would've hired her in the first place."

"You know this because?" Lee drawled.

"Because Abraham knew she was a hack, and he knew what she tried to do to me with that knife. He knew she brought problems with her wherever she went. Any job she works on never goes smoothly. She's disruptive, a troublemaker, and besides her crappy attitude, she's just not very good at the work."

"But tell us how you really feel," Lee murmured, and almost cracked a smile.

Jaglow nodded in amusement. "I hear that." He looked back at me. "So you and the La Beef woman have some history and all, but what does she have to gain by lying about you?"

"For Minka, it would be for the sheer joy of watching me squirm."

"That's some serious stuff," he said.

Lee was more philosophical. "Girls just want to have fun."

I walked into the town hall alone after watching the inspectors drive off. I'd offered them both some takeaway goodies, but they declined. Too bad. Lee could use the calories.

I was gratified to see Derek still cornered by Mary Ellen Prescott. He looked utterly desperate. I knew Mary Ellen, so I felt his pain, but I flashed him a broad smile and he bared his teeth at me. I'd be sure to remind him later that karma was a bitch.

I was headed toward the kitchen when someone called my name.

"Brooklyn, my dear."

I turned and saw Guru Bob walk toward me.

"Are you in a hurry, gracious?" he asked.

"Yes. Uh. No." He always left me tongue-tied. What did you say to someone who's supposed to be a highly evolved conscious being? I wasn't even sure what that meant, but I knew he was incredibly intelligent and perceptive. He could talk anyone into doing anything. I'd grown up trying to stay under the Guru radar and I'd been fairly successful for years. Then, when I was fourteen, Abraham showed him a beautiful family Bible I'd restored. That gained his interest.

It had been Guru Bob's suggestion that I go for the multiple degrees in library science and fine art, even though Abraham had thought it irrelevant. I'd always insisted to my parents that neither of their opinions mattered, but Guru Bob's encouragement had helped move my parents to fully finance my college and post-grad schooling, so I was grateful for that.

"I saw you speaking with the police, dear," he said.

Good to know someone had been aware of my situation out in the parking lot. The fact that it was Guru Bob caused my throat to go dry as sand. I reached for a water bottle from the nearby table, popped it open and took a long sip.

"You are distressed," he said kindly.

"No, I am fine," I said. "I am just very thirsty."

Guru Bob never used contractions and I tended to imitate him whenever I spoke with him. Weird.

"Water is life-giving," he said quietly as I drank.

He was a tall man with broad shoulders, but when he spoke with you, he would hunch over to appear less intimidating and more humble. He also spoke softly, believing his words would be better received than if he spoke louder. It worked. I definitely paid attention to him.

"The police upset you?" he asked.

"No, no," I said. "They were just asking me about Abraham and some statements one of my, er, colleagues made." Calling Minka a colleague left a bitter taste, but I didn't want to have to explain the whole thing to Guru Bob.

"There is no need to explain," he said, doing that creepy mind-reading thing he did sometimes.

I felt an urgent need to explain anyway. "It's just that this woman lied to the police and I had to tell them the true story. She's not really a colleague, Robson, she's really a . . ." I sighed. I couldn't say anything too negative to Guru Bob.

He touched my shoulder and I felt a tingle of energy.

"You are under a great deal of strain, gracious."

Guru Bob called most people "gracious." Mom said he liked to make them aware that they actually were full of grace. He was definitely a glass-half-full kind of guy.

"I will be fine," I insisted.

"Of course you will." He absently kneaded my shoulder blade and I felt a rush of something like electricity zing across my shoulders and down my spine. How did he do that?

"Take more potassium this week," he advised. "It will improve your ability to sleep and awake refreshed."

"Yes, okay."

"And eat oatmeal," he said. "It will boost your sex drive."

I choked on the water and he patted my back.

"Gotcha," he said, his eyes sparkling.

"Good one," I whispered between coughs.

"Anything that helps us remember the moment is a good one indeed," he murmured, then straightened to his full height, signaling that our conversation was over. Then he snapped his fingers, something I'd never seen him do.

He smiled and spread his hands. "You see, gracious, had I truly been in the moment, I would have remembered what I wished to tell you in the first place."

My eyes widened at his revelation, but I had no comeback and he didn't expect one.

"Gavin will be reading Abraham's last will and testament at four this afternoon in the tearoom. Your presence is required, of course."

Before I could protest, he brought his palms together as though he were going to pray, then bowed his head briefly. *"Namasté,"* he said, and walked away.

I needed a minute and took another gulp of water. Guru Bob always left me feeling completely charged but also kind of spacey.

"Sweetie." Mom stopped me right inside the kitchen door and pulled me over to a deserted corner.

"Mom, whoa. Watch the sweater. What's up?"

"Is that cashmere?" she asked, rubbing it between her fingers. "Nice."

I pried my sleeve away from her nervous hands. "What's wrong, Mom?"

"Why were the police here?"

"They just had a few questions."

"So they drove all the way to Sonoma? On a Saturday? That's very strange." She paced a few feet, then whirled around. "Don't you think that's strange?"

"I think it's good that they're working the case." And why was she so nervous? Had the police spooked her?

"What did you tell them? Are you in trouble?"

"Mom, it's nothing. A misunderstanding, that's all. Don't worry."

"I'm your mother. I get paid to worry." She folded her arms tightly across her chest and shook her head.

I smiled and rubbed her arms. "Mom, everything's fine. They just needed to clarify something and now they're gone. Everything's groovy."

"Groovy." She exhaled heavily. "Right. Good."

"Jeez, Mom, you'd think they were going to arrest me or something."

"Don't say that!" She grabbed a wooden spoon

from the utility shelf and held it out. "Knock on wood."

"Mom, this is crazy."

"Just do it."

I rapped the spoon with my knuckles and she tossed the spoon back on the shelf. Then she reached out and rubbed my forehead with her thumb to stimulate my third eye. This was supposed to open my clogged channels and allow me to tune into the right universal vibration in order to see the world from a higher place.

Or something like that. I grabbed her hand and squeezed it. "I love you, Mom."

I thought she would burst into tears. She grabbed me in her arms and held on tight. "I love you, too, sweetie. I'd just die if something happened to you."

I hugged her, but had to wonder why she was so nervous about the police being around. Was it because she was hiding her own reasons for sneaking into the Covington that night? Her behavior was making all my suspicious little nerve channels vibrate more than ever.

It was after two before I was able to sneak out the kitchen door and run down to Abraham's studio without being followed. I figured I had just enough time to search the place and be back for the reading of the will at four o'clock.

The studio was unchanged from the last time I'd seen it. Drawers were still opened with papers jammed in every which way or crumpled and thrown around. The stack of birch book covers was a jumble and there were shells and rocks scattered across the worktable and the floor. I started to pick them up, then realized I didn't have time to straighten things. I would try to get up here sometime during the week to take care of it, but right now, I needed to search for the missing journals.

It took almost an hour of meticulously searching through every drawer and cupboard and shelf, but I finally found the two journals that covered the work Abraham had done on the Winslow books. Why he'd kept them in plain sight on his desk, I'd never know. It was the last place I thought to look. There was no time to read them right now, so I shoved them into my bag.

I hadn't found anything that might be the missing item from the *Faust*. "GW1941." I'd done a quick check, but there was nothing tucked inside the journals, no slip of paper or directions or anything. I held out hope that Abraham had written down the details of what he'd found and where he'd put it. I'd know more tonight after I read the journals. Right now I had to get out of here and back to the ranch before someone came snooping around.

"Who the hell are you?"

I bolted, knocking my elbow against the solid brass book press. I whipped around, furious and in pain. "If one more person sneaks up on me, I swear I'll—"

"I saw you steal something."

I pulled the journals out. "They're mine. I work with Abraham. Now, who the hell are *you*?"

But I knew who she was. I recognized her by that headful of curly dark hair. It was Anandalla, the woman who'd left the cocktail napkin note. The woman who'd rushed out of the Buena Vista last night, causing me to run uphill in uncomfortable shoes. I'm not sure I could forgive her for that. She was even more petite than I'd thought. Also unforgivable.

Was she also a cold-blooded killer?

"What are you doing here?" I demanded.

"None of your business." She sounded like a snotty kid. But then she scooped up an X-Acto knife and waved it at me. "Answer my question first."

Snotty and dangerous.

I straightened up, happy to use the height card to intimidate and taunt, not that it seemed to be doing much good. "I'm Brooklyn Wainwright, Abraham Karastovsky's very good friend and colleague. I work here with him. I belong here. What's your story?"

She surveyed the room for a full minute, decidedly uncomfortable. Her gaze finally met mine and she said defiantly, "I'm Abraham's daughter."

Chapter 11

My mouth dropped open. "You are not."

She threw down the knife and planted her hands on her hips. "Am, too."

Okay, this was unexpected. I studied her for a minute, then wondered how I hadn't seen it before. The hair was a dead giveaway, the same curly dark mop as Abraham's. She looked about twenty-five years old, probably five feet two, short for someone who claimed Abraham for a father. Her mother had to be really short.

"I'm sorry," I said helplessly. "I didn't know Abraham had a daughter."

She blurted out a harsh laugh. "Yeah, well, neither did he till a week ago."

"You're kidding me. Where did you come from? When did he . . . hmm."

She shrugged. "I live in Seattle with my mom. She only told me a month ago who my father is." She grabbed a spool of sewing thread and rolled it between her hands. "She's, um . . . My mom's dying. Of cancer. Guess she figured it was time to come clean."

She put the thread down and rubbed her eyes. "I'm so tired. I've been staying with a girlfriend near Ghirardelli Square. She's kind of a night owl."

"Did you . . ." How did I ask this question? "Did you get a chance to meet Abraham?"

"Yeah." She smiled. It transformed her face and I realized she was even younger than I'd first thought. Late teens or early twenties, maybe.

"He's a big bear, isn't he?" she continued, chuckling. "We had a great dinner in the City; then I came out here the other night to meet him, see his place, but he wasn't here. I left him a note but he didn't call."

She looked perturbed. "He told me all about you, even showed me your picture."

"My picture?"

"Yeah, the one he carries in his wallet." She said it like an accusation. Hey, it wasn't my fault if she was miffed. But why was she talking about him in the present tense? I was getting a bad feeling.

"Anyway," she continued, "I told him I'd meet him at the Buena Vista last night but he didn't show up. Then all of a sudden you were there. I recognized you and I—I didn't know what to do, so I took off." She waved her hands helplessly. "Probably a chickenshit reaction, but it was weird to see you there. I felt a little threatened, I guess. Fight or flight, you know? So I ran."

"Yeah, I know."

"So I thought I'd try to snag him here today, but no such luck. And here you are. Must be my lucky day."

I would've risen to the sarcastic bait but I couldn't. She didn't know. Now what? I really wished my mom were here. She would handle this so much better than I could.

"I'm sorry, Anandalla," I said, clasping my hands tightly. "Abraham died a few days ago."

"What?" She shook her head. "No, I just saw him. What's today?"

"It's true," I said softly. "I'm sorry."

Her eyes were wide, filled with shock. "No, no, I'm supposed to . . . um, no."

"I'm sorry."

"That's not possible," she whispered. "You're lying. You're just . . ."

She blinked a few times and gulped. Then her face crumpled as the tears started. She buried her face in her hands and her shoulders hitched as she cried silently.

I grabbed a stool and forced her to sit. She laid her head on the surface of the worktable and continued to cry with heart-wrenching sobs. I rubbed her back but felt completely useless. I rifled through my purse and found a packet of tissues and shoved one into her hand.

I couldn't believe it. After a lifetime of not knowing, this girl finally had a chance to meet her father. And now he was gone. And her mother was dying, too. How could anyone survive that much pain?

My heart broke for Abraham, too. What a happy shock it must've been to find out he had a daughter after all these years. At the same time, I felt a spurt of anger for Anandalla's mother. How could that woman have kept them both in the dark for so many years?

And I suddenly realized this must've been what Abraham had been talking about the night of the Covington opening. "Life is good, Brooklyn," he'd said, hugging me. "I didn't think it could get any better, but it can."

At the time, I thought he'd been referring to the overwhelming success of the exhibition. Now I realized he'd been talking about his daughter. It was so unfair.

Anandalla's sobs echoed in the room and reached right inside me. As always, no one cried alone when I was nearby. I wiped my damp cheeks as I put my hand on her arm.

"I'm so sorry, Anandalla," I said. "He was a good man and I know he would've gone to any lengths to find you if he'd known. I—I don't know what else to say. It's just a tragedy."

Anandalla sat up, took in a big breath and let it out. She hopped off the stool and absently pulled at the cuffs of her jacket. "Yeah. It sucks."

"That pretty much sums it up," I said.

After a moment, she blurted, "You can call me Annie."

"Annie?"

"My mom tried to be Hindu for a while, so that's where I got the name."

"There was a lot of that going around back in the day."

She snickered. "Yeah. After a few years, she went back to being a legal secretary and I've been Annie ever since."

"I like the name Annie."

"Thanks. So I guess I'm going to be an orphan,"

she said with a chuckle, but it set off a fresh bout of tears and another round of heavy sobs.

I pulled her into my arms and held her. After a few minutes, she stopped sobbing but began to gasp with heavy jerks as she tried to catch her breath.

"Easy," I said. "Take it slow." I patted her back. Her breathing slowed, deepened, softened.

Finally, she stepped away. "I'll be okay."

"I don't know how," I said. "I'd be a complete disaster."

"Denial helps. I'm hoping it'll kick in any minute now."

"Well, I can promise you one thing."

She dabbed the tissue along her wet temple. "Yeah? What?"

"You'll never be an orphan. Not while you've got the Fellowship around you."

"The what?"

I sighed. "I guess your mother never told you about that, either."

She took a defensive step back. I was making an educated guess that her mother had kept Abraham from her because of his connection to the commune and Guru Bob. To an outsider, Guru Bob had often been mistaken for a cult leader. But he wasn't, just as his followers weren't held captive and hypnotized into drinking Kool-Aid.

"What exactly didn't my mother tell me?" Annie asked as she swiped her eyes dry with her knuckles. Some of her Goth eye makeup smeared across her cheek and I handed her another tissue.

"I could try to explain but it would take hours." I grabbed my bag. "Why don't I show you instead?"

*   *   *

The three hundred or so assorted family and friends still partying at the town hall were overwhelmed by the news that Abraham had a daughter. But never let it be said that the members of the Fellowship for Spiritual Enlightenment and Higher Artistic Consciousness couldn't rise to the occasion and welcome a newcomer into the fold.

Literally.

They closed in, encircling Annie in a warm, loving, sugary sweet human sandwich as they plied her with good wine and platefuls of delectable treats, then began peppering her with nosy questions and sentimental stories.

After twenty minutes, Annie was able to catch my eye. I almost laughed at her unmasked look of sheer terror. She was in serious danger of frying from happy face overload. I took pity on her and worked my way through the crowd to rescue her, but I was too late. My mother had cleverly intervened. She assured everyone they'd have their chance for a one-on-one heart-to-heart with Annie, then tucked her firmly under her wing and whisked her away to our house.

It was pretty much guaranteed I was about to inherit a third sister. I needed another sibling the way I needed a sixth toe. Or a twelfth toe. You know, an extra one on each foot. Never mind.

Three hours later, as the lights of the City cast a foggy glow on San Francisco Bay, I headed west on Highway 37 toward home. I gripped the steering wheel and tried to concentrate on the road. It wasn't easy and it had nothing to do with the darkness or the fog. No, I was blown away by the fact that I was six million dollars wealthier than I'd been this morning.

Six. Million. Dollars.

Except for a generous bequest to his housekeeper and assorted knickknacks to friends plus a few rare books to Guru Bob, Abraham had left his entire estate to me.

Me. I got it all. His house, his business, his library of books and papers, his portfolio of property and stock investments, which, his lawyer hastened to assure me, were extensive.

The daughter of his heart, he'd called me in his will. After hearing that, I'd run through the rest of my packet of tissues.

After the will was read, my father had to hold me up as we walked outside. I was in a daze. I had to escape. I couldn't go to my family's house. I didn't want to talk to anyone, especially Annie.

As soon as I'd promised my dad I'd call when I got home, I jumped in my car and escaped Dharma. I felt guilty leaving but knew it would only get worse if I had to look into Annie's sad eyes and know she was wondering what might've happened, if only.

If only her mother hadn't lied. If only Abraham were alive.

It was obvious Abraham hadn't had a clue Annie existed until a few days before he died. Her name was never mentioned in the will.

I shook my head as I swung onto the 101, still in shock over the full disclosure of Abraham's net worth. I knew property values in Sonoma were high and everyone who'd invested in the commune and Dharma had made money over the years, thanks to smart fiscal planning by Guru Bob and my dad and a few others.

Naturally, Guru Bob had presented a cosmically correct reason for making sound investments since the more money one had, the less negativity one suffered. Maybe that theory didn't translate out in the real world, but in Dharma, people were pretty darn happy and grateful most of the time. At least, that was the goal. But just in case they forgot, Guru Bob was always there to remind them to be joyful, damn it.

So, Abraham was loaded. Who knew? And I was in a quandary. What was I supposed to do with Abraham's stuff now that Annie was in the picture?

I could sign his house over to her. I didn't need a house in Dharma. There was no mortgage to worry about and Annie might be happy to live there once her mother was gone. She might enjoy the small community that would envelop her as one of their own. But that was a decision she probably didn't want to think about for a while.

It was too much for me to think about right now, too. As I hit the bridge, then drove through the Fast Track lane at the bridge toll plaza, I made up my mind to call a family meeting next week. My sibs and parents would probably agree that Annie should have Abraham's house. I would also find a way to give her some money or a portion of the investments. I didn't think she'd care about Abraham's books or his business as much as I did.

My brother Jackson, always the pragmatic one, would insist that Annie undergo a paternity test. So would the lawyers. But if anyone had a doubt that she and Abraham were related, they'd just have to look at all that hair.

The poor girl would need a chunk of Abraham's money just to support the hair products she'd require for the rest of her life. And I think Abraham would be pleased to know she was roaming around in that big house of his.

I dashed away the tears. I couldn't afford to lose it right now, not when this portion of 101 twisted and narrowed as I drove through the Presidio toward the Marina district. And not while a gas-guzzling SUV was zooming too fast toward me. It stayed right on my tail, flashing its brights to effectively blind me.

I had a moment to wonder whether this was just your everyday jackass or someone so angry that they'd actually threaten me on the open road, before they gunned their engine and roared past, kicking up road dirt and tiny rocks that pinged against my windshield.

I let out a breath. Just your everyday jackass, after all. But I was seriously tired of being frightened to death at every turn. And now that Annie was in the picture, my determination to find Abraham's murderer took a seismic leap. I wouldn't give up until the bastard was brought to justice.

I'd been home ten minutes when someone knocked at the door, and then I heard my neighbor Vinnie call out, "Halloo, Brooklyn? You are home?"

Oh no. I'd forgotten to feed the cats this morning. Were they dead?

I hurried to the front door, only to discover I'd left it unlocked. Vinnie was poking her head inside, looking around.

"Come in," I said. Had I truly been so distracted I hadn't locked my door? How dumb was that?

Vinnie walked in holding a straggly green plant in a pot. "We wish to thank you for taking good care of Pookie and Splinters." She bowed her head slightly, then handed me the pot. "We are so grateful."

"Oh, how pretty." I took the plant and bowed before I could stop myself. "But I didn't . . . "

Was I really going to confess to neglecting her beloved felines? Um, no.

"You didn't need to do this," I said feebly. "The cats were great. No problem at all."

"It meant so much that you cared for them," she said. "They are our children. Suzie worried all weekend."

The door opened and Suzie sauntered in. "Yo, hey, Brooks."

"Hey, Suzie."

She thrust out her knuckles and I bumped mine against hers. She was such a guy. She wore tight jeans and a black T-shirt with the sleeves ripped off to reveal a tattoo on her upper arm of a snake wound around a woman's curvy leg. Her bleached hair was chopped and spiked and she had a dozen tiny steel hoops hanging from each ear. Vinnie gazed at her in adoration.

Suzie jerked her thumb toward the plant. "Thing needs some CPR. It was trapped in the car for five hours. Just water it. It'll come back."

Vinnie beamed. "Yes, it will be so pretty, we promise. It is a stargazer lily. It already has a few buds ready to flower. You will be pleased, I think."

"I'll take good care of it," I promised.

"Come on, babe," Suzie said, grabbing Vinnie's arm. "Thanks again, pal."

"Anytime," I said. I carefully locked the door behind them, then stared at the lily and sighed. It would be dead within forty-eight hours. I might not be great with pets, but I was even worse with plants. No matter what I did or how much care I gave it, it would die. Really, I was only safe around books. Books I could take care of. Living things, not so much.

I left my house at seven thirty Monday morning, determined to get an early start at the Covington.

It was hard to keep my eyes open and my mind on the road because I was exhausted. I'd spent Sunday evening skimming Abraham's journals but had found absolutely nothing enlightening or instructive anywhere. Well, except for the fact that he didn't like the Winslows. There were notations on almost every page indicating their ignorance of art and process.

I'd winced as I read a few passages. Abraham had become obsessed with the Winslows, possibly to the detriment of his work. There was almost nothing written about the *Faust*. Not one reference to the secret panel he'd found behind the endpapers covering the front board. No slip of aged paper clipped to any of the pages with a stickie attached that said "This is the secret document you've been looking for." Nothing.

Needless to say, I hadn't slept well. The shocking confrontation with Annie, then the news of the inheritance, then that weird moment on the road Saturday night when I thought some SUV driver was going to kill me, all weighed heavily on me. Then at some point during the night, I realized I'd lost track of Derek

Stone up in Dharma. Maybe he'd joined Mary Ellen's Church of the True Blood of Ogun. I would miss him but he'd obviously found his true calling.

By midmorning, I was shaking. I couldn't concentrate on the *Faust*. When I wasn't wondering about Derek, I was thinking about Abraham. And Annie. And six million dollars. And some missing link that might reveal Abraham's killer. Abraham's dying words continued to haunt my thoughts and I wondered whether the devil he'd been referring to was a part of the book's text.

It made me crazy that all these distractions were interrupting my work since I had only this week to complete the restoration. To concentrate, I grabbed a 3 Musketeers bar from my bag, unwrapped it and took a big bite. It helped, as always, and I hunkered down to work.

I'd already unsealed the black leather cover from the boards and separated the text block. I'd dissolved the glue and carefully pulled the threads out, separating the signatures in order to clean and repair those that needed attention.

I spent some time examining the pages with the worst wear, then tried to read the text for some clue to the genius that was Goethe. Unfortunately, I didn't know enough German to understand all the words, and it didn't help that the text itself was written in an Old English–style font.

The book was written in the form of a play, with the characters' names written out before their speeches. As I studied the page, one short exchange jumped out at me.

MEPHISTOPHELES: Ich bin's.
FAUST: Herein!

The words alarmed me. Even my rudimentary knowledge of German was enough to know that with one word, the arrogant Faust had doomed himself to an eternity in hell.

It is I, the devil says.

Enter, says Faust.

"Yes, do come in," I muttered. "Take my soul in exchange for immortality and destroy everything I've ever loved."

That was the devil's plan all along, wasn't it?

Remember the devil.

Did Abraham's last words have anything to do with Goethe's masterpiece? I kept forgetting to pick up a paperback copy, but in my defense, I'd had some distractions to deal with. I made a note to do it after my meeting with Enrico this afternoon.

For now, I concentrated on the foxing I'd seen on a number of the pages. Foxing referred to the small, reddish brown spots of mildew or dirt that appeared over time on the pages of old books. There were different techniques for removing the spots. Most of them involved solutions of bleach or peroxide or other chemicals that could ultimately damage the fibers in the paper. I couldn't take that chance with the *Faust*, so I had decided to experiment with something I'd seen on one of my online loops.

I pulled a slice of white bread from the cheapest loaf I'd found at the market, then tore off the crusts and squished the slices together to make a ball.

The theory was that the bleached flour would help whiten the spots without damaging the paper itself. The e-mail poster had warned that the results wouldn't be perfect but there would be some improvement.

After gently rubbing in a circular pattern, I was amazed to see the white ball of bread turning darker and crumbly. It was actually pulling the dirt out of the paper. The spots didn't completely disappear, but they were much lighter than before.

"That was amazing," I marveled as I tossed the used bread in the wastebasket and pulled out another slice. All this bread reminded me that I'd been going on two lattes and chocolate since I'd left home this morning. I was starving. I supposed I could munch on the white bread, but that seemed pathetic somehow. Maybe I'd grab a sandwich at the Covington tearoom.

I pushed the stool away from the table, stood and stretched. Without warning, my neck muscles cramped up.

"Loafing on the job as usual," Minka said as she walked in. She wore leopard-skin leggings, a tight black turtleneck sweater and sparkly red heels. I don't make this stuff up.

"Didn't I warn you to stay out of my workroom?" I asked, dismissing any pretense of politeness as I rubbed away the kink in my neck caused by her proximity.

"What bug crawled up your ass?" she said, her nasal voice fraying my nerves.

"I'm busy, Minka." I made a show of grabbing the white cloth and covering the book, afraid her cooties might infect it. Childish, but it worked for me.

She snorted. "If I'd just inherited a shitload of cha-ching, I'd be in a hell of a better mood than you are."

My mouth fell open. How had she heard about Abraham's will? I hadn't mentioned it to anyone. It was as if the woman had extrasensory psychosis.

She studied her half-inch-long fingernails, then nibbled at a hangnail. "I had a little talk with the police yesterday."

"What a coincidence. So did I."

Her brows knit together. "You did?"

"Yeah. Except in my case, I told the truth."

"I don't lie," she said, offended.

"Yes, you do," I said. "You lied about Abraham and me, remember? About us fighting the night he died? That was a lie."

She cocked her head. "Really? My bad."

It was probably unkind to despise someone so stupid, but I did. My bad.

She glanced at me through blue-mascara-caked eyelashes. "I bet the police would be interested to hear about all that money you got."

I took a breath and counted to five. It wouldn't do for another murder to occur at the Covington within a week of the first one.

"I'm sure they would," I said. "That's why I'm calling them this afternoon to tell them."

She blinked. "Really?"

"Yeah, really."

"Whatever." But her lip curled. I'd stolen her thunder.

"I should apologize, though," I said. "I didn't realize you hadn't mentioned to the police that Abraham fired you from your job."

Her eyes grew wide. "That had nothing to do with—"

"With murdering him?"

"You shut up."

"They think that's a great motive for murder."

"You're such a liar."

"Now, that's the pot calling the kettle late for dinner."

"What?"

"Never mind." I waved my hand at the table. "Go away, Minka. I'm busy here."

She folded her arms tightly under her breasts and glowered at me. "You think you're so smart."

I thought about that. "I guess I do."

"We'll see who's smarter when you're standing in the unemployment line."

"Is that a threat?"

"Maybe."

"Fair enough." I moved closer. "But if you say one more word about me to the police, I'll make you sorry you ever crawled out from under that rock and started screwing with my life."

"Is that a threat?" she mocked.

"Yeah, it is."

"God, you're such a bitch."

"And that's a bad thing?"

She turned on her heel and stomped out, pushing Ian out of her way before he could move aside.

"Bye-bye," I called.

Ian stood at my door, watching Minka storm down the hall. "What was that all about?"

"The usual girl talk. Come in and close the door."

He did so, pulled up a stool and sat. "I wanted to talk to you yesterday at the memorial but you disappeared."

"You're the one who did the disappearing act," I said. "Right when the cops showed up. What was that all about?"

"Hey, I didn't want to get in their way. But then I looked for you a while later and couldn't find you."

"Sorry. You want some water?"

"No, thanks."

I grabbed a bottle from the cupboard, popped the top and drank. "Girl talk makes me thirsty. What's up?"

He adjusted and readjusted the knot in his tie.

"Ian?"

"I saw you talking to Enrico Baldacchio at the memorial service."

"Oh yeah." I took another sip of water. "I was surprised to see him there since he and Abraham were less than friends. But I really think Enrico might be—"

"He's dangerous, Brooklyn," Ian blurted. "Stay away from him."

Chapter 12

I put the water bottle down and reached for the candy bar. "What do you mean, dangerous? I've known Enrico Baldacchio forever."

"You don't know him as well as you think. He's a liar and a thief."

Whoa. Harsh words from someone who defined political correctness in this business.

"Why, Ian? What did he do?"

"I guess you didn't know that the Winslows hired Enrico first, before they ever came to the Covington."

I put the water bottle down. "You're right. I didn't know. What happened?"

He held up his hands to make a disclaimer. "Keep in mind, this is all secondhand information."

"Fine. Just tell me."

"Things were great for a while. They just wanted some books rebound."

"How did they find him?"

He chuckled without humor. "In the phone book. His name is listed first under bookbinders."

"You're kidding me."

"No. You can look it up."

I would. "Wow, who uses the phone book anymore? I thought everyone used Google."

He folded his hands together on the table. "Not everyone."

"Apparently not." Then I noticed Ian gritting his teeth. "You're probably not here to talk about the Yellow Pages."

"No," he said.

"Right." I smiled. "You were saying about Enrico?"

He looked uncomfortable and I almost offered him some of my chocolate, but figured I needed it more.

Ian sighed. "Some book-savvy friends of the Winslows were concerned that Enrico wasn't doing a good job. They'd seen some of his avant-garde leather work on several antiquarian books and were horrified. They insisted the Winslows bring their books to the Covington before Baldacchio destroyed the integrity of the collection. These friends convinced them—well, Sylvia anyway—that they had an incredible collection and needed a conservator and restoration experts to work with them."

"Smart friends."

"Doris Bondurant and her husband."

I smiled. "I love her."

"Yeah, she's great."

My stomach growled again. "I'm starving. Do you want to talk while we walk to the Rose Room?"

"Sure."

I ignored his amused look, grabbed my purse and walked out, locking the door behind us. Outside the main library entrance, we made a right turn and followed the wide path around the building, then wound our way through the camellia garden to the small Victorian building that housed the Covington's elegant Rose Room, named for the famous terraced rose garden it overlooked.

I turned and stared at the view from here at the top of Pacific Heights. The wind was brisk and the sky was a shade of blue no paint could replicate. From here, we could turn in three directions and see most of the City and the bay. It was spectacular. For a moment I felt at peace. This was the best place in the world to be.

"I'm buying," Ian said, snapping me back to reality as he held the door open.

I looked at him. "I'm just going to grab a sandwich."

"No, let's sit and talk."

I checked my watch again. Almost noon. I had plenty of time, but sitting around doing nothing was the last thing I wanted to do. Still, he was the boss and there was eating involved, after all.

It was early so we got a table by the window overlooking the sea of colorful roses spread across several acres. A swath of coral, ribbons of white, rows and rows of perfect pink, glorious deep reds.

A waitress arrived with a pot of tea, took our orders and left. Ian poured tea for both of us.

"So the Winslows brought their collection here," I said as I reached for my cup. "Why didn't you bring Enrico along to finish the restoration work?"

"Are you kidding?" Ian said in a furious whisper. "The man is a hack. The last time he worked here, he took a priceless Shakespeare quarto and turned it into rags."

"Why am I just hearing this? He's supposed to be a genius."

"Oh, come on. Didn't Abraham tell you stories?"

"Well, yeah. But I figured it was because they were rivals."

"But once Abraham came to the Covington, he heard the full story. He still didn't tell you anything?"

I squirmed. "We, you know, hadn't talked in a while. I'd just moved to the loft, and business was booming. Then I flew to Paris for a week before starting the class at L'Institut in Lyon. I hadn't seen him in six months."

He nodded in understanding. "He was a difficult man."

I wrapped my hands around my cup for warmth. "So I guess Enrico didn't take it well when they took their collection away from him."

"He was enraged. He warned the Winslows they'd lose money on the deal."

I laughed. "Well, duh. They were donating their entire collection, right? Not much money in that. Unless you purchased it. Did you?"

"We weren't in a position to purchase the collection," he said discreetly. "But we might if it does well."

Translation: if it brought in crowds. And it might, if they twisted the advertising toward the lurid. Focus on the *Faust* curse, the Hitler connection and all that good stuff.

"Okay, so Enrico's right," I said. "They won't be cashing in on eBay."

"Which was exactly what Enrico had in mind."

"You're kidding me. EBay?"

He shrugged. "A lot of dealers work through eBay."

"I know, but a collection like theirs? They could've found a reputable dealer to work with."

"Enrico assured them he could handle the whole business."

"And they bought it." I shook my head. "He probably used his cheesy Italian accent on them."

Ian absentmindedly stirred his tea. "People don't understand the book world."

"Conrad Winslow did admit he was pretty clueless when it came to books."

Ian just shook his head.

"I thought he was nice," I said.

"Right."

I laughed. "Ian, tell all."

He grimaced. "He's always bugging me about money. He wants to sell the collection and I don't know what to tell him. Of course I know dealers, but I want to show the books here. And it's important to keep the collection together. The show hasn't even opened yet, but if I have to put up with his threats much longer . . ." He didn't finish, just shook his head.

"It's not like the Winslows need the money."

"No, they don't," Ian said, staring into his teacup. "But he's got a bug up his butt about making money all the time. He doesn't get the whole nonprofit thing."

"Who does?"

He chuckled. "Isn't that the truth."

"Maybe you should start dealing with Sylvia," I suggested. "She seems to be the more savvy of the two."

He nodded. "Not a bad idea. But he's the one who comes around."

The waitress arranged our plates in front of us, checked the pot of tea, then left us. I'd ordered the curry chicken sandwich and they served it cut in four triangles around a delicate baby lettuce salad. I scooped up a triangle and devoured it.

After a few bites, I slowed down. "So essentially, your only beef with Enrico is over the quality of his work?"

"No." Ian took a sip of tea before continuing. "I've heard from a few dealers about some deals they've come across recently on the Internet, for finely bound rare German books."

I bit into another triangle and chewed as Ian spoke.

"One of the books is an extremely rare Rilke first edition, autographed. His *Duino Elegies*, I believe. The dealer paid an outrageous sum of money and when he received it, he found an ex libris with the Winslow insignia on the inside cover."

An ex libris is an ornate label pasted inside the front cover of a book with the owner's name or family crest.

"That was silly," I said. "Why didn't he remove the bookplate? He's just asking to get caught."

"To remove it would've devalued the book."

"Maybe," I allowed, but knew I could've finessed the label off without ruining the endpaper. "Maybe he just doesn't care."

"He certainly doesn't worry about getting caught. I suppose he's got a fake company name with a P.O. box, the whole deal. So far, six rare books have been traced back to the collection."

I tried to do the math. "So we're talking ten, twenty thousand dollars?"

"Try two hundred thousand," he said, looking at me with pity. So I didn't excel in math. Or market economics.

"Do the Winslows know?"

"I had to tell them."

"Yikes. What did they do?"

"Meredith wanted to take out a contract on him, but Sylvia calmed her down by suggesting the police run a sting operation. I think that's what the authorities have in mind."

I took a bite of salad. "I'm sure Enrico figured nobody would miss a dozen or so books out of hundreds in the collection."

"I'm sure," Ian agreed. "But the world of rare books is small. He'll get caught eventually."

"Minka told me Enrico was working with a new collector now. She wouldn't tell me the guy's name but said he made them sign a confidentiality agreement. I wonder if—"

"Wait. Minka's working with Enrico?"

"Apparently, but—"

"That's a pile of crap. What does he need an assistant for?"

"I've never seen you so fired up," I said. "He must've really burned your butt."

"You have no idea." He finished off his last triangle and wiped his hands on his linen napkin.

"But listen," I said. "Maybe this confidentiality agreement guy is part of the government sting you're talking about."

"I can only hope," he said. "But that's another reason why I don't want you to have anything to do with him."

"Thanks for the heads-up," I said. "I promise I'll keep my distance."

Starting sometime after two o'clock this afternoon.

It was one thirty by the time I took off for Enrico's house in the exclusive neighborhood of Sea Cliff. This enclave overlooking China Beach was known primarily for its famous celebrity residents, but the area also had a view of the Golden Gate Bridge from the ocean side looking into the bay that was more breathtaking than any I'd ever seen.

I guess I was an unabashed fan. I did love my City.

Lunch with Ian had been enlightening, but I couldn't help but wonder if there was something more personal in his disgust for Enrico.

Enrico had said he had something to show me and now I wondered whether he'd show me other books he'd taken from the Winslow collection. Would he be that bold? I hoped so.

I found his house and parked a few doors down. It was one of the smaller homes on the block but still lovely, with manicured hedges and freshly planted flowers lining the walkway. I climbed the brick steps to the front door and rang the bell. After a moment, I rang it again, then glanced around the neighborhood. It was completely deserted in the middle of the day. No gardeners, no kids, no signs of life.

After another minute, I knocked on the door.

"Enrico?" I called. "Are you here?"

Maybe he was in the back. I walked around to the side of the house, but the high gate was locked and

I couldn't see whether there was a back house or studio.

I returned to the front door and knocked again. I hated to think I'd driven out here for nothing. Without a clear thought, I tried the doorknob. It turned easily and I pushed it open a few inches.

"Enrico?" I called again. "Anybody home?"

I peeked inside. I couldn't hear a sound. I pushed the door open a foot and stepped inside. "Enrico? It's Brooklyn. Hello."

Was I actually walking into his house without an invitation? But he *had* invited me. Maybe he'd left the door open for me. I glanced around the small, fussy foyer. An arched entry led to the living room and after closing the front door, I ventured in farther. If he came home, I'd be sitting on the couch, waiting for him.

Yeah, that would work.

A large desk in the corner of the room was stacked with bills and papers. I glanced through a few, wondering whether I'd see any notices of sale or e-mails about his eBay business. It wouldn't hurt to look. Well, unless I got caught. But if I could find some evidence of his thefts, I could bring the Winslows some justice.

I heard a noise out on the street and glanced nervously over my shoulder. I could handle Enrico coming home to find me sitting on his couch but not rifling through his private papers.

A small vertical file held a stack of bills and checks, and I thumbed through them. They were all made out to Enrico Baldacchio, no fake name. I recognized a few of the check writers, some booksellers and an antiquities dealer.

One name jumped out at me.

Ian McCullough.

I stared in horror at Ian's check, payable to Enrico in the sum of five thousand dollars. The memo line said "Services."

My first thought was blackmail. Was this the real reason Ian was so angry with Enrico? But that was absurd. It was more likely that Ian had paid Enrico for something tangible, like a book.

Perhaps a stolen book?

And there went my mind, circling back around to blackmail.

I slipped the check into my jacket pocket. Now what? I was trying to figure out my next move when I heard the scuff of a heel against the concrete walkway out front.

Crap. I froze for one long second, then scanned the room for a place to hide. There was nothing. No closet, no room to hide behind the couch.

So much for my plan to relax on his couch. I didn't want to be discovered going through Enrico's house, especially by Enrico. Not since I'd found that check from Ian.

I raced through the alcove dining room and into the rustic gourmet kitchen. Along with a back entry, there was a laundry room and another door leading to a full pantry. In the middle of the kitchen was a butcher block island with a stainless steel pot rack hanging from the twelve-foot ceiling. What a great kitchen. Too bad I couldn't stay.

I dashed through the laundry room to the back door, but it wouldn't budge. It was dead-bolted with no key, no latch. Damn Enrico for taking normal security precautions. Desperate, I slipped into the full pantry and closed the door, just as someone entered the house.

I was shaking. I folded my arms tightly across my chest to control it. If this was Enrico coming home, I would have some explaining to do. Now would be a good time to think of a plausible reason why I was hiding in his pantry. I was being followed? I suspected foul play? I was hungry?

Heavy footsteps traipsed back and forth between the living and dining areas. I could hear papers being shuffled, drawers being opened and slammed shut. Someone was looking for something. The same thing I was looking for? Whatever that was.

Glass shattered in the living room area and I jolted, then tried to breathe again.

I didn't think Enrico would be stomping around breaking things, rifling carelessly through his own stuff. So who was out there? I hoped they would hurry. It was dark as hell in the pantry and my imagination was going crazy. I could smell peanut butter and I'd swear there were mice in here. I shivered, uneasy about sharing space with rodents.

Footsteps moved into the kitchen and I started to panic. They were too close. I was going to be discovered. And the mice. I could hear them breathing. A scream built in my throat.

A wisp of breath on the skin beneath my ear was my only warning before someone slapped a hand over my mouth and grabbed me from behind.

Chapter 13

I was trapped in the viselike grip of my assailant. He'd wrapped one strong arm around my torso to prevent me from hitting him, but if I was about to die in a pantry closet, I refused to go meekly. I didn't dare make any noise, but I squirmed and tried to bite the palm of his hand. I only managed to gnaw some skin, which almost made me gag. I twisted to get free, but there was no room to maneuver in the confines of the pantry closet.

"Shhhhh," he whispered, as though he were trying to calm a colicky baby. I could smell his spicy scent and wondered how I hadn't realized he was hiding here from the moment I stepped inside this space. It wasn't mice I'd sensed, just one big rat.

"Damn it, Derek," I hissed, but with his hand clamping my mouth, it sounded like "Mrkmr, rruk."

"Shut up," he whispered roughly.

I was truly going to kill him. For now, though, I nodded slowly to let him know I was on board with the plan to keep quiet.

He eased the pressure of his hand on my mouth but kept his other arm tight around me. As the footsteps grew closer to the pantry, I stopped breathing altogether. I was jammed up against Derek's hard chest and stomach, not to mention his thighs. Oh my. Now that I knew it was him, part of me, okay, *all* of me wanted to rub up even closer and purr like a satisfied kitty cat. This probably wasn't the best time to be thinking along those lines, especially in light of my recent decision to kill him.

I sucked in a breath as Derek reached between me and the door to grasp the handle, seconds before the intruder tried to open the pantry door. I could feel Derek's muscles vibrate with tension as he held the door handle so tightly, the intruder had to think it was either stuck or locked.

Either way, the guy on the other side of the door finally uttered an oath and gave up.

As his footsteps moved away from the pantry, I let out a slow breath. The intruder crossed the kitchen and retreated down the hall, his footsteps growing fainter as he moved toward the back of the house.

Just as I thought I might collapse in relief, a door slammed somewhere down the long hall. I tensed again as footsteps pounded down the hardwood floor of the hall and raced out the front door.

There was nothing but silence for a moment; then a car engine started up and tires squealed as the intruder took off.

After ten more seconds, Derek shoved the door open and we escaped the pantry.

After first sucking in the air of freedom, I turned

and smacked his arm. "What the hell were you doing in there?"

He dusted off his jacket. "Waiting for you."

"Very funny. Did you follow me here? I mean, not *follow* me, exactly, since you were here first. But, you know, did you? Follow me?"

"I haven't the slightest idea what you're talking about."

I stomped my foot, then felt like an idiot. But I was irate. "How did you know I was coming here?"

He grabbed my arm and headed for the front door. "We can talk later. Right now we're trespassing."

I whipped my arm away. "I have an appointment with Enrico."

"Call to reschedule." He pointed to the door. "Let's go."

I skirted him and headed the opposite way, down the hall. "I'll just be a minute."

"What the hell are you doing?"

"I'm looking for something. I'll be quick."

"God, you're a pain in the ass."

I glowered at him. "You should talk."

I heard him sigh as he followed me, coming up close behind me as I surveyed the first room. Twin beds, nightstand, dresser. No frills. It appeared to be a guest bedroom. There were no books, no boxes, nothing that indicated a bookselling business was being operated in there. And nothing that indicated it might be the missing "GW1941."

"Did you see Enrico leaving?" I asked.

"No."

"He must've forgotten I was coming."

"Yet he left the door unlocked."

"Maybe he just ran out for a minute."

"Which means he'll be home any second to find us trespassing."

"I was invited. What's your excuse?"

"I told you, I was waiting for you."

"I didn't tell anyone where I was going," I insisted.

"You're not exactly subtle," he said.

"What's that supposed to mean?" The room across the hall was empty except for an ironing board and a television set. I couldn't see Enrico standing here ironing his shirts while watching *Oprah*. Maybe he had a housekeeper.

"I overheard your conversation with him at the memorial service. You said you'd meet him at two."

I put my hand on my hip. "You were supposed to be talking to Mary Ellen Prescott."

He thought for a moment. "Ah yes. Lovely woman. Completely insane."

I chuckled. "I was hoping she'd convert you."

"She worships someone's blood. I envisioned goats on an altar."

I smiled. "You're close. Chickens."

"Good Lord."

"It's okay, nothing's wasted. They eat the chickens after they're sacrificed."

He put up his hand to stop me. "More than I wish to know about dear Mary Ellen."

The next door on the left was closed. I opened it and found Enrico's library.

There were shelves of leather-bound books from floor to ceiling on all four walls with cutouts around the two windows and the closet. Two brown leather chairs sat in the middle of the room with a mahogany table in between. More finely bound books were stacked on the table. The chairs looked lived in, comfortable and cozy. The rug beneath was an elaborate Persian style with swirls and curlicues in multiple shades of blue and black and beige.

I focused again on that stack of books on the table.

"Ah." I stepped into the room and picked up the beautifully bound book lying on top. It was Plutarch's *Parallel Lives*, bound in burgundy calfskin, heavily gilded, nearly five centuries old, in perfect condition. Nearly priceless.

"What is he doing with this?" I turned to show it to Derek, and that was when I saw Enrico lying in the corner, curled up on that fabulous rug. A dark halo of blood puddled around his head.

"Oh no. Oh God." My vision wavered; then Enrico's head telescoped out, in, then out again.

I tried to scream but it sounded like a whimper.

Derek grabbed me, shook me, then pulled me close. "No fainting."

"He's dead," I mumbled into Derek's shirt.

"Yes," he said crisply. "Pull yourself together. We've got to get out of here."

"But . . ." I looked at him. "We should call the police."

"We will."

How long had he been lying here, dying? The whole time I'd been poking through his desk and his papers? All that time I'd been hiding in the pantry with Derek while another intruder ransacked the house? Had Enrico still been alive when I walked through the front door? If I'd found him earlier, could I have kept him alive? Called for an ambulance? Would I feel guilty about it for the rest of my life? Right now I thought I might.

"I should've—"

"No."

"But I might've—"

"No." He drew me back into his arms.

"He was here all along," I whispered.

"Yes."

"You knew."

"No."

I was relieved to hear him say it whether he was telling the truth or not. He moved his hands up and down along my spine.

"Come on, let's go," he said quietly.

"Shouldn't we—"

"No, we'll call from elsewhere."

"We might've helped him."

"I'm certain he was already dead."

"You don't know."

"Yes, I do." He placed his hand on the back of my head and eased me closer to him. It shouldn't have felt so good, but it did. I felt completely enveloped, secure. Loved. An illusion to be sure, but nice for the moment.

Finally, I leaned back to look at him. "You honestly didn't know he was back here?"

"Honestly."

"Then how do you know he was dead when we—"

He looked me straight in the eye. "The fact that he's got a bullet hole in his head makes me think he died rather quickly. And since we heard nothing . . ."

He let it go at that.

I tried to swallow past the sudden lump in my throat. "Right. You're right. I'm sorry."

He hung his head, in defeat or contemplation, I couldn't say. But when he looked at me again, it was with determination. "Come here."

Call me weak, but I went willingly back into his arms.

"I'm tired of finding dead bodies," I whispered after a moment.

"It does get tiresome."

I must've been going into shock because I giggled at that. Taking a deep breath, I vowed to keep it together. Enrico was dead, murdered, and I was standing three feet away from his body. "We'd better get out of here."

"What a good idea."

I realized I was still holding the Plutarch and slipped it into my purse. "I'm taking this with me."

"Fine. Steal another book." He grabbed my hand and I allowed him to pull me down the hall toward the front door. "We'll call the police from the nearest restaurant."

"The Left Hand."

"Beg your pardon?"

"The Left Hand. It's a vegetarian restaurant about two blocks away, on California Street."

He stared at me. "Why am I not surprised you know every eating establishment in this city?"

I shrugged. "I like to eat."

"I've noticed."

I reached for the front door handle, but Derek pulled me away. "Wait." He went into the front room and stared out through a crack in the curtains. From over his shoulder, I caught a glimpse of a funky old black sports car pulling up to park.

There was a small explosion as the car backfired and trembled to a halt. A woman climbed out from the driver's seat and headed for the front door.

"It's Minka," I said, feeling a chill that had little to do with the dead body down the hall.

"This place is worse than Heathrow for crowds," he muttered. "And let's not touch anything else." He pulled a handkerchief from his pocket and used it to wipe the front doorknob and throw the bolt into place, then grabbed my hand and pulled me into the kitchen. "We'll go out through the back and around the side."

"Back door's got a dead bolt. I already checked."

"Bloody hell." We looked at each other. I would panic in just a minute.

"We could break the window," I said.

"If we must. Let's look for a key first."

I gulped again. "Maybe they were in his pocket."

His eyes narrowed as he thought about it. "Or maybe he empties his pockets when he arrives home." He jogged into the living room and I followed. He scanned the room, finally spying a small bowl on the short bookshelf near the foyer. Sure enough, there was a bowl holding a set of keys and a pile of coins, a cell phone and a wadded tissue, as though he'd stood right there and emptied his pockets.

"Brilliant," I said.

"We men are a predictable lot."

He grabbed my hand again and we raced through the kitchen to the back door, just as the front doorbell rang. I could hear Minka shouting Enrico's name from the front step. She sounded like a fishwife—not that I'd ever heard a true fishwife yelling. It didn't matter. I had no doubt Minka's annoying bellows would qualify.

Derek tried the first key and in seconds we were out of the house.

"Enrico, I've got my key," Minka hollered. "I'm coming in."

"She's got a mouth," Derek said. "The entire neighborhood's going to be alerted."

We tiptoed around the side of the house just as Minka went through the front door. I could still hear her shouting out his name a few more times.

"Don't run," Derek warned as we reached the front sidewalk. "Don't make eye contact with anyone. Walk as though you belong here. Then drive to the restaurant and park at least a block away. I'll follow you."

I didn't argue. I wanted to be miles away when Minka found Enrico's body. I walked briskly to my car, started the engine and took off. A few blocks later, I turned right on California Street, found a space and parked.

I could barely catch my breath.

What had I been thinking, walking into Enrico's house? I had been trespassing on private property. It didn't matter that I'd had an appointment with Enrico. I didn't belong there. And all along, he'd been dead in the back room.

I rubbed my arms to fight the chills. Someone had been angry enough to kill him in cold blood. With a gun. Just like Abraham. Why? What had Enrico done? And more importantly, *who* had he so totally enraged that they'd taken a gun and shot him in the head?

It had to be the same person who had killed Abraham. It couldn't be a coincidence.

The killer hadn't ransacked Enrico's home, so maybe they hadn't been looking for anything but him. That could mean the Winslows were involved. Once again, I pictured little Meredith in that pretty orange jumpsuit.

But maybe Derek's arrival had scared the killer off and he planned to return to search the place. Which meant that the person searching the house while Derek and I were hiding in the pantry could be the killer.

What was the real connection between Abraham, Enrico and the murderer? Books, to be sure. But which books? One of the Winslows' collection? Something from the Covington? Or something to do with the old grudge between the two men?

I had no doubt there was a connection between the two deaths. Find that connection and I would find the murderer.

I would find the murderer? I shuddered. No, thank you. I was going back to my loft and hiding under my bed.

Derek's black Bentley pulled up half a block in front of me. As I watched him approach my car, his gait purposeful, his eyes studying me as a wild cat might scrutinize his quarry, three things occurred to me.

Number one, Derek Stone was really hot.

Number two, Minka didn't kill Enrico.

Number three, I knew who the intruder was.

Chapter 14

I'd recognized the intruder's voice when I heard him utter the oath outside the pantry door.

I stared at Derek as he came closer. I couldn't tell him what I knew. Not yet. I needed to think, needed to figure out whether to confront the intruder privately, let him know I knew he'd been in Enrico's home. I debated whether to tell him I knew what he'd been looking for.

Which reminded me, that check for five thousand dollars was burning a hole in my jacket pocket.

I shook my head as I climbed out of my car. Who in the world besides Ian McCullough would've said "Feather buckets" when he couldn't open a recalcitrant door? I'd heard him say it a hundred times over the years. He'd once explained that when he was a boy, his very proper parents had forbidden him and his brothers to curse in the house, so "feather buckets" was the young boys' coded way of saying "fuck it."

I couldn't believe he still used that stupid phrase. Of course, he probably hadn't expected an old friend to be hiding just behind the very thin door of that pantry when he uttered those words.

I had no doubt Ian had been looking for the five-thousand-dollar check I'd found and now I was absolutely certain Enrico had been blackmailing him. But why? What had Ian done to make himself vulnerable to someone like Enrico Baldacchio?

I really couldn't see Ian being a killer. From what I'd heard from inside the pantry closet, Ian had literally stumbled onto Enrico's body, then torn out of the house as if he'd seen a ghost.

The bad news was, Minka couldn't have killed Enrico, either. Unless she was an extremely good actress, I seriously doubted her ability to shoot the man in cold blood, drive away, then return a while later, shouting his name like the aforementioned fishwife. Even *I* was forced to admit she wasn't *that* stupid.

So who killed Enrico Baldacchio?

I was suddenly paranoid about walking around this part of town, so I found an old Giants cap in my glove box, wrapped my hair up and shoved it under the cap. I climbed out of the car and met Derek on the busy sidewalk. This section of California Street in the Richmond District catered to the wealthy residents of Sea Cliff. There were boutiques, a cheese shop, a butcher, two bakeries and several chic restaurants.

Derek looked at my cap and nodded in approval, but call me surprised when he put his arm around my shoulder and hauled me in close.

"We'll call the police from that petrol station," he said, discreetly pointing out the ARCO station across the street as we walked.

"They'll probably have a pay phone inside the restaurant," I said.

"Not a good idea," he said, nuzzling my neck.

"Oh, right." I could barely think. "Uh, because they'll trace the call."

"They don't have to trace anything. The location pops up on the screen as soon as the dispatcher picks up the call."

"Ah. Good to know." Why didn't I know that? Maybe because I'd just embarked on this new life of crime and still didn't know all the ropes.

Derek whispered, "We'll order something first, then call."

It seemed wrong to put off the call. Maybe not wrong, exactly, but calculated certainly. Enrico was dead and probably wouldn't care, but it made me feel callous somehow to allow his body to lie there on the carpet, alone, ignored, while I ordered lunch.

Then again, I didn't want to be connected to his death any more than I already was. Derek was helping me set up a firewall, so to speak. I should be grateful.

My eyes widened as his jaw brushed my chin. I inhaled deeply and caught the scent of his skin. I wasn't complaining, but what was going on here? Had all the danger and excitement gotten to him?

I guess it had gotten to me, too, because I stared up at him and my mouth went dry. My appetite for food was history and trust me, that never happens.

"What do you think you're doing?" I asked. "I'm not going to faint, you know."

"I didn't think you were," he said quietly in my ear.

I trembled from the breathy contact. "Then what's going on here?"

He bent his head to gaze at me. "We're pretending to be completely enamored, of course. If the police think to interview anyone around here, they'll vaguely recall seeing a couple in love walking down the street. They won't be able to describe a gorgeous blonde and the handsome buck by her side."

I took a few seconds to appreciate the *gorgeous blonde* comment. Then I slugged him. "You're truly a jerk."

He laughed and hugged me tighter. "I love it when you call me names."

I smiled and touched his cheek. "In that case, you're a complete ass."

"Mmm. Music to my ears."

I grabbed his lapel and whispered, "For a cop, you know a lot about larcenous behavior."

"It's part of the training."

"I think you live closer to the edge than you let on."

He gave me an innocent smile before pulling the restaurant door open and pushing me inside.

"I need a drink," I said, breaking away from him.

"Fat chance of finding alcohol in a vegetarian restaurant," he complained.

"Hey, vegetarians drink wine," I insisted, taking off my jacket as we passed through the foyer. "It's like the staff of life or something."

"Isn't that bread?"

"Whatever."

Despite the sunny day outside, the restaurant was as dark as a cave, its walls and ceiling lined in thick redwood panels. The darkness suited my mood.

"Ah, delightful," he said, and led me to the fully

stocked bar that ran the length of the room on the far side. We grabbed two stools and sat, the only two customers in the bar.

I studied the wine list and finally decided on a glass of the 2004 Concannon Petite Syrah. Derek ordered a very dry Belvedere martini with a lemon twist, shaken, not stirred. Why was I not surprised?

We didn't speak until our drinks were served. As soon as the bartender walked away, I turned to Derek. "Maybe Minka already called the police. Don't you think we should lie low for a while?"

"Lie low?" he said with a smirk. "Now who's living on the edge?"

"It was just a thought."

Derek took one sip of his martini, then said, "From everything I've heard about this Minka, we oughtn't depend on her to do the right thing."

"Good point."

He pushed his barstool away and stood. "I'll go make the call."

I grabbed his arm. "No, I'll make the call."

"It's no problem." He tapped his head. "I know the number. Nine-one-one. See?"

"Very funny," I said. "Don't you think it should be an anonymous phone call?"

"It will be."

"Not if you make it," I said. "When Inspector Jaglow plays the dispatcher's tape back and hears a distinguished British accent, he'll know it's you."

Derek smiled crookedly and patted his chest. "I'm touched you think I'm distinguished."

"I didn't say *you* were . . . Oh, never mind."

"I won't be long." He started to walk away.

"You stay right here." I jumped off my stool. "All you need to do is open your mouth and they'll know it's you."

"I'm perfectly capable of disguising my voice," he said imperiously.

"Right, Double-O." I shook my head in disbelief. "Shaken, not stirred. Give me a break."

He pulled me back. "All right, listen. I'm not calling anonymously. I'm telling Jaglow I overheard your conversation with Baldacchio and went to see him before you got there. I found the body."

"Oh." That made sense. "But what about me?"

"What about you?"

"Are you going to tell him I was there?"

He pierced me with a look. "Are you going to do everything I tell you to do from now on?"

"Probably not."

His lips twisted. "Then I'll have to think about it."

"That's blackmail."

He grinned. "Such an ugly word, but yes."

"All right, all right. Just go." As I watched him walk away, I realized I didn't care whether the police knew I'd been there. The most important thing right now was that they took care of Enrico and tracked down Abraham's killer.

As soon as Derek came back, he said, "It's best if you go back to work this afternoon."

I took a hearty gulp of wine. "As though nothing happened?"

"Exactly," he said as he paid the bill.

"I'm not sure I can lie about this."

"I'm well aware of your status as the world's worst

liar," he said. "And I know you had nothing to do with his death. But if the police find your fingerprints, it could make things difficult. Are you prepared to deal with it?"

As I pushed the barstool back I thought about it. "I know I'm innocent so I'll deal with it. I just want the police to find this killer before he strikes again."

I made it back to the Covington in less than twenty minutes. Ian was nowhere to be found and I was just as happy not to have to confront him this afternoon. I'd give him a day to calm down. Not to mention I could use a day to calm down, myself. Of course, there was a strong chance Ian would grow more frantic once he realized the police would be going through Enrico's house looking for clues—like a five-thousand-dollar check with Ian's name on it, for example—with a magnifying glass and tweezers.

I left him a voice mail message, telling him I had some good news for him. I didn't mention the check, but I hoped my exuberant tone would keep him from jumping off a ledge somewhere.

I tried to carry on my normal activities, but it wasn't easy. People were dying around me. Two of the City's most prominent bookbinders had been brutally murdered. I'd seen their dead bodies with my own eyes. I hadn't been close to Enrico, hadn't even liked him. But I'd known him. I'd seen him curled up on his antique rug, shot through the head by some insane killer. I couldn't get the sight out of my head.

"Enough!" I protested aloud. I pushed away from the table. I needed to move around, shake myself up, do something to distract myself from the pictures of blood and dead bodies that kept playing over and over in my brain like some broken movie reel.

I stretched my arms and rotated my wrists and did a few jumping jacks and deep knee bends—which really hurt so I only did two.

I pushed my hair back into a ponytail and sat down again. I didn't have time for any more distractions. I had to finish this book, and this last process of repairing the tears I'd found would be time-consuming and problematic.

It wasn't the repair itself, which involved ripping a small piece of thin, fibrous Japanese tissue paper and gluing it over the tear. The problem came when you introduced moisture, in the form of glue, to paper. If your timing was off or you used too much glue or you didn't dry the page properly, your page could ripple and buck.

To dry each page flat, I'd place it between two pieces of glass with a sheet of blotter paper to soak up any excess moisture.

I could use the drying time to clean and polish the rubies from the front cover.

Ian wanted the book finished in time for the official public opening of the exhibition this Saturday. I knew I could make it—if good-looking security experts and various dead bodies would stop interrupting me.

I'd just stirred up my first batch of wheat paste glue and was about to apply it to the repair tissue when I heard the sound of high heels tapping madly down the hall.

My door swung open and Minka pointed at me.

"Killer!" she screamed. "Murderer! She killed him! I saw her car at Enrico's house. Arrest her."

I was relieved to see Inspector Lee step closer to Minka and clutch her upper arm. "Ms. La Beef, keep it down."

"Check her hands for gunshot residue," Minka added shrilly as she yanked her arm away. "Do your damn job right so she won't kill somebody else!"

"Now, look, Ms.—"

"And for the last time, my name is La*Boeuf*, not La *Beef*!"

Oh, for God's sake.

Minka charged in, Inspector Lee hot on her heels. I stood and braced myself for whatever else she was about to spew, but nothing could've prepared me for her vicious slap across my face.

"Ohhhh." I fell back against the counter from the force of the blow.

"Wait a damn second!" Inspector Lee grabbed Minka from behind.

I leaned one elbow heavily on the counter, clutching my jaw, breathing deeply, staring sideways at the two of them as they grappled for power.

Had I thought the presence of a cop would keep Minka in line? Big mistake.

I looked beyond Minka at Inspector Lee. I could tell she'd been taken aback as well, but she still managed to subdue her. Physically, anyway.

"Killer!" Minka shrieked again.

"Shut up," Lee shouted, then looked intently at me.

"I didn't kill anyone," I said, rubbing my cheek and jaw where her meaty hand had connected with my face. "But I could always change my mind."

"Okay, you shut up, too," Lee said, still struggling with the writhing maniac.

I tried to move my jaw back and forth. It didn't feel broken, not that I knew what a broken jaw felt like. I just knew it hurt like hell.

Lee's lips twitched, and not in amusement. She'd had enough of Minka's squirming and one-handedly shoved her to the floor, then reached behind her back for handcuffs and snapped them onto Minka's wrists. "Shut up and don't move."

Minka growled and squirmed on the floor like a pissed-off alligator. "You're arresting *me*?" she cried. "She's the murderer!"

"And you're under arrest for assault," Lee told her, clucking her tongue. "Right in front of a police officer. That's just stupid."

I figured it wasn't a good time to give Inspector Lee a high five, but I was definitely impressed with her style.

The side of my face was starting to burn and I wanted to go home and sleep for a week.

Lee glared at me. "You want to start talking?"

"About what?" I tried to look innocent but probably only managed to look bruised.

She shook her head as she pulled her cell phone out and pushed a few keys. "I need backup," she snarled into the phone. "Now."

She flipped the phone shut. Apparently, she'd heard enough bullshit for one day.

Meanwhile, I could feel my cheek swelling.

After two uniformed officers took Minka off to jail, Inspector Lee asked me to follow her back to police headquarters for a little talk. And when I say she "asked" me to follow her, I was fairly certain she meant I could follow her to headquarters on my own or I could take a ride in the back of a squad car.

Minka's assault must've slapped some sense into me because I was more than willing to tell the truth about being at Enrico's. Lying about it had just gotten my face bashed in.

My cell phone rang and I grabbed it, hoping it was either Derek or Ian. I'd left more than a few voice mail messages for each of them.

"Hi, sweetie."

"Mom."

"I'm planning a barbecue next Saturday because Austin's bringing Robin home for dinner. Isn't that sweet? Savannah will be in town, too, and I left a message for Ian. I understand there's a nice English fellow you've been seeing. You can bring him if you'd like."

That nice English fellow who was ignoring my calls? Not a chance. And who had told my mother about him?

"I'm not sure Derek can make it, Mom," I said.

"We'll be barbecuing filets," she said to tempt me further.

"Savannah's eating a steak? I wouldn't miss that for the world."

My youngest sister was a fruitarian. I didn't even bother trying to understand what that meant. The girl insisted she got all the protein she needed from coconut milk and raw nuts. If you asked me, she'd consumed one too many nuts.

"Oh, she'll eat a mango or something," Mom muttered; then she perked up again. "Dad has a new cabernet he wants you to try. You know he trusts your taste buds more than anyone's."

It was blatant flattery but it worked. "I'll be there, Mom. But I'll have to let you know about Derek."

"Super dandy," Mom said. "So, what are you up to, sweetie? How are your chakras?"

I turned right on Fillmore and waited for a break in traffic in order to make the left turn onto Oak. "Well, if you must know, my chakras and I are on our way to police headquarters."

"What?" she cried in alarm. "Sweetie, that's not funny."

"Sorry, Mom. I'm just going down to answer some questions."

"Oh my God."

"Don't worry, Mom. I'm okay. Well, I think so, anyway. But see, first Abraham was murdered and now they've discovered Enrico Baldacchio's body. So they want to talk to people." I jammed my brakes at Geary as the light turned red. The action jarred my tender jaw and I groaned aloud.

Mom groaned, too. "Oh God, they're arresting you."

"Mom, no."

"Oh God," she said again. "I knew this would happen."

"What do you mean?"

She moaned, then abruptly began to chant. *"Nam myoho renge kyo nam myoho renge kyo nam myoho renge kyo nam myoho renge kyo—"*

"Mom, stop. They won't arrest me. I didn't do anything. They don't have any evidence."

"Not yet," she cried, and chanted even louder. *"Nam myoho renge kyo nam myoho renge kyo."*

"Mom, they just want to talk to me because I knew both men."

She was chanting so loudly now, I didn't think she heard me. *"Nam myoho renge kyo nam myoho renge kyo nam myoho renge kyo nam myoho renge kyo."*

For a Unitarian, the woman sure could belt out a Buddhist chant.

Dad had always talked about the time he and his buddy Norman ran out of money. Since they were hungry, they decided to chant for food. Twenty minutes later, Mom showed up with two bags of groceries. She believed in the power of the chant.

"Nam myoho renge kyo nam myoho renge kyo nam myoho—"

"I'll call you when I get home, Mom," I shouted, unsure whether she could hear me anymore. "Please don't worry."

I disconnected the call, but I was pretty sure Mom would keep chanting until either world peace was declared or I broke out of jail.

I sat on a folding chair in a small interrogation room in the police homicide division, located inside the Hall of Justice Building. Inspectors Lee and Jaglow had started the interview but had been called away, leaving me alone for the last hour and forty minutes. I knew they were trying to unnerve me by making me wait, and it was working. I was ready to confess all my sins. Fortunately, murder was not one of them. So far. I was hedging my bets where Minka was concerned.

I tapped my fingers on the table and stared at the

strangely attractive taupe walls for the three hundredth time. As usual when I had time on my hands, my brain circled around Abraham's murder. But instead of the usual visions of dead bodies, blood and books circling my brain, I kept going back to my last meeting with Abraham the night he died. He'd been so warm and jovial, so positively reflective, so excited for the future.

"We won't be strangers anymore," he'd promised. And "I plan to live in the present and enjoy every minute."

I swiped away angry tears and repeated my vow to find the person who killed Abraham's chances to enjoy his life. That person had destroyed my opportunity to rebuild my friendship with my teacher and deprived Annie of the father she might've known.

The door swung open and Derek Stone walked in. "Did you confess all?"

"I haven't had the chance."

"Good." He looked around. "Nice room."

"It is pleasant, isn't it?"

"Ready to go?"

"I haven't talked to the police yet."

"That won't be necessary just now. They'll call you later and arrange a time to stop by your place."

"How do you know?"

"Inspector Jaglow told me."

"He couldn't tell me?"

"He's busy."

My eyes narrowed on him. "He had time to talk to you."

"Of course."

I sighed. "He could've said something."

"He's been occupied elsewhere. Somebody confessed to the murders."

I gawked at him. "You're kidding me. Who?"

He lifted his shoulders. "How the devil would I know? I listened to twelve hysterical messages from you, so I raced down here, only to be told that someone else had already confessed. Do you want to go or not?"

"Don't get snippy with me," I said, stalking toward the door. "I've had a bad day."

"Whoa," he said, gripping my shoulders to stop me. He stared at me for a long moment, then cautiously touched my cheek with his fingers. "What'd you run into, darling?"

"Very funny." I felt tears welling up, so I went on the offensive. "Where have you been, anyway? And by the way, I do not leave hysterical messages."

He wasn't cowed. Instead, he tucked my arm through his and led me down the corridor to the main entrance of the Hall of Justice, just as the double glass doors swung open and my mother was led inside by two police officers. Her hands were held behind her back.

"No," I cried, and rushed across the wide, linoleum-floored lobby. I hugged her and felt her trembling.

"Mother, what're you doing here?" I tried to ignore the flash of déjà vu from that question, the exact same thing I'd asked her the night Abraham was murdered.

"Oh, sweetie, you're safe," Mom said, then focused in on my bruised jaw. "They beat you!" she cried, and burst into tears.

* * *

Derek walked with me the two long blocks to the parking structure and waited until I was in my car with the doors locked and the window opened.

I hadn't said a word, too worried about my mother confessing to two murders in some cockeyed scheme to protect me. My need to find Abraham's killer, now, today, had just accelerated into hyperspeed. I couldn't let Mom spend the night in jail for something she didn't do.

"You know my mother didn't kill anyone," I said.

"Well, yes." He folded his arms across his chest. "She hardly strikes me as a cold-blooded killer."

"Thank you." I sighed. "She freaked out. I was on the phone with her, telling her I was going to the police station, and she lost it. I'm sure she just confessed to protect me. The problem is, I'm the one who needs to protect her."

"Why must either of you protect the other?"

Oh, crap. I looked into his eyes. "I know you're working with the police but I . . . I trust you."

He nodded. "I appreciate that."

"Okay, what I'm about to tell you is never to go any further. If I find out you told someone, I won't rest until I've hunted you down and whacked you. I'll beat you until you're a bloody stump; then I'll destroy your—"

"Got it," he said, resting his hands on my windowsill. "Just get to the point."

"Fine," I said in a huff. "But you've been warned. My mother was at the Covington the night of Abraham's death. She had a meeting with him but he never showed up. The police don't know this. I ran into her on the stairs as I was going down to Abraham's workroom in the basement. It shocked the hell out of me. She wouldn't tell me why she was meeting with him. I'm afraid. . . . I think they might've been having an affair."

His lips twisted. "I don't believe it."

"It's true; she was there."

"Maybe she was, but I don't believe she was having an affair. She's not the type."

"There's a type?"

He shrugged. "A vibe, if you will."

I looked askance. "Are you saying my mother couldn't attract a man?"

He backed away from the car. "I refuse to have this discussion with a woman on the verge of hysteria."

"You want to see hysteria? Where are you going? Come back. What do you mean, there's a type?"

He waved as he continued to back away. "Drive carefully, darling. Put some ice on that cheek."

Chapter 15

No matter how self-sufficient and worldly a girl is, sometimes she just needs to talk to her dad.

I paid the parking ransom and drove out of the Bryant and Sixth Street garage, then punched the speed dial number for my parents' home. Dad picked up on the first ring, which told me he'd been expecting a phone call since he usually let the answering machine pick up.

I told him everything I knew. As usual, he refused to give in to fear or negativity.

"Mom's going to be fine, Brooks," he assured me. "She took a refresher course in Vedanta last week."

"Ah, Vedanta," I said, vaguely familiar with the ancient Indian philosophy that taught one to live life according to higher ideals in order to achieve inner bliss. "Why was I worried?"

"Exactly," he said, pleased that I appreciated the significance of Vedanta. "Still, I'd better get my butt down there."

That was the first note of stress I'd heard in his voice.

"I'll meet you there," I offered as I pulled into my building's parking garage, shifted to Park and turned off the engine. Homicide headquarters was nothing if not convenient to my place. I'd made it home in less than five minutes.

"No, no, you've been through enough. I'll call Carl and his pack of lawyers. They'll take care of everything."

"Dad, you know Mom's innocent, right?"

He actually chuckled. "Of course she's innocent. Your mother wouldn't knowingly hurt a flea. It would skew her karma and jeopardize her samsara for lifetimes to come."

"Why didn't I think of that?" I glanced around the cold, dark, deserted underground parking lot and made a mental note to insist on better lighting at the next homeowners' meeting.

"So, I'd better get cracking here," Dad said.

"Okay, but, Dad, I'm afraid Mom confessed because she's trying to protect me."

"Really? What did you do?"

"Nothing, I swear! But could you please tell Mom it's not necessary?"

"What's not necessary?" There was a pause; then he said, "I'm going to need to write this down, aren't I?"

I could picture him scratching the side of his head as he searched for a pad and pencil. I sighed. "Never mind, Dad. Just please call me as soon as you know anything, okay?"

"You bet your boots, honey. Peace, out."

"Uh, yeah, bye." My parents were nothing if not semicurrent with their lingo.

I limped to the elevator, unsure what Dad could do to get Mom out of jail after she'd come forward and confessed to killing Abraham. Short of confessing to the murder himself.

"Oh no, he wouldn't." It felt as if a tendril of ice were sliding down my spine, and I pushed that thought firmly out of my mind.

As I slammed the elevator gate shut and pushed the button for the sixth floor, different scenarios ran through my head of my mother being grilled by two determined homicide inspectors.

I could just imagine her giving them some half-baked reason for killing two men in cold blood. Then she'd flash them her Sunny Bunny Face and invite them to next Saturday's barbecue.

Now that I thought about it, the inspectors probably needed more of my sympathy than Mom did.

Dad was right. Mom would be fine, while I was on the verge of a nervous breakdown. The police really wouldn't keep her in a jail cell, would they?

As soon as I got inside and took off my shoes, I was going to call Inspector Lee.

The elevator trembled to a halt. I shoved the gate back and walked down the hall to my place, grateful for the skylights and wall sconces that kept the long hallway light and welcoming instead of dark and gloomy.

I was anxious to shut myself away and do what I always did when my world was going crazy—bury myself in work.

I turned the corner and staggered to a halt. My front door was ajar.

A thousand nerve endings pulsated, stabbing my

skin like so many needles. I tried to replay the day in my head. Had I really been so distracted when I left this morning that I'd—no. I never would've left my door open.

Someone had been inside my home. They might still be there.

Every rule in the book told mc not to go inside. And after a few seconds of debate, I complied. I ran to Suzic and Vinnie's place down the hall and around the corner. I hammered on their door, praying they were home.

"What the fagoo?" Suzie said as she opened the door. "Brooklyn! Whassup? Whoa, you look freaked. Come on in."

"No. I need to know if you saw someone go into my place today. Did someone—oh God. I think someone broke into my place."

"No fucking way," she said. Looking over her shoulder, she shouted, "Vinnie, stay in the house. Lock the door behind me."

Suzie grabbed my arm, said, "Come on," and pulled me all the way to my front door. "Shit, somebody punched the lock straight through."

"How?"

"You don't wanna know," she said grimly. "You ready?"

Damn, this girl was tough. I guess that was a prerequisite if you worked with chain saws all day.

"I'm ready," I said.

" 'Kay, we're going in."

I nodded firmly. "Let's roll."

She used her foot to push the door open and we walked inside. Or tried to, anyway.

I groaned. "No, no, no."

"Shit, man. This place is a mess."

That was putting it mildly. My studio was a shambles. Tools and brushes were scattered every which
way on the worktables and the floor. Paper was torn
and thrown everywhere. Piles of marbled endpapers
and rolls of cloth and leather used for making new
book covers were tossed across the room. Hundreds
of spools of thread that had been neatly sorted by
color and size into narrow shelves on the walls above
the wide sideboard that ran the length of the room
were now skewed every which way all over the floor.

"Oh no!" My carefully mapped diagrams and pieces
of the medical treatises I'd been working on were
shredded and tossed on the floor. I took one step into
the room to rescue my work, but Suzie pulled me back
by the collar of my jacket.

I fell against her and she wrapped me in a hug.
"Easy, girl. Let the police take care of that."

"But it's all ruined." Tears stung my eyes. I was so
angry. Who would do this? But I knew, and I literally
felt my blood run cold.

"Let's make sure they aren't hiding somewhere,"
Suzie whispered. "Then we'll call the police."

"No, let's call the police first."

"Yeah, okay."

I was shaking badly and probably sinking into a
state of shock so I handed my cell phone to Suzie.

"They'll be a while," she said after ending the call.

"Okay. I'm going inside."

"I'm right with you."

But I allowed Suzie to take the lead as we moved

furtively inside, then down the hall to my living area. I knew it was bad when Suzie tried to block my view.

"I need to see." I broke from her grip and took a step into the living room. The first impression was of complete disaster. The heavy glass coffee table was upended but not shattered, thank God. Sofa pillows were tossed on the floor and magazines were scattered about.

Then I saw the delicate ceramic vase smashed on the floor. Robin had made it for me as a housewarming gift.

"Bastards," I mumbled. We looked in both bedrooms, but there was no obvious damage back there. On more careful inspection, there was not much damage anywhere but the studio. Nothing appeared to be out of place or missing.

Whatever the burglar had been looking for, he'd apparently confined his destructive spree to my studio. Had he been scared off too soon? Maybe he'd seen my car pull up and escaped as I was talking to my dad. I scowled at the thought that I might've caught him in the act if I'd only come upstairs a few minutes sooner.

Of course, I might've been dead by now if I'd come home sooner.

As Suzie looked around, I felt my eyes water. This had to be the last straw in a truly sucky day.

First, the confrontation at lunch with Ian, then finding Enrico's body—after spending time in a dark closet with another intruder who turned out to be Derek, then being stalked by yet another intruder who turned out to be Ian.

I couldn't forget almost getting caught by Minka at Enrico's, then her surprise smack-down, followed by the summons to show up at Homicide headquarters to be interrogated. Oh, and being left to wait alone for two hours while my mother was being arrested for a murder she didn't commit.

I had to wonder if my father was currently confessing to the same crime that got Mom arrested. Oh God.

And now this.

I stared at my ravaged studio. I knew I could clean it all up and put things away, but someone had been here, touching my things, creating havoc. Someone evil, who had killed two people. I could only assume he was now focused on me.

"I wonder if anyone else in the building was hit," Suzie mused.

"I'm pretty sure this was personal, but we should—"

Heavy footsteps echoed down the hall. Suzie shrieked and clutched my arm, then cursed out loud when Vinnie stepped into the room.

"Mercy, Brooklyn!" Vinnie cried as she grabbed my other arm. "You are all right?"

"I thought I told you to stay put," Suzie shouted, as she jerked my arm possessively.

Vinnie's eyes narrowed on her. "You are not the boss of me."

Suzie shot back, "Well shit, somebody ought to be."

Vinnie pulled me closer. "You are disturbing Brooklyn with your foulness of speech."

"No, it's okay," I said, easing away from both of them. I'd never seen them bicker before and didn't want to be the cause of it now. And gads, my arms were starting to hurt. "We're all a little shaken."

"Did you lock our door?" Suzie asked in a slightly more subdued tone.

"Of course, you silly squirrel," Vinnie said crossly.

I traded looks with Suzie. We burst out laughing and I grabbed both of them in a fierce hug.

"Thank you for being here," I said. "I'm so lucky to have you as my neighbors."

"We are the lucky ones," Vinnie said.

"Cops should be here any minute," Suzie said.

Despite her warning, at the sound of another set of footsteps tapping against the wood floor, Vinnie yelped and threw herself into Suzie's arms.

Robin entered cautiously, clutching a brown grocery bag. She wore high-heeled boots that made her appear a foot taller, a red cashmere sweater and black pants.

"What the hell is going on here?" she asked, looking around at the damage. Then she focused in on the worst of it. "Oh, shit. My vase."

"I know, I'm so sorry," I said miserably.

"It is not her fault," Vinnie said staunchly. "There has been a burglary. We have barely escaped with our lives."

Robin looked at me, puzzled. I shook my head. "It's not that bad."

"But it could have been," Vinnie insisted. "We are all in mortal danger."

"No," I insisted. "Your place is safe. I'm certain this was a deliberate attack on me."

"That sucks," Suzie said.

"I'm so sorry, Brooklyn," Vinnie said.

"It's okay," I assured them. "The police will sort it all out."

"You're staying at my house tonight," Robin said,

then held up the brown bag. "I brought wine. I'll pour you a drink while we wait for the police."

I was surprised to see Inspector Lee show up at the door with two uniformed officers. They walked into the studio, carefully skirting the mess. One cop pulled out a small digital camera and started taking pictures. The other had a clipboard and began to write up a report.

Inspector Lee took out her cell phone and made a call, then joined me and the girls at the bar that separated my kitchen from the living room.

Lee raised an eyebrow as Robin offered her a glass of wine.

"Thanks but no thanks." She turned to me. "Fingerprint guys are on their way. You want to tell me what happened?"

She wrote in her small leather notebook as I talked. Since I'd just finished relating the whole story to Robin and my neighbors, they all took turns jumping in to fill in any details I'd forgotten.

Lee finally held up her hand to stop the chatter. "Is anything missing?"

"I have no idea," I said. "Nothing seems to be missing back here, but I haven't checked the studio yet. I didn't want to disturb anything before the police had a chance to do, you know, whatever they need to do."

"I know," Vinnie piped up. "They will diligently search for fibers and hairs that may reveal the DNA of the perp, then dust for fingerprints, which will later be processed through IAFIS to find a match. After this, they will go door-to-door in the building and around the neighborhood, conducting interviews in order to find any eyewitnesses, but no one will come forward to squeal like a pig."

Inspector Lee frowned at her.

Suzie drained her glass. "*Law and Order* junkie."

Vinnie beamed, her cheeks pink from the wine. "I particularly enjoy Mr. Ice-T. If any man can bring sexy back, I believe it is he."

Robin burst out laughing.

Lee was speechless.

Suzie grinned. "She's a trip, isn't she?"

"Yeah," Lee agreed, then turned to me. "So the heavy damage was pretty much limited to your studio?"

"Yes."

"Are your supplies and tools expensive? Would a burglar be able to sell them quickly?"

"I doubt it." I looked at Robin, who grunted in agreement. Both sculpting and bookbinding tools could get expensive, but I doubted they would generate much cash on the street. "I can't see some burglar coincidentally picking my place up on the sixth floor, just to make some easy money."

Lee gave me the raised eyebrow. "No, neither can I."

"Everyone in the building can hear when the elevator's moving," Suzie explained. "The stairwell takes a key to access. No other loft was broken into."

"So what do you think they were looking for?" Lee asked.

I frowned. "I don't know."

She tapped the pen against her notepad and studied me for a moment. "If there's something you've been avoiding telling me, you might want to reconsider."

I couldn't make eye contact. "Nothing I can think of."

She looked as though she might ask me something else, but instead, she slapped her notebook closed and reached for her purse. "Okay, we'll be in touch."

I followed her down the hall to the front room. "Inspector, did you let my mother go?"

She pokered up. "That's police business."

I fisted my hands on my hips. "My mother, my business. You know she didn't kill anyone."

"I can't discuss it."

"I thought we were friends."

She actually laughed. It sounded silly to me, too. She patted my shoulder, with some affection, I thought. "Be careful. I'll be in touch."

"Okay."

The two cops were still working in the studio as Lee opened the door. She took one last glance around. "You might want to consider staying somewhere else for a few days."

"I'll be at Robin's tonight." I wrote down Robin's phone number and handed it to her.

"Smart," she said. "Because if this was personal, they might be back."

"Good to know. Thanks for that."

She chuckled as she left. More cop humor?

I walked back to the kitchen in time to see the girls gathered at the west-facing window to watch the sun set.

Robin topped off my glass. "I called a locksmith. He should be here within the hour."

I almost collapsed with gratitude. I'd completely forgotten that little detail. I sat on the couch and watched as the sky filled with pink and coral streaks.

Vinnie broke the silence. "We are happy to have the morning sun on our side, but the evening sun is more dramatic."

"I love it," I said, and hated that someone had marred my wonderful home.

Robin put the bottle in the recycling bin. "Inspector Lee has great hair, doesn't she?"

"Very pretty," Vinnie said. "But she is too thin."

I took a big gulp of wine. "I was just thinking the other day that she needs a makeover."

"Yeah," Robin said, "but tonight probably wasn't the best time to bring up the idea."

"You could do me," Vinnie said, draining her glass. "I would very much enjoy a makeover."

Suzie stared at Vinnie, appalled, then looked at Robin and me. "I'd better get her home."

Robin insisted that I spend the night at her house and I didn't argue. I hated leaving my place unoccupied, but Suzie and Vinnie promised they would keep their eyes and ears open and alert our other neighbors to do the same.

I called my parents' house that night, but there was no answer. My father didn't own a cell phone, so I had no way of reaching him if he wasn't home. I called my sister China and my brothers, but they hadn't heard anything yet. I made them promise they'd call me as soon as they heard from Dad.

The next day I woke up to the smell of coffee and dragged myself out of bed. After examining my face and finding the bruise had turned to pale yellow, I stumbled to the kitchen, where Robin sat reading the newspaper.

She took one look at my worn plaid pajamas and said, "We could go shopping today."

"I don't need anything."

She snorted. "Yeah, you do. Appropriate sleepwear, if nothing else."

I poured myself a mug of coffee, stirred in a little half-and-half, and took a sip before responding. Then I took another sip and decided there was no suitable response.

"I'd better get moving," I said finally. "I need to finish the Covington job."

"I'll pick up something cute for you while I'm out."

"Sweet, but not necessary."

I showered and dressed in jeans, sweater, jacket and comfortable yet stylish flats. No more heels this week. My mangled feet and aching calves couldn't take it. I used some of Robin's makeup to cover the bruise on my face and thought I did a pretty good job.

Robin lived on the edge of Noe Valley, one of the nicer, upscale neighborhoods in the City, a land of attractive three-story flats, charming shops and baby strollers. Whenever we ate out in her neighborhood, Robin would warn me to watch my ankles. Those new mothers with their strollers played hardball.

After thanking Robin for safe haven and breakfast, I walked down the block to Twenty-fourth Street, where the Phoenix Bookstore had two paperback copies of Goethe's *Faust* in stock. One of them contained a convenient German translation on the pages facing the English text. I bought that one, determined to read it from start to finish for any possible clue to Abraham's last words. I also found a German-English dictionary and bought it for good measure.

I strolled back to my car, enjoying the cool, sunny weather. For the first time in a few days, I didn't get the eerie feeling that someone was watching me. But I did have a compelling urge to go home, see if my place was okay and clean up and reorganize things. The burglar had made a huge mess, but the fingerprint guys hadn't helped the situation. Fine black powder covered every surface.

After weighing the pros and cons, I figured I'd better put in a full day at the Covington and get back on track with the Winslow project. I pulled out of the parking space and headed north on Castro, then crossed Market Street. The lush, thick palm trees lining the center island at this spot along Market were always an impressive sight, but I was too uptight to appreciate them today. I checked my rearview mirror all the way across Market, up Divisadero toward Pacific Heights. As I came to a stop at Jackson Street, a homeless woman with leathery skin and tangled hair crossed in front me, shouting and cursing at no one in particular. The disturbed, ranting woman reminded me of Minka LaBoeuf going off on me yesterday, screaming to the world that I was a murderer. Okay, maybe she *had* seen my car on Enrico's street, but you'd never hear me confess it aloud.

I'd discounted Minka as the killer, but now I had to wonder why. She certainly was capable of violence. I touched my still-bruised cheek and rubbed the scar on my hand as if to hammer home the realization.

I doubted she was clever enough to *pretend* to show

up at Enrico's house after she'd killed him, but it could've happened.

But if Minka were the killer, she also would've been the one who ransacked my loft and studio. Regrettably, Minka had been in jail last night, so she was an unlikely suspect. Or was she? I made a mental note to check with Inspector Lee on Minka's whereabouts last night.

My hands trembled on the steering wheel. I still had plenty of unresolved issues when it came to my nemesis.

When the signal changed, it felt good to gun the engine and roar up the steep hill.

"Yoo-hoo?"

I looked up from my pasting job and saw Sylvia Winslow standing tentatively at the door.

"I know I'm interrupting," she said.

"Not at all," I insisted with a smile. "Come on in."

She stepped inside and closed the door, looking lovely in an elegant navy pin-striped pantsuit, her red hair tucked behind her ears to show off her diamond studs. Robin could've nailed the suit's designer and the size of those diamonds in a heartbeat. All I knew was that everything she wore was expensive and gorgeous.

"I just wanted to stop in and see how you're doing," she said. "Your work is so interesting."

"Come look."

"Oh my." She placed her clutch purse on the side table and stared at the vertical press that held the repaired signatures I was gluing. Her gaze slowly swept across the wide work surface, resting on the black leather cover for the *Faust* that was stretched and held in place at each corner by weights.

"It's all in pieces, isn't it? I never expected . . ." She wrung her hands. "Well, you obviously know what you're doing. I won't disturb you."

"Please don't worry." I stuck my glue brush into the jar of water and wiped my hands. "You've caught me at the perfect moment. The glue has to dry before I can do much else."

She wandered around the table to get a better look at the weighted leather cover, then looked at me, bewildered.

I explained the process of straightening the leather, showed her how the glue was drying on the signatures and how I'd fasten the refurbished leather cover to the new boards.

"It's fascinating," she said, but her lips were pinched with worry.

"What's wrong, Mrs. Winslow?"

"Oh dear," she said. "I hate to even bring up the subject. But I understand Enrico Baldacchio was found dead yesterday."

"Yes. It's horrible."

Her hand was trembling when she took mine. "I hate to speak ill, Brooklyn, but he was not a nice man. I didn't trust him in the least. But of course, he didn't deserve to die."

"No, of course not."

"I don't know what's happening," she whispered. "I wonder if it's our fault."

"What do you mean?"

"Our book is cursed," she said, forlorn. "I'll never forgive myself if we somehow—"

"No." I pushed my high chair away from the table. "I'm sorry, but a book does not go around killing people. You can't blame yourself for any of this."

She waved her hand in the air, flustered. "Oh, of course it's not really cursed. But so many awful things are happening. I don't like all this controversy hanging over our exhibit."

"Well, it'll certainly drive up ticket sales," I said philosophically.

She hid a smile with her hand. "That's very bad of you."

"I know," I said, biting back my own smile. "I apologize."

"No, you've made me feel better." She wandered along the side counter and ended up in front of the heavy brass horizontal press. She planted both hands on the wide wheel and barely budged it a half inch. "My goodness, that's impressive."

"Yes," I said, smiling. "Nobody can keep their hands off the book press."

"I can see why." She straightened her jacket and moved closer to the worktable. "Well, I didn't come here solely to waste your time. I actually had a question about books."

"I hope I can help."

"It's a bit distasteful." She laughed uncomfortably.

"I can probably handle it."

"It's about silver fish," she said, wringing her hands. I laughed. "I hate those little buggers."

"God, so do I. One of the maids found several on our bookshelves. I'm absolutely revolted at the thought of vermin in my house."

"I don't blame you," I said. "And they do love

books. Or rather, they love the paper and the wheat paste and the starch in the bindings."

"I knew you'd know about this. You're so clever. Tell me what I do. I'm determined not to bombard our home with chemicals, but how else can I get rid of them?"

"If I were you, I'd have your housekeeper empty the shelves and wipe the wood down with cinnamon oil."

"Cinnamon oil? Are you sure?"

"Some people love it and recommend it. I've never had to try it, but I know bugs don't like it."

"It sounds perfect."

I pressed my finger to the glued spine to test its dryness. Not quite. "I've heard of people using a drop of tea tree oil on the book paper, but it smells like antiseptic, so I'd try the cinnamon oil first."

I mentioned some places she could buy the oil and she clapped her hands in glee. "I knew you'd have the answer. I'll leave you in peace now. I've got to meet—"

"Mother?"

We both turned as the door opened and Meredith poked her head in.

"Here I am," Sylvia said gaily.

Meredith looked at me with distaste, then turned to Sylvia. "What are you doing in here, Mother?"

Sylvia winked at me. "Just checking up on things."

"We're going to be late," Meredith said peevishly.

"We'll be fine." Sylvia sighed, picked up her clutch and patted my arm as she passed. "Thank you, dear. We'll see you at the opening this Saturday."

Meredith threw me a poisonous look and stormed

off behind her mother. Instantly, all the pleasant feelings from Sylvia's visit dissolved. I was really growing tired of Meredith Winslow and her bad-tempered behavior toward me.

I'd been half kidding when I'd envisioned her in that orange jumpsuit, but now I seriously had to wonder if she had taken her hissy fits to another level by killing Abraham. I remembered Ian saying she wanted to put a hit out on Enrico. Was she capable of murder? Had she ransacked my studio?

I needed to walk off my anger and clear my head. Since I couldn't do much with the book until the glue dried, I decided to take a lunch break. I told the front desk where I was going and headed to my favorite hole-in-the-wall noodle house, the Holy Ramen Empire.

As I cautiously walked down the steep slope of Pacific toward Fillmore, that feeling that someone was watching me returned. I continually glanced around, but didn't see anyone I knew.

Safely inside the restaurant, I ordered the Singapore noodle bowl with shrimp and a small pot of tea, then set my tray down at a small table by the front window and dug into the noodle bowl with gusto. I opened my paperback copy of *Faust* and read while I ate.

It was . . . interesting. I knew it was a classic, considered by many to be the finest German work of fiction in history, but I couldn't help thinking that if he tried to sell it today, old Goethe might find himself out of luck. Still, I was surprised to find so much humor in the dialogue. Naturally, the devil got all the best lines.

I skimmed the translator's introduction and his words began to jump out at me. Alchemy, magic, necromancy. Temptation. The devil.

I rubbed my arms to ward off another bout of shivers, then glanced up as a man walked into the restaurant wearing worn jeans and ratty high-top sneakers. Despite the fact that his faded navy hoodie stretched so far over his head I couldn't see his face, he seemed familiar to me. I'd seen him somewhere before. In my neighborhood, maybe? Or earlier in Noe Valley? Had he been following me? I realized I was holding my breath and forced myself to relax.

Hoodie Guy checked out the menu on the wall above the cash register, then turned around and stared at the people in the room. He might've made eye contact with me. I couldn't tell. There was a black hole where the hoodie covered his face and eyes.

I tried to brush him off as yet another San Francisco burnout, but it wasn't easy. After all I'd been through lately, this weirdo was freaking me out. I stared at the noodle bowl and realized I'd lost my appetite.

Now I was really angry.

I kept my eye on Hoodie Guy, aware that too much ugly stuff had happened over the past week. I reminded myself that once I was through with the Winslow project, I would be able to put the finishing touches on two books I was eager to enter in the Edinburgh Book Fair competition.

In one short month, I'd be packing my bags and taking off for Scotland. I breathed in deeply and tried to picture myself in Edinburgh, walking along the Royal Mile, stepping into a pub on a cold day for a pint and a sandwich. I loved the city, loved the people, and the Edinburgh Book Fair was one of the best in the world. I would see old friends and have a blast.

I smiled at the thought. Edinburgh as a distraction

always worked for me. Determined to ignore Hoodie Guy, I scooped up another bite of noodles. My appetite—and therefore, my world—was righting itself.

A woman screamed at the front of the restaurant and I stared in horror as Hoodie Guy pulled out a gun and waved it around.

The woman at the counter cried out again and everyone in the room panicked, scrambling and screaming and dropping to the floor to avoid being hurt. Me, I was too stunned to move, but my blood and my temper were bubbling over.

"Shut up!" Hoodie Guy shouted, holding one hand over his ear as he brandished the gun with the other.

Two more people lurched off their chairs and scrambled to hide, using their meager fast food restaurant table as a shield.

I shoved away from the table, but the back of my chair was trapped too close to the chair behind me. The push caused the table to jostle and the noodle bowl bobbled precariously. I grabbed the bowl just as Hoodie Guy whirled around and pointed his gun directly at me. I let the bowl go. It hit the table and broke, sending noodles and broth and fragments of porcelain flying in every direction, but mostly all over me.

"Damn it," I yelled, and Hoodie Guy stared right at me. His eyes were still hidden, but I could see his teeth as he grinned, cocked his gun and slowly straightened his aim.

"No," I whispered.

He was a nanosecond from pulling the trigger when a man dressed entirely in black stepped inside the door and said, "What up, dawg?"

Hoodie was taken aback. It was just the distraction I needed. I grabbed the soy sauce bottle and threw it like a missile. It glanced off Hoodie Guy's ear.

"Motherfucker!" he shouted, and turned back toward me, just as Man in Black kicked the gun out of his hand.

The gun went soaring. Some people cried out in horror. Hoodie Guy yelled incoherently and Man in Black moved in, grabbed Hoodie's arm and wrenched it behind his back, then shoved him down on the floor.

Hoodie cried out as he writhed back and forth, trying to escape.

"Sorry, dude, does that hurt?" Man in Black asked.

"Yes! Oww!"

"Good." He pushed his knee into Hoodie's back and grinned harshly when the creep howled.

I stared at the surreal scene in utter shock. Everyone in the restaurant stayed completely still. The fear and confusion were palpable.

Who was this Man in Black? An accomplice? A savior? He was tall and wore a striking black leather duster that skimmed his long, lean legs and fit his broad shoulders like a glove. His shirt and pants were black and so were his boots.

He was frankly beautiful. His hair was black, too, thick and long, worn back off his forehead in a dramatic sweep that almost reached his shoulders. His eyes were dark as well, and when he grinned, two dimples emerged in a face more suited to an angel than any human.

A dark angel.

Broth seeped into my clothes, but I couldn't move from my chair, just sat there staring at Man in Black as he pushed his knee more forcefully into the squirming Hoodie Guy's back.

Man in Black scanned the room, then focused on me. I caught my breath as his eyes twinkled and his dimples teased.

"You okay, Brooklyn?" he asked.

Startled, I nodded. "I'm okay."

He winked at me and said, "Call the police."

Chapter 16

He knew my name?

Tall, Dark, Dangerous and Gorgeous knew my name?

Sirens wailed to a stop outside. I didn't have time to figure out how he knew me before six police officers converged on the room.

As one of them tried to calm down the counter woman, the restaurant patrons scurried out from under the tables. I stayed where I was. My chair was wedged too tightly into the space, but more important, my knees were wobbly. I was still staggered by the events that had just occurred.

I'd escaped sure death by less than a second. I knew it. Everyone here knew it, and they were all gathered in small groups discussing it. My only question was, who was Man in Black and how did he know my name? Okay, that was two questions but I wasn't up for quibbling.

As Man in Black released Hoodie Guy into the hands of two of the police officers, everyone applauded. He waved off their praise and moved out of

the way, over to the wall, where he leaned casually
with one booted foot crossed in front of the other.

One woman stared at him in stark adoration, shoot-
ing quick glances my way that plainly said she wished
she'd been the one about to die.

So who was this knight in black leather armor?

The police handcuffed Hoodie, pulled him to his
feet and pushed the hood off to see his face. He was
thin with pale skin and a shaved head. He had a tattoo
of a snake wrapped around his neck. The snake's fangs
were exposed and its forked tongue slithered across
the guy's bald head.

Ugh. My hands shook. He was just a kid, no more
than twenty. Needless to say, I didn't recognize him,
but I was pretty sure I'd never forget him.

Snake Boy—formerly known as Hoodie Guy—
turned and stared at me. "You."

One of the cops jerked him back around, but Snake
Boy fought him. "She has to die!"

The other cop holding him rolled his eyes. "We're
all gonna die, asshole. Let's move it."

"They told me," Snake Boy whispered. "She's
cursed. I have to kill her."

Cursed? Was this about the *Faust* or was everyone
going insane? Snake Boy seemed to be mentally de-
ranged, but now he knew about the *Faust* curse? Or
was that just another coincidence? I thought not, and
felt dread clear down to my feet. Had this sinister,
unbalanced street kid been sent to kill me?

"Get him out of here," one cop said to the other
two. The two cops maneuvered him out the door and
over to the parked squad car. I watched through the

window as they shoved his head down and angled him into the car. He whipped around to stare at me through those beady eyes. I looked away.

A third cop spoke to the woman at the counter, then turned to the rest of us. "Folks, I appreciate your patience. We'll need to get witness statements from all of you before you leave. Again, your patience is appreciated. I promise we'll move this along as fast as possible so you can all be on your way."

Man in Black met my gaze. He pushed away from the wall and wound his way around the tables until he reached mine. "Hi," he said, his voice low, deep and raw. Up close, I could see his eyes were a mesmerizing shade of dark green.

"Hi." I was half stunned that I could speak at all. "Thank you for what you did."

"Hey, you saved yourself. Nice arm."

"I was the pitcher on my high school softball team. I can't run to save my life, but I can throw." Was I blathering? I was no longer sure of anything. "I guess I'm a little freaked out."

"Don't blame you. Guy's a total whack job."

"That's not all that's got me freaked. You seem to know me. How?"

"We have mutual friends."

"And they sent you to meet me at a noodle shop?"

"No, the guy at the Covington told me you were here."

"So you followed me." I knew someone had been following me, but I never saw the likes of this guy.

"Yeah, I followed you," he said. "You've got something I want."

"That sounds ominous." With more strength than I thought I had left, I was able to maneuver my chair away from the table.

The front counter woman said something in a shrill voice and we were both distracted.

"I need to get out of here," I said. But when I tried to stand, my wet pants stuck to the plastic chair. I finally had to hold the chair down with both hands, bend forward and pull my butt up. It wasn't elegant but it worked, except that my pants made a loud sucking sound as I separated myself from the chair and stood. Rivulets of broth ran down my legs into my shoes.

My humiliation was complete.

"You're kind of a mess," he said as he flicked another noodle off my shoulder.

I glared at him. "Thanks for that astute observation."

"I'll see if they have a towel you can use."

As he walked away I stared at his wide shoulders, narrow waist, perfect backside, long legs. Man in Black was one gorgeous guy.

I followed him to the counter, handed one of the policemen my business card and showed him my driver's license. Then I explained about the soaked pants and he said he'd track me down later at the Covington.

Man in Black handed me a towel. "Keep it." Then he swept his arm out. "After you."

I went back to my table to get my purse and gingerly picked up the paperback copy of *Faust* from the table. It was soaked through, swollen to almost twice its size and puckering badly.

"Ruined," I muttered. Much like my afternoon. Someone had tried to kill me, I was covered in noodles and I was still hungry. All in all, this had been a truly unsatisfactory dining experience.

I sloshed away from the table, knowing I reeked of eau de soy sauce. I would never be able to eat another noodle bowl as long as I lived, and that was a thoroughly depressing thought.

As I walked out the door, I tossed the sodden book in the trash can and turned to Man in Black. "Thank you again. I guess I'll see you around."

"Yeah, you will. I'm going with you."

"Not necessary."

"Like I said, you've got something I want."

I looked up at him and frowned. "And like I said, it sounds ominous, and I've had it up to here with ominous."

But he followed me out and stayed with me the half block down Fillmore; then we both turned at Pacific Street. Man in Black had to slow his pace quite a bit to walk next to me. I recalled those long legs expertly kicking the gun out of that kid's hand and realized it was futile to try to talk him out of accompanying me.

He seemed like someone who could be dangerous, but he didn't seem inclined to hurt me. In fact, he was acting almost protective of me. Then again, I was probably going insane. Maybe I really was cursed, in which case, I might as well enjoy the moment. I was walking with a handsome man, it was a beautiful day in the City and I was alive.

So far.

"What's your name?" I asked as we climbed up Pacific Avenue toward the Covington.

"People call me Gabriel," he said.

"Gabriel, like the angel."

He bowed his head slightly. "If you wish."

"And people call you Gabriel because . . . it's your name?"

He laughed and my stomach took a dip, not just because it was so unexpected but because the deep, rich sound of his laughter combined with his amazing green eyes and those dimples, for God's sake, just about did me in.

So sue me, I was weak.

I glanced sideways at him. Hadn't I thought he looked like a dark angel earlier? A fallen angel, maybe. More devilish than angelic.

I took a deep breath and let it out slowly. "And who are these mutual friends of ours?"

He peered straight ahead. "I knew Abraham."

"Oh." I blinked. I wasn't sure what I'd expected him to say, but that wasn't it.

"And Ian McCullough."

I relaxed. "You're a book person?"

"Occasionally. I buy and sell things." He pulled a slim leather wallet from his back jeans pocket and handed me a business card.

I stared at the card. I knew paper and recognized that this was expensive stock. The color was Mohawk eggshell. His name was written in elegant script in the center of the card. "Gabriel." Just Gabriel. I glanced up at him. Who needed two names when you looked like every woman's dream man come to life?

Under his name was his occupation. Discreet Procurement. One phone number was listed. Probably an answering service. I turned the card over. Nothing.

Discreet procurement. Was that the politically correct term for thievery? Or was he a legitimate broker?

Impossible. He was too slick. Too damn gorgeous. I had no doubt he could get away with murder. And wasn't that a cheerful thought? I forced it right out of my head.

"So, Gabriel, what do I have that you want?"

He stared at me for a moment, then said, "A book."

I laughed. "I have many books."

As we started to cross the street at Pacific and Scott, I heard an engine revving up; then a dark SUV came racing down the hill right toward me.

I shrieked as Gabriel jerked the back of my jacket and pulled me back to the sidewalk.

"What the hell was that?" he shouted. "That guy tried to kill you."

I couldn't catch my breath. Maybe I should've been used to being the target of someone's wrath by now, but I wasn't.

"Are you okay?"

"Yeah," I whispered. "Just need a minute."

"Wow." He paced the sidewalk as I tried to calm my nerves. I felt completely vulnerable, standing on the sidewalk in broad daylight.

On the bright side, it was good to know my new friend Gabriel wasn't a stalking maniac killer.

He raked his hair back from his forehead. "That scared the shit out of me."

"You and me both," I said.

We slowly started back up the hill and he gave me another one of his watchful stares, then said, "Plutarch."

I flinched. Plutarch? How could he know I had the book from Enrico's study? "I beg your pardon?"

"That's the book I want. Plutarch's *Parallel Lives.*

Incunable. Ulrich Han printing. Gilt edged, illuminated. How much do you want for it?"

"Sounds expensive," I said carefully. "But I have no idea what you're talking about." Incunable referred to any book printed in the fifteenth century when movable type was first used.

He shook his finger at me. "Expensive didn't come close to describing it, and I think you know that. It's priceless. Magnificent. And my client is willing to pay any price for it."

"It does sound fabulous." I splayed my hands in front of me, all innocence. "But what would I be doing with a book like that?"

"Selling it to me," he said, adding one of his scrumptious grins for enticement.

It almost worked. My legs nearly turned to Silly Putty, but I was able to hold my ground. "I would if I could, but I don't have it. Sorry. But if I hear of anything, you'll be the first one I call."

"Oddly enough, I don't believe you," he said with a grin. "But don't lose my card in case you change your mind."

"I won't lose it." I patted the side pocket of my bag where I'd slipped his card. "I mean it, I'll call you if I get a line on this Plutarch."

His look was fierce. "Do that."

I smiled. "And thank you again."

"For what?"

"For pulling me back out of the street. That's twice you've saved me now."

"Great," he said, scowling. "One more time and I win a trip to camp."

* * *

As Gabriel and I walked through the door of the Covington, Ian was walking out.

"G'night," he said, and rushed off toward the parking lot.

"Ian, wait," I called out. I turned to Gabriel. "That's my boss. I'll just be a minute."

Gabriel grabbed my arm before I could race off. "No, I'll leave you now. Just wanted to make sure you got back safely."

"But—"

"You'll call me," he said. "Or I'll be in touch."

"When?" I asked, then wanted to bite my tongue.

"Soon," he said, and walked away.

I stared for a moment at those impossibly long legs and the black duster skimming his knees as he walked. All he was missing was a black hat and a Sergio Leone theme playing in the background.

I sighed. I still didn't have a real clue who he was.

Taking off on a jog, I caught up with Ian as he pressed his security key to unlock his car.

"Ian, wait."

"I don't have time right now," he said. I'd never seen him look so angry, but then again, maybe I didn't know him as well as I'd thought I did.

"You'll want to make time for this," I said as I rummaged through my bag. I found the folded slip of paper and handed it to him.

He opened it, stared, then looked at me. "How'd you get this?"

"I found it at Enrico's yesterday, right before you got there. That's what you were looking for, isn't it?"

"I don't know what you're talking about," he protested, his tone a combination of anger and denial. "Why would you—"

"Ian, please." I gave his arm a sympathetic squeeze. "I know you were there."

All his bluster slipped and he sagged against the car. "How?"

I gritted my teeth and confessed, "I was hiding in the kitchen pantry while you were searching the house."

I watched him as realization dawned. "That door was locked."

I shook my head but said nothing. I wasn't about to mention I'd been sharing that space with Derek.

Ian stared up at the sky. "This is all such a damn mess. Enrico was a bastard, Brooklyn. He knew I'd pay for his silence."

"How much did you pay him?"

"Five thousand." He rubbed his face. "A month."

"What?"

"For the last three months."

It was my turn to sag against the car. "You're joking."

He laughed without humor. "Hardly."

"But why, Ian? What secret is worth so much you'd pay someone to be quiet about it?"

He stared at the ground for a moment, then pushed himself away from the car and paced a few steps before turning to meet my gaze. "I don't know what you want me to say, Brooklyn. I was paying Enrico five thousand dollars a month to keep quiet. Do you really think I'm going to blurt out my big secret to you?"

"Blurt out what? That you're gay?"

His jaw dropped and he staggered back a step. "I'm

not—how can you—oh, Jesus." He collapsed against the car.

"Ian, who cares?"

He covered his face with his hands. "Does everyone in the world know? Am I that big a moron?"

"Not everyone in the world," I said lamely.

"Feel my confidence soar," he said peevishly.

"You're hardly a flaming soprano," I said, then quickly added, "Not that there's anything wrong with that."

He snorted a laugh, then let out a strangled cry.

I touched his shoulder. "To answer your question, no, not everyone in the world knows. Maybe nobody knows."

"But you knew." His head hung down in shame and my heart broke for him.

"Give me credit for something," I said. "You and I were engaged to be married. Don't you think I could tell something was off? It was just, I don't know." I sucked in a deep breath and blurted, "It was clear to me that I wasn't the Wainwright you wanted."

Ian had been best friends with my brother Austin. I'd always thought it was odd that he preferred to hang out as a threesome—Ian, Austin and me—rather than just the two of us.

"Oh God, Austin," he wailed. "Does he know, too? Does your whole family know?" He slid down the car and came to rest in a stooped, almost fetal position. His shoulders shook and I realized he was crying.

"Ian!" I stooped down to wrap my arms around him. "It's not that bad, honestly! It'll be okay. This is San Francisco! Everyone's gay! It's like a requirement or something. Really, you have to sign a gay affidavit just to move into some neighborhoods. The best neighborhoods, to be honest, which doesn't seem fair but there you are. This is a good thing, really. Please stop crying."

He shuddered in my arms and I held him tightly for a few more moments, then scuttled out of his way when he raised his head to gasp for air.

"Oh, Brooklyn," he cried as he wiped his eyes. "You're priceless."

"You'll survive this, Ian, I swear. You need to be strong. I can help. We'll go shopping."

He let out another cry, grabbed his stomach and fell to his side on the blacktop.

"Ian! What's wrong with you?" I jumped up and scrambled for my phone. "I'm calling an ambulance."

"Stop it, you're killing me," he said, as he rolled on the ground, laughing.

Laughing?

I nudged his shoulder with my foot. "Ian?"

He shook his head, waved me away. "I need a minute."

"You'll need a doctor if I find out you're laughing at me."

"I'm not, I swear." He lay flat on his back with his arms spread out, inhaling and exhaling raggedly. "Got to catch my breath." He gulped in more air, then looked up. "Why do you smell like Chinese food?"

I glared down at him, my arms folded tightly across my chest. "You are so dead."

He tried to steady his breathing, bit his cheeks to stop from smiling, then choked out another laugh. "Sorry, I'll stop. Any minute now."

I sniffed. "Frankly, I'm not even sure how gay you

are if you're willing to roll around on a dirty blacktop parking lot."

"Good point," he said.

I tapped my foot in annoyance. "If this is such a joke, why were you paying for Enrico's silence?"

He pouted. "You really are a killjoy."

"I'm just asking."

He rolled himself up to his knees, then pushed off the ground. Steadying himself against the car with one hand, he smoothed his hair back into place with the other.

"When the Covington hired me three years ago," he began, "they thought I was engaged to be married. Mrs. Covington likes her upper management to be steady and family oriented."

I frowned. "In twenty-first-century San Francisco, she discriminates against gay people?"

He sighed. "She's a conservative old biddy who doesn't approve of anything outside the norm."

"But gay *is* the norm here."

He chuckled. "You're preaching to the choir, babe."

"Okay, so get another job."

"But I love the Covington," he insisted. "I was born to run this place. And Mrs. Covington loves me. She's promoted me every six months for the last three years."

"Then talk to her. Maybe she'll understand."

"I was going to, I swear." He paced back and forth. "But then Enrico found out somehow and threatened to tell her before I could. I was just placating him until I could find the right moment to tell her."

"Placating to the tune of five thousand dollars a month?"

"I just needed time," he said, and continued pacing. "I needed to get her in the right mood. Serve up some martinis, then give her the news. As soon as I told her, I was going to call the police on Enrico and get my money back."

"I don't suppose you killed him."

He stopped midstep. "What? No!"

I frowned. "I didn't think so."

"You sound disappointed."

"It would make this whole thing easier to figure out."

"Can't help you."

I pulled my bag onto my shoulder and straightened my jacket. "I'd better get back to work."

"All right." He reached over, pulled something off my jacket and looked at it. A twisted, dried noodle. Then he looked at me. "You lead a strange and interesting life."

"You have no idea."

I took a shortcut through the camellia garden to get back to the Covington entrance. The huge camellia bushes were thick with flowers filling every branch. Their lush perfume hung on the air and gave me a break from my soy sauce stench.

I jogged silently down the mulch-covered lane, darting back and forth to dodge errant branches and overgrown bushes. The garden was world-renowned for showcasing more than a thousand different varieties of the flower, thanks to the present Mrs. Covington's great-grandmother-in-law who started the garden in the beginning of the last century. At least, that was what the guidebooks said.

But my favorite aspect of the camellia garden was what it hid in its center, a charming Shakespearean herb garden complete with the Shakespearean references of rosemary, tansy, lavender, chamomile and others, all carved in stone.

But I couldn't concentrate on the beauty of the garden. Instead, my mind wandered to Gabriel. He'd saved my life, so I owed him something, but I wasn't about to give up the Plutarch simply because some unknown "client" of his wanted it. Yes, so maybe I'd come into possession of the book through illicit means—okay, I took it—but that didn't mean I'd let it go without getting a few questions answered first. And besides, how did Enrico get his hands on it? Had he stolen it? Probably. But that didn't make my action any less wrong.

Did the Plutarch have anything to do with Enrico's death? Impossible. The book had been sitting in plain sight on the table. If that was what the killer was after, he would've taken it right then.

As I passed the ornate brass sundial in the center of the well-tilled herb garden, I heard a leaf snap somewhere behind me.

I wasn't alone.

My heart pounding, I whipped around, ready to face anything. Oh, who was I kidding? I was scared to death and my throat was threatening to close up on me. There was no one in sight, but that didn't mean anything. Someone was watching me. I ran faster than I'd ever run, all the way to the front door of the library.

I decided I'd work at home the next day. I knew I could finish the book faster if I had fewer interruptions, such as people attempting to kill me everywhere I went.

I found Ian's secretary, Marissa, in his office, organizing files. She called Ian's cell to get approval. Since the *Faust* was currently in a hundred different pieces, and fully insured, Ian gave his okay.

I spent another hour in the workroom, packing up the wood press that still held the *Faust* text block in its grip, boxing up all the pieces and all the tools I'd need tomorrow. I borrowed a small hand dolly from Marissa and lugged everything out to my car. By the time I got home, my body was down for the count. But when I opened the door and saw my studio still in shambles, I couldn't stand it.

I locked the door and parked the dolly next to my desk. As I removed my jacket, I caught a disturbing whiff of soy sauce.

"First things first," I said. Checking again that my front door locks were set, I headed for the bathroom where I peeled off my broth-soaked clothing and took a long shower. I dressed in sweats and a T-shirt, satisfied that I no longer reeked of Chinese noodle bowl.

Back in the studio, I noticed the red light flashing on the phone and played back the messages. Doris Bondurant had called to offer me a job rebinding a vintage *Alice in Wonderland* she'd found recently. I understood it would be a test to see whether I passed muster with her. I felt a pang of sadness, knowing Abraham had been responsible for my connecting with her.

There was also a message from Robin, who called to let me know she'd bought me some cute pajamas so I would no longer embarrass her on our sleepovers. The third message was from Carl, Abraham's lawyer, who wanted to meet and hash out my new financial condition. I made a face. I'd honestly forgotten I had a new financial condition. Not that I wasn't grateful, you understand. I could always use more money. But it still felt odd to be the lone recipient of Abraham's entire fortune.

I left Carl a message, putting him off for a week or two. I could only concentrate on one or two major upheavals at a time.

Grabbing a trash can and a broom, I began the cleanup. I threw away the stacks of torn and crushed endpapers, gathered my scattered tools and organized them precisely as they'd been before, picked up every spool of thread and put them back in color order in the narrow shelves I'd had built for that purpose. I rolled up the leather skins and stacks of cloth that weren't damaged and put them back in their rightful places.

An hour later, I looked around, pleased that things were almost back to normal. I would need to order more marbled paper and a new set of glue brushes, plus two of my bone folders were missing, but that was the only real damage I found.

Except for Robin's vase, which had been crushed to smithereens.

Despite that minimal damage, I could tell that whoever was behind all this destruction had been in an absolute rage, and that was the most frightening part of this ordeal. I just couldn't picture anyone I knew being capable of such behavior.

I thought of Abraham's studio up in Sonoma. Someone had gone through there in a similar fashion. But who? And what had they been looking for?

Whoever it was, they hadn't found it, and I guessed that was why they'd struck back with violence. But at least they hadn't destroyed my books. That would've been a lot more painful to me.

So whoever it was, they didn't know me. As strange as it sounded, that was a comforting thought.

I was exhausted and nearly half-asleep when I checked the locks again, then shuffled off to my bedroom. As I reached to pull back the bedspread, something on the pillow caught my eye and I jumped back.

On my pillow was a long-stemmed red rose. It looked fresh, with dew still clinging to its outer petals. An elegant note card was placed next to the rose. Without thinking, I picked up the card and read the one-word sentiment.

"Soon."

Chapter 17

I cried out in shock, threw the rose down and ran from the room. Shaking like crazy, I ran from room to room, checking the locks on every window and the front door. I ran up the narrow stairs that led to the rooftop garden to make sure that door was secure.

It wasn't. The door had been jimmied open.

I started to panic. Was the killer still inside my loft? Was he hiding up on the roof? I wasn't about to walk out there.

Summoning every ounce of courage I had, I ran down the stairs, found my cell phone and called the police.

The dispatcher said it would be about a half hour since the intruder wasn't on-site. How the hell did she know?

And just because I'd checked the entire apartment and knew in my gut there was no one here but me, it didn't mean I felt safe.

Soon.

What the hell did that mean? I thought of Gabriel and the last word he'd said to me earlier that day. No,

I refused to believe he'd had anything to do with this. I'd known him for only an hour, but I knew in my heart he wasn't warped enough to break into my place just to leave a rose on my pillow. Maybe to steal the Plutarch, but never—

"Oh, hell, the Plutarch!"

I grabbed my keys and ran to unlock the hall closet. In the old corset factory, this closet had housed a rope-and-pulley shelving system that moved supplies up and down between the floors. Like a dumbwaiter, I guess. Now the dumbwaiter function was disconnected and nobody would ever know about it unless they studied the building blueprints. But the metal floor panel still slid back to reveal a shallow space where I hid important papers and extra money.

And the Plutarch.

I let out the breath I'd been holding. It was still there. That didn't rule out Gabriel as the intruder, of course, but I knew it wasn't him.

I paced around, wondering whether Vinnie and Suzie were home. But they'd had enough of my traumas lately. I didn't want to wear out our neighborly relationship. I'd never minded being alone until this moment.

I knew who I wanted to see. Summoning up a few more ounces of courage, I found the business card and made another phone call.

He answered on the first ring. "This better be good."

"It's Brooklyn."

"What's wrong?"

"Someone broke into my house."

"I'll be right there."

I stared at the phone, hearing nothing but a dial tone.

Having taken some action, I felt more relaxed. I looked down at my threadbare pink kitty jammies. Robin would be appalled. I needed to change into something normal.

As I rounded the bar toward my bedroom, I heard the floor creak behind me, then something hard and heavy smashed into my head. My thoughts evaporated as I crumpled to the floor.

"That's it, baby. Come on, open your eyes."

I drew in a breath and smelled the most delicious scent of leather and forest and springtime rain.

My eyes flickered open, then closed again.

"That's it, you can do it," he whispered, his voice warm and rich like whiskey sweetened with caramel-flavored hot chocolate.

I was either dead and gone to heaven or suffering serious brain damage, because I vaguely recalled waking up to that same voice in my ear once before.

I mentally surveyed my situation and surroundings. I wasn't dead. That was a good thing. I was on my couch. The cushions felt like clouds under me. My head felt as if a train had collided with my skull. A cold cloth covered my forehead.

I opened my eyes. Derek held my hand and stroked my cheek. I was safe.

"Thirsty," I managed to whisper.

"I'll get you some water."

I opened my eyes, saw him cross the living room to the kitchen, then return a moment later with a glass of water.

"I brought you a painkiller. I found the prescription bottle on top of your refrigerator."

"Thank you." I still had some Vicodin left over from the evil dentist I'd seen last month.

He carefully lifted my head and held the glass for me to drink. "There you go."

"Thanks," I said again, then focused beyond him. The coffee table was at a right angle to the couch and the overstuffed red chair was pulled into the space. He sat there, about two inches away from me. "Did you rearrange my furniture?"

"Yeah."

"Odd."

"I take liberties where I can."

He helped me lie back down until I jolted from something icy on the pillow.

"It's a bag of frozen peas," he said. "Lie down."

"I have peas?"

"Surprisingly, yes. I found them in your freezer behind several dozen packages of pizza and ice cream."

"Don't judge."

"Lie back. The peas will help with the swelling."

"Good news." The thought of my head swelling up was not appealing. I carefully laid my head down on the frozen package. It was cold, but after a few seconds it began to numb the pain.

"Better?" he asked.

"Seems to help." Trying not to move my head, I squirmed around to adjust the cushions and yank the hem of my pajama top down until I was more comfortable. Figures I was still wearing my provocative pink kitty jammies. "How'd you get in?"

"Good question," he said, sitting back and filling the big red chair nicely. "Your door was wide-open."

"I was afraid of that," I whispered. "Did you call the police?"

"They're already here."

"Good. Maybe my neighbors saw someone."

"I take it you saw no one."

"No, of course not."

"The door to your front coat closet was open."

"I checked all the closets." But that closet was stuffed with coats, so I supposed someone could've hidden themselves behind them.

I struggled to sit but gave up as soon as my head started to pound. "Did you find my baseball bat? They might get prints off it."

"Still playing at crime-busters, I see." But he said it mildly, without a hint of sarcasm.

"I guess," I said wearily.

"I'd better make my report, then."

"What report?"

He held up his hand. "First off, the blood you found on the book belonged to Abraham."

"Oh."

"The fingerprints found in Abraham's studio were his."

"No one else's?"

"No. And the only prints found at Baldacchio's house were his own."

"Oh." My shoulders relaxed. "I guess that's something." And the fact that he'd shared that information caused my heart to beat somewhat erratically. Or maybe it was the frozen peas.

"Indeed, it is." He leaned forward, rested his elbows on his knees and took hold of my hand. Warmth spread up my arm as he said, "Now, why didn't you call me last night when your place was ransacked?"

I frowned, and the small move caused shards of pain to skitter across my skull. "Feels like so long ago."

"It was less than twenty-four hours ago."

"Right." So much had happened since then. I'd almost been killed in a noodle house. I'd almost been killed in my *own* house. And what about the mysterious Gabriel? Good guy? Bad guy? Good Samaritan? Clever opportunist? Had he left me a red rose or was that the killer's calling card? My head was spinning. "I should've called you."

"But you didn't."

"No need to rub it in. I admit you're right."

"Ah, music to my ears." He twisted his lips in that annoyingly attractive way I'd grown used to, which usually meant he was trying not to laugh at me. "We're in this together, remember."

"We are?" I didn't see him wearing a bag of peas on his head.

"Of course," he said. "It's all connected, don't you agree?"

"Absolutely." Maybe it was the crack on the head or maybe it was the way his blue dress shirt fit his muscular torso, but I completely agreed with him. "It's all connected to Abraham's murder."

"So we're agreed."

"Yes."

"And where does the wilted red rose on your pillow fit in with the story?"

My eyes widened. "That's why I called you. I found it on my pillow and it freaked me out."

"I don't blame you. It's rather Gothic, isn't it?"

"That's one way to put it."

"Before I conclude that our killer left it as a warning of some kind, I suppose I should ask if there's someone in your life who might've left it as a romantic gesture."

I thought of Gabriel. If he'd wanted to break in and steal the Plutarch, he would've done so without playing the rose-on-the-pillow game.

Derek coughed. "Was that a yes?"

"Oh, sorry," I said, coming back to the room. "No, there's absolutely no one I know who would leave a rose on my pillow."

"All right."

"That's why I called you," I explained. "I was scared."

"And when the studio was ransacked last night, who did you call?" he asked, not ready to let go of that point.

I waved my hand lamely. "Last night I ran to my neighbors' place; then Robin showed up and we drank a lot of wine and I spent the night at her house."

"I see." Was it possible he was genuinely hurt?

"I'm sorry," I said. "I didn't call you because it didn't cross my mind that you might be . . ." I couldn't finish the sentence.

He could. "Interested? Concerned? Insane with fear for your safety?"

I bit back a smile. "Insane? Really?"

"You needn't sound so pleased about it." He placed

his hand over his heart, but his blue eyes shimmered with mirth. "I'm suffering clear to my soul."

"Oh, please." I laughed softly. "That's probably heartburn."

His eyebrows went up. "Smart mouth. As soon as you've recovered sufficiently, remind me to punish you."

I laughed again. "I'd like to see you try."

"You're in no condition to bait me."

"I hate that you're right." The surge of energy brought on by our friendly bantering was dwindling. My brain was losing the battle of wits and my eyelids were giving up on their fight with gravity. "Well, thank you for being here tonight. I'm sorry I didn't call you last night."

"You're forgiven," he murmured, moving closer to the edge of his chair as he traced lines along my fingers and the palm of my hand.

The sensation of his touch went straight to my solar plexus. I watched him watching me and knew he knew exactly what he was doing to me. If I were in better shape, he wouldn't stand a chance. For tonight, though, I had to cop out.

"I think you might've saved my life." I hated being so weak. I was used to saving my own life, thanks. Or better yet, not having to save or be saved in the first place.

He patted my hand. "It's all part of the job."

"Yes, of course. The job." Right. He had a job to do. So much for our little flirtation. What had I been thinking?

He continued some kind of massaging thing up and down my arm that was starting to affect my ability to concentrate. And the Vicodin was definitely kicking in.

"I told you from the start I'd be watching you like a hawk," he said. "Did it slip your mind?"

"Everything's slipping my mind," I admitted. "Except I do recall that you said you'd be watching me because you thought I'd murdered Abraham."

"Only for a moment," he insisted.

"More like a week," I nitpicked.

His lips curved. Then he nudged some ayurvedic energy point on my inner arm and I lost track of the conversation.

". . . and then there was the fact that you were behaving rather suspiciously," he was saying. "What else was I to think?"

I yawned. "Sorry."

He tilted his head at me. "You need to sleep."

"Yes."

"You probably won't remember much tomorrow."

"I'll remember you're the hawk." Had I said that out loud? How silly.

"Yes, remember the hawk." He moved off the chair and knelt on the carpet next to the couch. "Before you drop off to sleep, there's one thing I must do."

"Yes?"

"Highly inappropriate behavior on my part," he said, putting his hand on my cheek. "But it seems it can't be helped."

"Well, if it can't be helped . . ."

But his lips were already brushing mine. His tongue outlined my bottom lip and electricity shot straight through me. My eyes glazed over as he moved his mouth along my chin, nibbling, planting light kisses, grazing my jaw, my ear, my forehead, with his lips as though he were memorizing the shape of my face. A nip here, a tiny lick there. It was torture. It was heaven.

Footsteps sounded in the hall and I tensed, then tried to sit up, but Derek stopped me.

"It's all right," he murmured.

"Commander," an officer said. "We'd like your opinion out here."

"Yes, of course." He ran his finger along my jaw, then stood. "You'll sleep now."

"Could you . . . would you stay for a while?"

"I had no plans to leave."

I awoke slowly, opened my eyes and was completely disoriented. I recognized the red chair, but why was it cockeyed? My table was out of whack, too. Plus, I hurt everywhere and wanted to cry.

But wait, I smelled bacon. Maybe life was worth living after all.

I pulled back the fuzzy blanket and sat up. And immediately lay down again. My head was about to explode.

"Oh, that's not good." The night before came back in a rush. The attack. Derek. The police. The kiss.

Oh yes. The kiss.

I let out a breath and tried to sit up again. So far, so good. I waited a few seconds, then pushed myself up to stand. I had to hold on to the arm of the couch for a minute, but I took halting steps and finally made it across the room.

I checked the kitchen and found bacon strips wrapped in paper towels and aluminum foil, sitting inside the warm oven. Coffee was made. A yellow sticky note was stuck to the refrigerator that read "Stay home and recuperate." It was signed "The Hawk."

I smiled as I poured a cup of coffee, then padded to the bathroom, where I took two pain relievers and stepped into the shower.

The hot water revived me enough to dress myself. The Hawk—Derek—was right. I'd already planned to work at home today, finish the *Faust* restoration and maybe get a head start on some other projects that I was behind on.

I dressed for comfort in jeans, a T-shirt and a warm sweater. Wool socks and my Birkenstocks completed the ensemble.

As I munched on bacon and read the paper, I couldn't help smiling. The Hawk kissed like a dream. *Remember the hawk,* he'd said. I wasn't likely to forget him any time soon.

"Remember the hawk," I said, and chuckled as I took another bite of bacon and turned to the sports page.

Remember the devil. The words popped into my head unbidden.

"Whoa." Something clicked and I jumped up. A spasm of pain vibrated across my skull and I sank back into my chair and clutched my head in my hands.

"Oh God." I had to breathe through the pain. But the words began to spin around. Remember the hawk. The devil. Remember. Remember.

Remember the devil.

"Oh, you dimwit." I stood more slowly this time, then walked as fast as I could to the studio, straight to the bookshelf where the blue leather cover shone like a beacon.

Wild Flowers in the Wind.

I pulled it from the shelf. The soft leather felt cool in my hands. I splayed the covers and the book fell open to page 213.

Pilosella aurantiaca. Hawkweed, otherwise known as the devil's paintbrush.

Remember the devil.

Old memories came rushing back as I groped for my desk chair and sat. I was eight years old and I'd chosen the wildflower book from a shelf full of decrepit tomes Abraham kept for the purpose of practicing craft. He'd scoffed at my choice and had begun reading out loud the descriptions of some of the more noxious flowers as I'd gathered tools to start my work. I'd laughed with him, agreeing that it was silly that someone actually considered these ugly-looking plants to be flowers. But I'd still wanted to work with this book because the title was so pretty.

Wild Flowers in the Wind.

Abraham had regaled me with the shortcomings of the dreaded *Pilosella aurantiaca.* Its stiff leaves and petals were covered in short, rigid hairs, its stems and leaves were black, and the flower itself was the color of rust. And it smelled bad.

"No wonder the devil uses it for a paintbrush," he'd said with a laugh, and succeeded in charming his too-serious, rather needy eight-year-old apprentice.

The poor devil plant hadn't deserved our derision, I supposed. But it was one of those shared moments between teacher and student I would always treasure.

"Some treasured memory," I said, mentally flogging

myself, wondering why I hadn't remembered it until this minute.

My mother would've told me the truth wasn't meant to be revealed until this moment, but that dubious bit of wisdom didn't assuage my remorse.

I shook it off. My feelings didn't matter. The fact was, I'd just found what I'd been searching for since Abraham was killed.

Chapter 18

I ran my fingers over the aged, deckled paper. There, wedged between pages 212 and 213, next to the fuzzy photograph of the devil's paintbrush, were several pieces of notepaper, thinned and yellowed with age.

My hand shook as I pulled the pages out and unfolded them. It was a three-page letter, written in German.

The date written on the first page was 8 September 1941. The ink was faded but the handwriting looked feminine to me. I checked the last page and saw that the letter was signed "Gretchen."

This had to be what Abraham meant by GW1941. But who was Gretchen?

Perhaps after reading the letter, I would know. Beyond excited, I found my bag, pulled out the English-German dictionary I'd bought to help translate *Faust* and settled down at the worktable to decipher the correspondence.

The letter was addressed to "Sigrid" and at one point in the text, Gretchen referred to her as "*liebe schwester*" or "dear sister."

Forty minutes later, I closed the dictionary and pushed away from the table. My excitement had turned to distress. I powered up my laptop and spent a few minutes online, Googling additional information. Then I walked around the room, lost in thought. After a few minutes, my stunned silence grew to vocal anger and I pounded the worktable a few times.

"Gretchen, you stupid coward."

Saying the name aloud gave me a jolt. In Goethe's *Faust*, Gretchen was the virtuous young woman destroyed by Faust, but her real name was Marguerite. As I'd just learned, "Gretchen" was a common German diminutive for Marguerite. A nickname.

Heinrich Winslow's wife's name was Marguerite. Also affectionately known as Gretchen. But unlike her fictional namesake, Heinrich Winslow's wife was all too real and completely responsible for so much destruction.

And no wonder someone was willing to kill to keep these papers hidden.

My translation abilities weren't perfect, but they were close enough. I hadn't mistaken the words or the sentiment.

It definitely explained why Abraham had been killed. Not that the explanation was fair or acceptable, but it certainly clarified things.

Such as, who the killer had to be.

I'd always considered myself a good judge of human character, but obviously my judgment was flawed. I'd actually spent time with and *liked* the killer. I rubbed my arms against the chills that skittered across my skin. Maybe I needed my head examined. Or maybe I needed my Vata-Dosha tweaked. Maybe when this whole nasty episode was concluded, I would take my mom up on the chakra cleansing day at the Ayurveda spa. I might spring for the deluxe mani-pedi while I was at it.

I shoved the personal grooming issues out of my head. I needed to call Inspector Lee. But first, I wanted the person who'd destroyed the life of my friend and mentor to suffer, just for a little while.

I owed that much to Abraham.

I searched my bag for the right business card, then stared at the name of Abraham's killer for several long moments. Could I do this? Could I call this person, this killer, and actually sound calm and assured as I made my accusations?

I needed a minute.

I was scared, really scared. I wasn't sure I could do it. I looked at my worktable. Pieces of *Faust* were scattered about, waiting for me to put them back together. Maybe if I worked for a while, buried myself in the book, I could trick myself into casually picking up the phone and making the call.

For courage, I opened a small bag of candy corn, then blocked out everything but the *Faust* restoration. The individual repaired pages were dry, so I pressed the text block together and stitched the signatures back together. I applied a coat of PVA glue to consolidate the text block. While that dried, I affixed the cleaned and polished black leather cover to the new boards.

This was what I'd needed. Busywork. Doing what I did best. Here, I knew exactly what to do. No questions, no mysteries.

When the glue was not quite dry, I used a hammer

to pound the sewn ends and thus create a rounded edge to the spine of the text block. I put the block back into the press and added another thin layer of glue to hold the newly rounded shape. Then I added decorative black and gold silk endbands at the head and foot of the spine.

The glue would have to dry, which meant I could take a break. I glanced at the clock, then stared at the phone. It was now or never.

I sat at my desk, clutching the business card. I composed myself, then made the call. It went to voice mail, so I left a clear message. "I have what you're looking for and I'm willing to hand it over for the small sum of two hundred thousand dollars."

I felt like Dr. Evil. I should've demanded more, but since I was bluffing anyway, did it really matter? I checked my watch.

"It's two o'clock, Tuesday afternoon," I continued on voice mail. "If I don't hear from you by six o'clock tonight, I'll call the police."

I hung up and immediately called Inspector Lee. Yes, I'd lied to the killer about waiting until six to call the police. My bad.

Inspector Lee wasn't in. I didn't feel comfortable talking to Inspector Jaglow, so I asked the operator to transfer me to Lee's voice mail. I left another detailed message, telling her what I'd found and the name of the person I was convinced had killed Abraham Karastovsky and Enrico Baldacchio.

I hung up the phone, feeling a tiny bit guilty. Maybe I shouldn't have teased the killer with my threat of blackmail, but I'd worked my way back to full anger. That bastard had killed my friend, killed Enrico, plundered and pillaged Abraham's studio, broken into my home and ransacked my studio, destroyed Robin's beautiful vase and knocked me unconscious. I had the right to demand some frontier justice, such as it was.

I made two more quick phone calls and had to leave messages both times. Where was everybody today? The first call was to Derek, explaining what I'd discovered and asking him to come by whenever he could. The other call was to my dad, telling him I was absolutely certain that Mom would be released later today.

Then I folded Gretchen's letter, wedged it back into the wildflower book, and shoved the book back into place on the shelf.

Now there was nothing to do but wait for the phone to ring. I nibbled on noodles but I wasn't really hungry. On any other day, that would've been cause for alarm, but today I was hyperaware of the source of my anxiety.

So I got back to work, first testing the glue on the spine. It was dry. Time to put it all back together.

Adjusting the Armageddon painting back into its pastedown/flyleaf position, and using Mylar and waste sheets to shield the pages from any excess glue, I rolled the text block onto the glued, refurbished cover boards and sealed the book.

I cleaned and polished the rubies until they sparkled with new life, then glued them back into place on the front cover.

It was gorgeous if I did say so myself. Next, I covered the jeweled front cover with a layer of protective foam, then wrapped the entire book in thin cloth and slid it between the plates of the book press for thirty seconds to seal the deal.

I would take pictures of the finished binding tomorrow. I hoped that someday I'd have the time to replicate the intricate design with its gilded royal crest and fleur-de-lis finishes. But in the meantime, the photos I took would be uploaded to my Web site with a detailed description of the work I'd done to complete the restoration.

The book itself gleamed in the fading light, a rare and beautiful work of art, but what it represented was tarnished and ugly. So much for its legendary curse. The curse didn't exist—unless you considered arrogance, greed, fear and stupidity a curse.

The light in the studio had grown dim as I'd worked, so I turned on some lights. It was only four o'clock but the fog was rolling in. The phone hadn't rung and my head was beginning to pound again.

I felt the painful lump on the back of my head, a dull reminder of the attack last night. I needed some aspirin and my stomach was growling. I'd left the bowl of noodles virtually untouched. My world was truly cracked.

Checking that the protective foam and cloth were still wrapped tightly, I secured the *Faust* between two pieces of smooth plywood and put a ten-pound weight on top. I would keep it wrapped and pressed overnight until the glue was completely dry and the aged black leather was securely fastened to the boards.

The restoration was complete.

I celebrated by sticking a piece of leftover pizza in the microwave, then popping two aspirins while I waited for the pizza to heat up.

Ten minutes later, the pizza was history and I was feeling more like myself, no longer suffering hunger pangs and now wondering whether it was too early for a glass of wine. Unfortunately, there was some pesky business to deal with involving a killer and the police, so sobriety was called for until further notice.

I was washing my dishes when the phone rang. I dried my hands and grabbed it on the third ring.

Conrad Winslow lost no time getting to the point of his call. "What the hell are you trying to pull?"

"Hi, Mr. Winslow."

"You're trying to blackmail me?"

"Abraham Karastovsky is dead and now I know why."

"And blackmail is your way to handle it?"

"No, that was just a little joke," I said, rubbing my head where I'd been coshed last night.

"What the hell are you talking about?"

My doorbell rang. I figured I had the killer on the phone, so I didn't have a second thought about whipping the door open.

Sylvia Winslow stood there, looking fresh and elegant in a peach suit and matching heels.

"Hello, Sylvia," I said. "This is a coincidence."

"Hang up the phone," she said, lifting her hand to reveal a small but lethal gun pointed directly at me.

"Uh, good-bye," I said into the phone, and put it down on the desk. She followed me inside and nudged the door shut with her hip.

She glanced around. "You've cleaned the place up."

"Yeah," I said as I carefully backed away from her. "Some slob made a real mess of things."

"You're pretty funny for someone facing the wrong end of a gun." She waved it for emphasis. "Give me the letter."

"I don't have it."

"We both know you're lying."

"Why do you think I have it?" I backed up another step, closing in on my worktable where I knew I'd left at least one knife and several bone folders I could use as a weapon. Not that a flimsy bone folder would be much of a match against a gun. And I had no illusions that she wouldn't use it, since she'd already killed at least two people.

"Because you left a clear message on my husband's voice mail," she said. "Must we play this game?"

"You screen your husband's voice mail?"

"Yes, I do. Otherwise, nothing would be done on time or correctly."

"Why did you kill Enrico?"

She sighed. "Why do you care? The man was a pig."

"I'm just wondering what he did to you."

"He stole from me."

"You could've called the police."

Her laugh was laced with contempt. "That was Conrad's solution. Men."

"Yeah, men are funny."

"Brooklyn dear, just give me the letter." She smiled tightly. "I might decide not to kill you if you cooperate."

"Oh, right." My heel grazed the leg of the stool. "I hand you the letter and you go your merry way. Why do I not believe you?"

"No, I don't suppose you should." She waved the gun in a blasé manner. "But can you blame me? I don't like being blackmailed."

"And I didn't like seeing my beloved friend die in my arms."

"Ah, your beloved friend, the blackmailer. You saw how far that got him and yet, here you are, trying the same thing." She shook her head in disappointment. "Just give me the letter now and let's be done with this nonsense."

Staring at the gun, I could feel my knees shaking. I could barely swallow, my mouth was so dry. I backed up slowly. She wouldn't kill me without getting her hands on the letter first, would she?

"Why should I give you the letter when you're just going to kill me anyway? Besides, do you think I'd be dumb enough to keep it here in my house?"

"You'll give it to me," she said.

"But I don't have it."

"You're lying. It's what you all do. Lies and black-mail. Do you really think I'd allow my family to be blackmailed by the likes of you and that big ape, Abraham? How dare you try to ruin the good name of my family with your little scheme?"

"Actually, I didn't intend to blackmail your family," I said as I sidestepped the stool and eased my way back against the worktable. "I just wanted to make you squirm awhile until the police arrested you."

"Do you think I'm an idiot?" she said with a hiss. Her cheeks were turning an angry shade of red. "You didn't call the police. You're a grasping, greedy bitch, trying to make money off the pain of others."

"I take it Abraham tried the same thing." I was stalling, leading her on, waiting for a miracle. To keep her talking was all I could think to do.

"He tried—and failed miserably."

In Gretchen's letter to her sister Sigrid, she'd be-moaned the fact that Heinrich was putting his own family in jeopardy with his grandiose schemes to save mankind. "Jews, Sigrid, can you make sense of it?" Gretchen had written. "He risks our lives to help Jews!"

Gretchen had gone to Heinrich, insisting that he stop. Otherwise, she wouldn't be responsible for her actions. In the letter, Gretchen had suggested that the gardener's shed held everything she'd need to complete a certain unpleasant but necessary task.

I'd Googled the details of Heinrich Winslow's death and discovered that he'd died of arsenic poisoning. The date of his death was three days after the date of Gretchen's letter. The poison was traced to a box of weed killer. Wikipedia claimed that Heinrich's grieving wife and children went to live with her sister Sigrid in Denmark after his death.

Somehow, Gretchen's letter had found its way into the secret pocket inside *Faust*. In my heart, I liked to think her sister Sigrid wanted the truth to be revealed someday.

"I guess it wouldn't help Heinrich's heroic reputation," I said, "if the world knew his wife had been a cowardly anti-Semitic murdering bitch."

"You think?" Sylvia said snidely. "Oh, I don't blame her for what she did, but the world would consider her evil. My family's honor and reputation would be ruined. We would be persona non grata everywhere we went. I can't allow that."

"No, that would be unacceptable. Much better just to kill off a few people and hide the truth."

"Don't patronize me," she snapped. "The man didn't care about his own family. He had to be the big hero, saving all those Jews."

"You make it sound like that's a bad thing."

"What if he'd been caught? He would've been killed on the spot or sent to a camp. Gretchen would've been shunned, ridiculed, and left alone to raise four children. Or who knows? Maybe they would've sent her to the camps with him. He left her no choice."

"But to kill him?"

"Yes, and good for her."

"But she was still left alone anyway," I said.

"But this way," Sylvia argued, "her husband died a hero and a good citizen instead of being gassed to death as an enemy of the state. Her reputation was saved."

"And reputation is everything," I said.

"Despite what you and my daughter think, yes, reputation is everything."

I straightened my shoulders. There was no need to be insulting, bunching me in with Meredith. But it was disappointing to know that Meredith was actually a pillar of dignity and honor compared to her mother.

"So if you already read the letter," I ventured, "why didn't you destroy it?"

Her nostrils flared like an offended little bull's. "I didn't read the letter," she conceded as she strolled calmly through a patch of sunlight coming through the blinds. "Karastovsky read it over the phone to my husband, then demanded money."

"And Conrad . . ."

"Panicked. He told me what the letter said and I told him to calm down. I had to take care of everything."

"A woman's work is never done."

"Exactly," she said with a sneer. "I called Karastovsky back and told him I'd bring the money the night of the opening."

"But you didn't bring money. Just a gun."

"Right again," she said. "That big, stupid ox. Did he think I'd allow my family to be shunned and ridiculed because some loathsome *cobbler* thought he could manipulate us?"

"Cobbler?"

"Oh, whatever." She waved her gun hand impatiently. "You work with leather. Your hands are dirty. You're low-class craftspeople."

Craftspeople. Ouch.

Beyond the insults, none of this made sense. Abraham was wealthy. He didn't need the money. Why would he resort to blackmail?

A thought sprouted and grew. According to Minka, Abraham and Enrico had begun a collaboration shortly before Abraham was killed. Had Abraham revealed the contents of the letter to Enrico? Had Enrico been the one to attempt blackmail, using Abraham's name since he'd already burned his own bridges with the Winslows?

The scheme had Enrico's name all over it.

I wondered.

"So, when you confronted Abraham with the gun the night of the opening, when you accused him of blackmail, what did he say?"

"He denied everything," she said scornfully. "Said he'd never made the phone call, never demanded money. He whined and cried like a big baby girl. It was disgusting. I'm glad I could put him out of his misery."

My hands bunched in fury. Abraham had talked about Enrico betraying a confidence. It had to be about Gretchen's letter. I was virtually certain Enrico had found out about it and hatched the scheme without Abraham's knowledge or approval. Which meant Sylvia had killed Abraham for no reason at all.

I could see the whole scenario clearly. Enrico had wanted to get even with the Winslows for cheating him out of his source of easy money. He really was a scumbag, but even he hadn't deserved to die.

As she spoke, I continued to face her but carefully, gradually brought my arms back and leaned against the worktable. I reached farther back to feel around for a weapon. My fingers wrapped themselves around something long and thin. A bone folder.

"I assume you sent the guy with the snake tattoo after me."

"Willie," she said, and rolled her eyes. "He's a little fellow who occasionally does odd jobs for me. Not all that dependable, but it was worth a shot."

"Aren't you afraid he'll implicate you?"

"I give him little gifts and he's thoroughly devoted to me," she said. "Besides, he's completely off his rocker. Who would believe him?"

She had a point. Then something else occurred to me. "Do you own a dark SUV?"

She gazed at her fingernails. "My housekeeper drives one but I borrow it occasionally."

"And the rose on my pillow?"

She chuckled. "A tender gesture, wasn't it? I overheard your gorgeous male friend telling you he'd call you 'soon.'" She grinned. "Boy, if I had a nickel for every time I'd heard those words. Am I right?"

Was this girl talk? Was she kidding?

She sighed, continued. "You came home sooner

than I expected, so I was stuck in your coat closet for a while."

I was stymied and finally blurted, "How in the world do you know how to break into houses?"

"It's a gift," she said with a cocky grin. "I didn't always live on Nob Hill, you know. I grew up on the streets, learned to survive. Otherwise, I would've died out there."

I clutched the bone folder more tightly.

"Hey," she said, taking notice of my movement. "Back away from the table."

I took a step closer to her, then threw the bone folder. It was absolutely useless as a weapon—but very effective as a diversion. Sylvia screamed and pulled the trigger at the same time. The bullet went wildly off course. We fell against each other and I pushed the gun away. She grabbed my chin and raked her nails down my neck.

"Ouch!" I knocked her back and reached for the gun. She tried to aim it toward me, but I grasped hold of her wrist and we fought for power.

"You stupid cow, let me go!" she cried as she smashed my face with her other hand.

"Damn it!" She was getting in plenty of smacks and slaps, but at least they weren't bullets.

The door burst open and my mother dashed in carrying a huge pizza box, just as Sylvia smacked me in the ear with her fist, then grabbed for the gun.

Mom used the only weapon she had to protect her daughter. The pizza. She flung the box and struck Sylvia in the head. Sylvia squealed in fury as the gun went flying and the pizza tumbled to the floor.

Derek rushed in behind Mom, grabbed Sylvia by

the back of her peach jacket and hauled her to her feet.

"Don't step on the pizza," Mom cried.

I looked up and grinned at Derek, delighted to see them both. He rolled his eyes and stepped a few feet away, out of pizza range, dragging Sylvia with him.

"You son of a bitch, take your hands off me!" she cried, twisting and struggling to free herself.

Mom scampered around to rescue the pizza. "It's your favorite, sweetie. Mushrooms, onions and garlic."

"Extra cheese?" I asked.

"You betcha." She put the heavy box on the work-table and burst into tears. I grabbed her and we hugged tightly.

"I love you, Mom," I whispered.

"I know, sweetie," she said, sniffling as she stroked my hair. "I love you, too."

Footsteps pounded outside in the hall and my studio was suddenly crowded with cops. Inspector Lee followed them in, clutching her gun with both hands. She holstered it as soon as she saw Derek gripping Sylvia's arms behind her back.

"You got my message," I said.

"Nope," Lee said. "Conrad Winslow called to report his wife."

"That bastard!" Sylvia shouted.

"Men," I said, shaking my head.

Derek released Sylvia to one of the cops and Inspector Lee suggested we clear the area. I grabbed the pizza box and led the way back to the kitchen, where she questioned me for the next half hour.

As soon as she left, I poured three hefty glasses of wine as Derek explained that he'd heard my message, called the police and swung by headquarters to spring my mom. They'd picked up a pizza and were on their way over to surprise me.

"Why did you confess to the murder, Mom?" I asked as soon as I'd fortified myself with several stiff gulps of wine.

"Sweetie." She glanced at Derek, then back at me and whispered, "I was trying to protect you."

My jaw dropped a few feet. "Me? Why would you—"

She smiled self-consciously but said nothing.

"Wait," I said. "You thought I killed Abraham? Why?"

"Because you hated him," she explained.

"I did?"

She nodded solemnly. "You found out he and I were having an affair and you blamed him for destroying our marriage."

I bobbled my wineglass, dumbfounded. "Y-you and—and Abraham were having an affair?"

"Oh, heavens no." She took a dainty sip of wine.

"But . . ." I looked at Derek, who was biting back a smile. He seemed to be enjoying the show.

I took a deep breath and let it out slowly. "Mother, what are you talking about?"

"Your friend confided in me the day of Abraham's memorial," she said. "She told me everything."

My eyes narrowed. "What friend was that?"

"The chubby one in the leopard gloves? What's her name? Minky? Monkey?" She waved the question away. "You know the one. Anyway, she told me how worried she was about you. How she hoped the police didn't find out how much you hated poor Abraham."

Minka. I gnashed my teeth as I planned my revenge. I was seriously going to destroy her. I just had to figure out how.

"Oh, I assured her it wasn't true about the affair," Mom continued. "But I was afraid the damage had been done. When you told me the police were hauling you in, I decided to take matters into my own hands."

"It wasn't necessary to go to jail for me, Mom," I said softly.

"Better me than you, sweetie." She took a quick sip of wine, then put her glass on the counter and nonchalantly cracked her petite knuckles. "I've been in jail and know how to survive. You wouldn't last a day."

I leaned back and drained my wineglass, then reached for the bottle, determined to be good and tanked before this conversation was over.

Epilogue

A month later, on a warm afternoon in Dharma, Mom and Dad celebrated their thirty-fifth wedding anniversary with seven hundred of their closest family and friends.

Mom looked beautiful and rested after spending a week at the Laughing Goat sweat lodge. After detoxification, she'd shared in the sacred pipe purification ceremony, which had allowed her to channel shamanic drum meditations and astral travel to Alpha Centauri with her spirit guide, Ramlar X.

Dad beamed with love as Mom reminisced.

Guru Bob offered the use of his elegant hilltop home and terraced patio for the occasion. He made a heartfelt toast, and then I presented my parents with a nicely bound leather photo album containing pictures and keepsakes of their life together, from the Deadhead days to the present.

There were photos of all of the kids along with pictures and mementos of the various Grateful Dead concert sites or weapons facilities protest marches we'd all been named after.

For the album, I had experimented with a flamed-heat iron to brand an embossed grapevine pattern into the thick leather cover. The stock was thick, acid-free paper, deckled and interleaved with delicate sheets of rice paper. I hoped it would become a family heirloom.

Mom cried like a baby when she saw it, so I know she liked it. Dad's eyes swam with tears and he couldn't speak for twenty minutes. It wasn't as grand as the first-class tickets to Paris my brothers surprised them with, but I think they loved it just as much.

A month before, the night Sylvia Winslow was taken off to jail, Mom had sat me down and begged me to put the album together. She'd confessed that Abraham had been her original choice to do the project she wanted to keep a secret from our family.

"I don't believe it!" I'd said when she'd explained what she wanted. "That's why you were meeting him at the Covington that night? To sift through family photos?"

"It was his idea to meet there," Mom explained. "He'd been so busy, but he knew that once the exhibit opened, he'd finally have a free minute or two to go over my plans."

"That's crazy."

She frowned. "What's crazy is me waiting in the wrong workroom for almost an hour."

I shivered. "That mistake probably saved your life."

"I never even heard the gunshot," she wailed. "I was practicing for my cosmic bilocation class."

"I would've done the same thing," I'd assured her.

Now we raised our champagne glasses and toasted

another round for my parents. They kissed and the crowd applauded.

"They're the most wonderful people in the world," someone said next to me.

"I couldn't agree more," I said as I turned and did a double take. It was Annie, Abraham's daughter. She was completely transformed. Instead of the kohl-eyed Goth look she'd sported when I met her, she wore no makeup except lip gloss. She looked like a happy teenager with her dark hair fluffed softly around her face. She wore a long, sage green cotton skirt with a matching tie-dyed tank top, and oh, dear Lord, Birkenstocks. Dharma had claimed another convert.

"Look who's gone country," I said.

"Thanks, I guess." But she smiled as she said it.

"Did the move go okay?"

"Yes, thanks to your mom and dad," she said. "I really like it here, you know?"

"I'm glad. I was sorry to hear about your mom."

"Thanks. It wasn't unexpected, but still." She shook her head. Annie's mother had died a few days after Sylvia Winslow was arrested.

After the paternity test results had come through, verifying that Annie was indeed Abraham's daughter, I'd signed papers making Annie and me joint tenants of Abraham's house and surrounding property. The lawyers took some of Abraham's holdings and set up a trust that would pay Annie an allowance until she could figure out what she wanted to do with the rest of her life.

"Your mom's been introducing me around," Annie said. "She's amazing."

I glanced over at Mom, who was currently doing the funky chicken with my four-year-old nephew. "Yeah, she is."

"I guess I owe you," Annie said with a half smile. "But don't expect me to kiss your ring every time I see you."

I sipped my champagne. "Not every time."

She grinned and walked away.

I looked around for Robin and saw her at one of the wine bars, talking to Austin. He beamed at her and she laughed. The sound was so sweet, I felt a big twinge of happiness for them.

Ian approached with a full bottle of Brut Rosé and topped my glass. Now that he was "out," Ian was so much more relaxed than I'd ever seen him. I said hello to Jake, Ian's boyfriend, whom I'd met at the official opening of the Winslow exhibition.

The opening had been a blockbuster event. News of the curse and the murders and the notorious Winslow women had hit the headlines and the crowds were intense.

I was thrilled that Ian had taken my advice and displayed the *Faust* on its own pedestal, encased in Plexiglas so that the cover, the text and the Armageddon painting could all be seen by the public.

Even Meredith Winslow, who'd attended the opening with her father as a show of public strength, agreed the *Faust* looked "okay, whatever." And even though I'd never achieve my dream of seeing her behind bars wearing an orange jumpsuit, her words were music to my ears.

Ian and Jake moved on to talk to Austin. I sighed and took another sip of the Brut Rosé.

"Are your bags packed?"

I struggled to catch my breath, not because Derek Stone had snuck up on me but because that mellow British accent of his never failed to give me a start.

I would've loved to think he'd come all the way from London to Dharma because of me. But the truth was, he and Mom had forged a bond the night Mom flung her kung fu pizza box at Sylvia Winslow's head.

Derek had surprised Mom when he showed up last night and she'd burst into tears of happiness. There was a lot of that going around lately.

"Packed and ready to go, bright and early tomorrow," I said with a smile.

"You're flying nonstop to Heathrow?"

"Yes, and I took your advice and sprang for first class." And why that made me more nervous than the flight itself, I couldn't say. Spending all that extra money on my own comfort was likely to give me hives. But hey, I needed something new to obsess over now that the murders of Abraham and Enrico had been solved.

"Why would anyone travel any other way?" he said.

Said the man who rented a Bentley wherever he went.

My suitcases were indeed packed for my trip to the Edinburgh Book Fair. I'd just received news the day before that one of my books was a finalist in the book fair competition. I was antsy to go but hated to leave.

And speaking of antsy, I'd been drinking champagne for the past two hours and needed to find a restroom. "Would you watch my glass for a minute?"

"Only for a minute," Derek said with a grin, and took my glass.

I stepped inside Guru Bob's house to find a restroom. As I passed the spacious living room, something caught my eye and I moved toward it.

"Oh my God." It was a genuine Vermeer on the wall nearest the foyer. I walked across the soft pale carpet for a closer look and stared for a minute at the painting of the young woman writing at her desk. "Beautiful."

"A superb study of light and shadow."

I whipped around and saw Guru Bob watching me.

"I'm sorry, Robson," I said awkwardly. "I was looking for the restroom, but I saw this and had see it up close."

"Please do not ever apologize for enjoying beautiful things, gracious," he said with a slight bow. "I enjoy having my home filled with friends and my art viewed by those who can appreciate it."

"You have so many lovely pieces," I said, glancing around the elegant room. My gaze settled on a startling Rembrandt portrait of a young boy.

"Holy cow," I said under my breath, and approached the painting with reverence. "Unbelievable."

"I am blessed." He walked beside me as I looked.

"Thank you for letting me take a peek around."

"You are always welcome, gracious."

I passed a stately three-door glass display cabinet that had to be an original Louis the Something. It was so very French and heavily laden with gold ormolu and beautiful parquetry. Not my style, but it fit perfectly in this room that was both strongly male while being light and spacious.

I almost missed it.

Guru Bob stood nearby, his finger pressed to his lips as he watched me stop, then turn back. There in the display cabinet was the five-hundred-year-old edition of Plutarch's *Parallel Lives* I'd taken from Enrico Baldacchio's library. The book sat on a small easel on the center shelf. The unusual green morocco binding and distinctive gilding was unmistakable.

In utter shock, I whirled around. "How?"

His smile was sweet as he admired the book. "It is simply exquisite, is it not?"

The extraordinary book was supposed to be stashed away in my secret hiding place at the bottom of my closet. I'd discovered that the book hadn't belonged to the Winslows, so over the past month, I'd kept it hidden while I made discreet inquiries through the Covington and several reputable booksellers to find the true owner of the Plutarch. So far, I hadn't had any luck. Which was why the book was still in my closet. Or so I'd thought.

"Gabriel," I whispered.

"A dear friend."

"How in the world?" I said.

"Ah, gracious," Guru Bob said gently as he took my arm and led me out of the room. "The gods work in mysterious ways."

Ready to find
your next great read?

Let us help.

Visit prh.com/nextread

Penguin
Random
House